CW01511522

The RED QUEEN

DIRK DRAULANS

translated by

SAM GARRETT

The RED QUEEN

a novel of

THE WAR BETWEEN THE SEXES

st. martin's press
new york

A THOMAS DUNNE BOOK.
An imprint of St. Martin's Press.

THE RED QUEEN. Copyright © 1998 by Dirk Draulans. All rights
reserved. Printed in the United States of America. No part of this book
may be used or reproduced in any manner whatsoever without written per-
mission except in the case of brief quotations embodied in critical articles
or reviews. For information, address St. Martin's Press, 175 Fifth Avenue,
New York, N.Y. 10010.

This publication was realized with support of the Administratie Kunst van
de Vlaamse Gemeenschap.

Design by Maureen Troy

Library of Congress Cataloging-in-Publication Data

Draulans, Dirk.
    [Rode koningin. English]
    The red queen / Dirk Draulans : translated by Sam Garrett.
        p.   cm.
    "A Thomas Dunne book."
    ISBN 0-312-15636-7
    I. Garrett, Sam.
PT6466.14.R38R613   1998
839.3'1364—dc21   97-8806
                                                     CIP

First Edition: January 1998

10   9   8   7   6   5   4   3   2   1

for Kristina

With thanks to Anita, Anna, Lieve, Mieke and Ria,
and to the professors Jean-Jacques Cassiman, André De Leenheer,
Henri Dumont, Peter Marijnen and André Van Steirteghem

P r e f a c e

This book is based on the most recent scientific insights into evolution, parasites and sex, and the relationship among them, as related in dozens of books and articles in these fields. Most of the scientific elements found in this book, therefore, actually exist. The "new" science is largely the brainchild of Professor Jean-Jacques Cassiman of the Center for Human Genetics at the Catholic University of Louvain. In this case "new" does not imply "trumped up." The details needed to make the plot practicable will likely be available by the end of this century. That is why this novel is not strictly a work of science fiction.

Everyone's out to get you, motherfucker.

—BECK, *Mellow Gold*, 1994

The RED QUEEN

ELLEN'S STORY

RED IS NOT THE COLOR OF SHAME. RED IS the color of excitement, a signal, subtle yet in marked contrast to everyday grayish blue or white. Red speaks of an extraordinary openness, a willingness to make contact, to interrupt the comforting routine of living alone by means of an intimate, tactile exploration, heralding a period of obligatory involvement. The color red opens up an unaccustomed world of contact.

The mating rituals of herons seem so romantic. As though realizing they were not made for vocal courtship, the birds usually remain silent. They clack their red beaks open and closed along the throat of their chosen one, shake their heads and their long crown plumage, bend their necks in submission. The movements are repeated for hours, as though they wish to draw out the only contact they will have in the course of the year, to enjoy it for as long as possible.

A misconception. The herons don't want to draw out that contact as long as possible, they want to get it over with. The hour-long rituals are needed to make the move to physical contact, to reproduction, the animal's only motivation. The beak and legs turn red to indicate that, for the time being, they will not be used as a weapon. The raw, aggressive shriek is muffled to a discreet gurgle. The neck is not extended to make the animal look larger and more threatening, as during a normal encounter, but bent in submission.

Once the pair has formed, they even work together. One of them will come bearing twigs, day after day, humbly presenting them to its partner, who weaves them diligently into their love nest. Copulation itself is brief and businesslike, no frills, wings spread wide, legs on the back, a bit of scrambling to gain position, a few seconds of contact. There is no afterplay. A fluffing of the feathers, an extensive preening, and it's over. No more rituals, for rituals serve only to reach this point. After the mating and the laying of eggs, it's every bird for itself and its offspring.

Differences are seen in male and female behavior during this brief mating period, but equality is the name of the game during the rest of a heron's year. Both sexes look the same: there are no differences in plumage, size or behavior. Together they build the nest, brood on the eggs, feed the young. At first the bird sitting on the eggs or keeping the chicks warm is relieved several times a day, but soon both animals go their own way, searching for food for themselves and their young, in accordance with a predictable rhythm, but independent of each other.

Yet even then they act as a team: that is the mystery of the heron couple. They tend to stay away from the nest for equal periods of time, to feed the young equally as often, as if knowing that their interests are served by an equal investment in their offspring, by not betraying their partner by desertion and leaving to him all the work of feeding. They no longer meet at the nest, yet still remain attuned. The week-long mating ritual does more than grant access to a female's back: it ensures that the birds' rhythms become synchronized and indicates how much they are willing to invest in their offspring. Two individuals who couldn't care less about each other force themselves to undergo a week-long ritual of contact, pledge themselves to work together for months in accordance with a schedule of mutual consent.

The measure of this temporary partnership is the young herons themselves. If things go badly, then the youngest of them will die, usually driven over the edge of the nest by the sharp bills of the older chicks. If things go very badly, then they will all die, one by one, from the youngest up. When one of the parents gives up, the partner also loses the returns on its investment in the offspring. If one of the two invests more heavily than the other, it is the swindler who benefits, for its stake produces proportionally higher returns, its efforts are expressed in terms of greater success: more progeny for fewer turns at feeding. Such behavior is taboo; it must be genetically punished to keep misrepresentation and fraud from gaining ascendance and ultimately paralyzing the heron population.

The heron's red beak and rituals fit perfectly within the reproductive design nature has worked out for it: a blind and programmed faith in the success of absolute equality.

My life revolved around herons once. Beautiful animals, loveliest in their treetop colonies, a focal point in their lives, a crossroads that creates the impression of a social existence but is nothing more than a meeting place for animals faced with a choice, birds that have to find a partner as prepared to invest in new life as they are. The more individuals that come together, the greater the chance of finding such a kindred spirit.

I spent years of scientific work and dogged observation on those birds, and I came to know them as individuals with their own personalities, peculiarities and habits, until I gradually realized that the colony served as a glorified singles' club, where contact was meant not to dispel loneliness—loneliness being what these animals treasure most—but to allow them to reproduce. Years of intensive field study on ponds, in steeples and blinds, years of tagging and measurement, of dangling from the tops of tall trees, of deskbound thought and calculation, resulting in a five-hundred-page tome full of figures and conclusions that have probably all been forgotten by now.

But my memories of the fieldwork remain, especially of the people I worked with. Like Jos, the bachelor birdbander who could manipulate five nestlings at a time in those huge filthy mitts of his, without hurting a feather. Each fall he would spend months living in the hut close to the nets he had spread to catch migratory birds. His sister had to bring him a meal now and then, because he was always forgetting to eat.

Or Walter, the toothless taxidermist who would take huge swigs from his mineral water bottle full of gin every time we had a picnic, and who never felt like washing himself during the nesting season, because he would only stink of birds again the next day. He was the one who taught us to catch herons.

Or Jan and Gert, and the rest of the youngbloods, who became excellent climbers after a few years and would argue about who got to go up in the trees the older men—with their heightened awareness of the risks involved—no longer dared to climb.

And not to forget gabby old Gust, with whom I spent many talkative hours in or hanging under a heron's nest, waiting until the crew on the ground had finished tagging and measuring the nestlings we had lowered down to them in a bucket. It was Gust who had developed the most efficient climbing technique of all: swaying the trees, which were usually quite thin, back and forth, and then stepping from crown to crown. The sublime thing about it was the time and energy it saved in climbing down and then back up again. Fortunately, the accidents associated with the "Gust method" had led to nothing more serious than a few bruises, and the growing realization that the technique was not devoid of a certain risk.

Jos, Walter, Jan, Gert and Gust had all died. Not so very long ago. Only the memories remained, of them and of the others. The fear had stayed too. It resurfaced at regular intervals, especially when the loneliness became hard to bear. Fortunately, I had soon learned to live with it. And I had learned to cultivate the ties I once had with nature but had neglected as the years went by. I talked to the birds and played with the butterflies; I sought out familiar places, not because they made me feel at home, but because I could find my way around there, and the cities had become too dangerous.

The panic, on the other hand, had disappeared, the despair of those first few years when it became clear that death was lashing out on a grand scale and I would have to flee. The routine struggle for survival, a struggle without weapons and therefore tough as nails, had relinquished despair to the background. And the increasing futility of trying to stay alive had also driven out the fear of dying.

Who or what did I have to stay alive for? For myself? It seemed so senseless. Sometimes a kind of resignation settled over me, fear made way for fatalism. I no longer cared about going on with head unbowed. Who or what would I bow to? To those women? Not a chance. I struggled with the vague premonition that giving up would make my life a hell, that giving up meant pain, intense pain. I had learned to respect my intuition for what it was worth, and it forced me at such moments to overcome my weakness and tear myself free of the rapture that sometimes welled up around the easiest of solutions: surrender.

I had gradually become used to surviving on my own. Only that first winter was truly difficult, especially being cold all the time, but now I could easily make it through even the coldest days with only a sweater. My body had adapted to a different range of temperatures. And if I couldn't find enough food on my own, there were enough villages around where I could steal it. Things were a bit more difficult in winter, but my old poacher's tricks were deeply ingrained, and the force of necessity brought them to the surface and whetted them on experience.

It was surprising how quickly I became used to a primitive life, without a house, without the convenience of running water and electricity, without the mass of appliances that an extensive distribution network had once brought into our homes almost unnoticed. I'd never thought I could do without them, but strangely enough I never really missed them. There was barely enough time to reflect on what I did miss, on the luxury of books and leisure; I had to eat and maintain a minimum of hygiene and safety. When there was time to muse, like now, and I hadn't fallen asleep from exhaustion, I would spend hours marveling at what had happened to the world.

I was lying at the edge of a heronry, flat on my back on a thick bed of moss, half dreaming. Suddenly the birds in the treetops stretched their necks. I pricked up my ears. Animals were an invaluable warning system; their senses hadn't been blunted by centuries of contact with sophisticated technological prostheses. The birds flew up, croaking. Far, far away I heard the irregular rumble of a straining engine. I cursed wholeheartedly, stood up and slunk off.

It had been so peaceful. I was already hoping they had given up. I hadn't gone close to the villages, where the risk of being spotted was greatest, for a long time. That had been hard to do, because surviving without raiding the villages was almost impossible. I was safe in the woods; almost no one ever ventured so far from home.

I withdrew deeper into the colony and lay down behind some brambles, in among the blueberry bushes but close enough to the edge to see what was happening. Ten yards away was the creek, lying in a hollow through which I could escape from the heart of the colony if necessary.

The roaring grew in intensity, the engine whined. The vehicle was having trouble climbing the slippery path up the hill. It was that dirty white Landcruiser again, a Mad Max–like vehicle with a heavy machine gun mounted on the back. A woman was standing upright in the bed of the Landcruiser, holding on to the gun; four others, clutching their automatic rifles, were seated on a bench in the back. Once, they would never have ventured off the road, but they would undoubtedly change their tactics if they knew I was around. Then they would search until they'd found me. Fortunately, they didn't seem to be paying much attention to the surroundings. Maybe they weren't even looking for me; perhaps it was a routine patrol.

No such luck. The vehicle drove past, only to stop further up the road, almost at the top of the hill. The women jumped out and stood with their rifles at the ready, covering all four corners of the Landcruiser. The herons screeched and went gliding away from the colony, their lives worth more to them than their offspring. I held my breath, ridiculously enough, for the women were too far away to hear me. It was a reflex I couldn't suppress.

The doors of the Mad Max swung open and two women climbed out. One of them was the stately blonde I'd seen earlier on one of these patrols. Even from where I lay I could feel her presence, she radiated that much personality. A rifle dangled loosely from her shoulder. The women never wore uniforms. The blonde was dressed in jeans and a loose-fitting, light-blue shirt. She was clearly in command, for when she gave the signal the woman operating the machine gun swung the barrel of the weapon toward my part of the woods. She hung her rifle on the car door, took a pair of binoculars from the front seat and began peering in my direction.

It was the first time she'd ever done that. She was on to something, that much was clear. I forced myself to keep down, not make a dive for the creek, and lay as low as I could.

The screen was filled with a preposterous wriggling, a mass of minuscule cells that squirmed past each other aimlessly, cutting sharply left and right, alert tadpoles with vibrating tails to propel their shiny heads. Their endless ramble and scatter was a search for the substances they were programmed to find, but couldn't locate in this artificial environment: the sterile medium drove the cells wild.

They were perfectly equipped to do the one thing they were made for. Their tails were exactly the right length to carry them through their long journey at optimal speed, and with a minimum of stress for the scrambling cell head itself. Just long enough to develop enough velocity without weighing down the cell with any superfluous mass.

But in the sterile medium, the cells didn't know what to do. Their precision-tuned velocity took them nowhere. Nothing they found meant a thing to them, there was no tube from which they were forcefully sprayed, no moist darkness in which beckoning molecules lured them to meet the siren. So the lashing tails and searching heads would run in circles, until their energy was exhausted, until they fell still and died a fruitless death. Nature isn't stingy with cells. Especially not with male reproductive cells.

Then suddenly, there was commotion on the screen: a flood of purplish blue heads with white edges rushed in to mingle with the translucent cells. The activity became feverish, the cells agitated, yet they continued to swim around aimlessly . . . until a ripple passed across the screen, and the picture changed. Now the cells struck at each other with trilling tails, the movement slowed, heads knocked together, vibrating cells wrestled at loggerheads, became stuck to each other, tore loose, reopened their chaotic attack, cells from one mass against those of the other.

This could go on for hours, Kristina knew that by now. She had seen the phenomenon before, but it always amazed her, the tenacity, the stamina with which the cells kept up the attack until their energy pumps cut out and tail could no longer propel head to a new attack in service of the collective millions with a single goal: seeing to it that one of their own was first to reach the divine siren, to the greater glory of the whole.

"Purple-white's going to win again," the woman slouching in front of the screen predicted. "I'm starting to get a picture of the hierarchy within the system. Unfortunately, though, we still have no idea what the mechanism is behind it. It must be something simple, something fairly straightforward, without too many variables; the results are always the same."

Kristina rested her hands on the woman's shoulders. Jasmine was fascinated by the kamikaze hypothesis, even though it was a male discovery and already a decade old, but the theory had never achieved general acceptance and men had never grasped its ramifications. It had been a classic case of the old vicious circle: lack of interest in the hypothesis had obstructed the search for its experimental evidence, thereby stunting any further interest. But Jasmine had revived it. She had found the key to experiments that produced results: the addition to the sterile medium of the chemical lure produced by the ovum to show sperm cells the way. As soon as this substance was added, friendly cells became enemies.

Jasmine saw her experiments with the kamikazes largely as a finger exercise. They served more to amuse her than to provide any additional insight into the principles that interested her. But they were fun to carry out, and she'd added a bit of color to it all by setting up a contest between the samples at her disposal. She was always varying the dyes she used to mark the specimens; that gave the experiment a cheery touch.

She squeezed out a tiny drop of lure onto the edge of the glass slide, and saw on-screen how the cells turned in unison to face the same direction. An enzyme with irresistible powers of attraction. Then she touched a key on the console in front of her. The movement on the screen slowed, then quite literally froze; the combative sperm cells had been frozen into their substrate. An assistant would later magnify a number of samples on the screen and count the number of cells rendered inviable by enemy attack. That would be the final score.

"I still can't figure out how nature ever arrived at such a waste of cellular material," Jasmine sighed. "Somewhere in the course of evolution there must have been a sort of arms race of unparalleled proportion. Individuals who produced more cells per ejaculation must have had the competitive edge in fertilization, and in passing their capacity as cell-producer along to following generations. And it must have been because they were better at eliminating enemy cells; after all, only one cell is needed for fertilization itself. Billions of sperm cells were sacrificed in the male struggle for insemination. It's mind-boggling."

Jasmine's obsession with the kamikaze hypothesis was fueled by her hope of sorting out the mechanism behind it, and so of finding an acceptable explanation for why nature had chosen such a wasteful option for the survival of the human species. The tens of millions of sperm cells that were squirted into a woman at ejaculation, and which then scrambled posthaste up the fallopian tubes, were obviously not all destined to achieve fertilization. The masses acted as a unit, like a single tissue of individual, fast-moving cells linked together by simple chemical substances. When the group's chemical feelers detected a foreign signal, an enemy, most of the cells stopped paying attention to the sweet allure of the fertilizable egg and just flung themselves on their hated rivals, even into the darkest recesses of the female uterus.

Men weren't the only ones who acted crazy when it came to the exclusive possession of a woman; their cells also went berserk when they came across the residue of contact with a stranger. The sharpest heads bored into the largely defenseless bodies of the cells left behind in the uterus after an earlier ejaculation. If that had been a few days beforehand, the struggle was over soon enough; the older cells no longer had the vitality to defend themselves against the upstarts, who failed in turn to realize that they had probably arrived too late anyway.

A prostitute's loins must once have been the scene of a daily massacre at the cellular level, a gruesome struggle between the sperm cells of a handful of horny men. The sperm that ran down the legs of a whore must have been full of murdered cells, tangles of drilled-through heads, cells gone haywire in the suicidal attempt to clear the way for that one cell that was faster than the mass, one cell which, if it succeeded in fertilizing the egg, would also bear the others' genes on to the following generation.

Kristina, who was no scientist but something of a sports enthusiast, compared the kamikaze sperm to another case of machismo: American football, in which the role of most of the unit was to eliminate the opponents standing in the way of the man with the ball.

"Did you want to talk to me?" Jasmine asked when she had stopped looking at the screen.

Kristina sat down. "We've been getting fairly regular reports for some time now about sightings of a non-inactivable, around thirty miles from here," she said, "but we've never been able to get a fix on him. I'm afraid he's well adapted and that he'll be hard to catch. I just wanted to know if you needed him for any reason, otherwise I won't take any risks."

Jasmine thought about it for a moment. "Maybe your informants are wrong," she suggested. "Some women are still seeing things."

Kristina didn't think so; the reports were too consistent, and came from too many different villages. They didn't seem at all like the persistent rumors that had caused her so much trouble elsewhere. By now she had learned how to recognize a potential problem when she saw one. This year she hadn't been mistaken once. And people were gradually becoming used to the new developments: they realized that the situation was under control, and they would come to no harm, even if problems did show up here and there. The information they passed on was accurate. But it hadn't always been like that, especially not at first. There had been a few incidents with a few innocent victims back then, and people had been too scared to cooperate.

All things considered, though, they had gotten through it quite well, Kristina felt, and she planned to keep it that way. But for the first time since she had started doing this work, she felt unsure of herself. All signs indicated that a non-inactivable was roaming around the area where the alert had been given, but they'd found no trace of him. There was a chance that he'd been trained to survive under difficult conditions. She was afraid of running into a Rambo, someone who could wreak havoc all on his own; with her limited experience, she wasn't sure she could handle that.

Jasmine caught her worried look and put an arm around her waist.

"Don't get too worked up about it," she said. "Just see what happens. Let me know as soon as you have some more information. I can always decide then whether I want to have him. But don't you want to attend the next performance by our revered matriarch? It would be a chance for you to see how she works in real life. Her cycle is about to recommence."

Kristina sighed. When would Diana stop pestering the public with her doctrinal blather? Until she stopped doing that, people could never forget the traumas her program had stirred up. It was time for her to start leaving well enough alone. People had suffered enough.

"The writer Virginia Woolf knew all about it. She was a sensible woman, way ahead of her time. Back in 1929, in her book *A Room of One's Own,* she posed the following questions: *'Have you any notion how many books are written about women in the course of one year? Have you any notion how many are written by men? Are you aware that you, perhaps, are the most discussed animal in the universe?'* An animal, yes indeed, as classified by the aloof observer, the male. And do you know how Woolf characterized Professor Von X, author of the standard work *The Mental, Moral and Physical Inferiority of the Female Sex*? As a fellow who would 'jab his pen on the paper as if he were killing some noxious insect as he wrote.'

"Isn't it striking that Lucy, our oldest known human ancestor, was a woman who lived three million years ago? And that females are therefore associated with primitive human life, while more recent curiosities, such as Pharaoh Ramses of ancient Egypt or the hunter Otzi found in the Austrian alps, were men; indeed more than men, conquerors and hunters?

"Did you ever realize that the Greek scholar Aristotle, universally lauded as a genius until only recently, once described the female sex as a freak of nature, too cold to transform its menstrual blood into sperm? In his view, only the male contributed to the essence—the form and objective—of the life being incubated in the womb, while the woman did nothing more than provide the physical space for it to live.

"Did you know that the Enlightenment-era thinker René Descartes, the pioneer of modern science, still thought that the human soul was derived from sperm?

"Has anyone ever told you that the seventeenth-century botanist Rudolf Camerarius, who first demonstrated the existence of sexes in plants, stressed that he had awarded the *noble name* of the male reproductive organ, and an active role in reproduction, to the stamen, while the female pistil had to make do with a passive role and no name?

"Have you read that Cesare Lombroso, the famous nineteenth-century Italian physician, dared to write about women? *Women allow themselves to be operated upon as though their flesh is the body of another. At childbirth they experience relatively little pain. They also undergo dental operations with greater ease than men, who lose consciousness more readily under such circumstances.* Did you pick up on that: *lose consciousness?* For women, the term would undoubtedly have been: *fall into a swoon.* And make no mistake about it, Lombroso was not out to demonstrate that women are braver than men. On the contrary. He considered tolerance to physical stress to be a vestige of the ability of lower species to regenerate lost organs. A capacity apparently lost by the higher species, though remnants were supposedly still found in the lower races and the lower social classes—meaning women and children. Our courage was not courage, but indifference. Our strength was not strength, but insensitivity.

"Do you recall the most important theorem of the Victorian scholar James McGrigor Allan, who wasn't simply some hack wordsmith, but a highly respected man of his day? *In the animal and vegetable kingdoms we find this invariable law—rapidity of growth, inversely proportionate to the degree of perfection at maturity. The higher the animal or plant in the scale of being, the more slowly does it reach its utmost capacity of development. Girls are physically and mentally more precocious than boys. The human female arrives sooner than the male at maturity, and furnishes one of the strongest arguments against the alleged equality of the sexes. The quicker appreciation of girls is the instinct, or intuitive faculty in operation; while the slower boy is an example of the latent reasoning power not yet developed. Compare them in after-life, when the boy has become a young man full of intelligence, and the girl has been educated into a young lady reading novels, working crochet, and going into hysterics at the sight of a mouse or a spider.'*

"Do you have any idea how some Victorian thinkers referred to motherly love, which was nevertheless regarded at the time as the highest thing a woman could achieve? They called it *'a ridiculous, overworked fuss about a product brought into the world through the excretory conduits.'* "

Diana paused, her face flushed with suppressed rage. Her own monologues could make her hysterical in no time. She seldom, if ever, engaged in a dialogue. She tended to just ramble on, sprinkling her meandering arguments with lengthy quotes, then stopping to remain sunk in thought. She rarely listened to what visitors had to say. That was common knowledge by now, so most people said nothing when they were around her.

By now Kristina was familiar with a few of the scientific classics herself. Since the war, almost everyone had become somewhat versed in the principles of evolutionary theory and genetics. Among the authors she had read was Thomas Huxley, fervent defender of the once muchmaligned theories of Charles Darwin, the founder of evolutionary science. When the American Civil War was over, Huxley noted that although the slaves had now been freed, the female half of the world's population remained in bondage. *"Their hair shall curl no less gracefully merely because they have brains in their heads,"* was his comment on women and men's dealings with them. But Kristina held her tongue as well. Diana had no tolerance for arguments that didn't suit her.

For someone with her responsibilities, Diana looked quite ordinary. Small and slender, slightly rounded shoulders, reddish brown hair with—even though she was barely in her forties—a good deal of gray, granny glasses and an inconspicuous way of dressing: the classic pegged skirt and plain blouse. It was a look she had adopted on purpose—very few of Diana's actions were unintentional. She had explained her reasons in a speech dealing with the spiral of beauty into which women had been forced by men, the drive to become ever more beautiful, and so live up to the world's expectations. The attitude was based on the sexual selection theory of Charles Darwin, who had been badly mistaken when he claimed that the power over natural selection was in the hands of men, and that women could use beauty to their own advantage.

Diana's drab appearance was in sharp contrast to the lavish furnishings of her flat at the laboratory. Beneath the glass dome there was a luxurious armchair, almost the only piece of furniture in a huge room otherwise filled with statues and cast models of black butlers in green or red livery, statues she rearranged often, as if to create the impression that these servile men truly walked about in her home.

During her tantrums, which were becoming increasingly frequent, she would throw the entire collection to the ground, then walk away and leave her assistants to clean up the mess, set the fallen pieces aright, replace the broken statues with new ones. The little studio that made them had its hands full: great care was taken to keep Diana supplied with enough butlers on whom to vent her rage.

On one occasion she had gone berserk in the laboratory itself; her bloodlust had destroyed years of scientific effort. And, of course, everyone knew how she had reacted to what she saw as an insulting lack of scientific recognition: she had turned the world upside down.

Amid the butlers was a small tublike container, and a podium with a music stand and a chair. Diana was wild about the harp and the cello, both instruments that were played between the legs. To Kristina, the posture had something erotic about it, but she wasn't sure if Diana felt that way too. The musicians she invited were always very discreet about their experiences. Almost none of them were known for their stunning renditions. Cultural excellence had declined in status the last few years.

"I just want to warn both of you that the problems with the experiments must not be allowed to get out of hand," Diana said suddenly.

Kristina braced herself. Every time Diana had spoken specifically about the way the program was going, there'd been trouble. When she drifted along, as she usually did, she was simply hopeless; but at least she wasn't dangerous as long as she had her head in the clouds. To a certain extent, she remained fairly abstract even when she became specific; the real problem was her refusal to listen to reason. Silence was the answer, as long as possible, and then hope that the storm would blow over without doing too much damage.

"We're making no progress at all in isolating the pheromones and hormones we need," Diana stated, "and we've reached a dead end in the search for the genes that play a key role in keeping the program going. I want that to change, and fast."

Kristina felt Jasmine go tense. She hoped she would be able to control her anger. The delays in the studies Diana was referring to were partly the result of her own destruction of a number of experimental subjects, during one of her tantrums, ruining a set of promising data and forcing Jasmine to start her observations all over again.

Unfortunately, suitable subjects were becoming harder to find. To make things worse, most of them exhibited defects that could compromise the results.

Diana was, of course, aware of the problem. She spoke to Kristina. "I want you to intensify your hunting parties. Your unit has been bringing in fewer and fewer men lately. Every non-inactivable you locate should be captured alive. It's the only way we can definitively round off the program as planned. Double the number of Warriors. It's ridiculous that there are still non-inactivables running around free."

Good thing there still were a few, Kristina thought: at the rate Diana was going through experimental subjects, the program would become stranded anyway, due to a lack of suitable study material. But still she said nothing.

And no one asked her opinion. Or Jasmine's, even though she was the laboratory supervisor. Diana had delivered her message; the rest was irrelevant. She put on a coat and gestured to them to follow. Obviously to the building's TV studio, where she was about to begin a new segment of her series, her brainchild: the program she had named after herself, DIANA.

Kristina had always been disgusted by stupid or megalomaniacal people who christened their achievements with their own first name: Freddy's Burgers, Jim's Marketing. Diana claimed, however, that the program *wasn't* named after herself, but after the goddess of the hunt. Because it was about the greatest hunt in human history. And the most successful.

Diana began this installment with the same footage as last time. She hadn't even bothered to update the text. She really was becoming lax. What would people think about this?

Kristina sank down in an armchair and listened for the umpteenth time to the familiar sentences, spoken in a monotone punctuated by brief pauses.

Diana stared with no apparent emotion into the camera, barely blinking. She could just as well have been a robot. Fortunately, she had enough charisma to cover up her lack of rhetorical skill. Besides, there was always the chance that she would add something new to her discourse.

"In one of his plays, the Greek dramatist Euripides gave the stage to the antihero Hippolytus . . . a man who hated sex, and who became the symbol of the cult surrounding the single-parent concept . . . or, to be more precise: the debate surrounding the indispensability of mothers. . . . In a long monologue, he confronted the god-king Zeus with his problem. . . . He wanted to know why Zeus had created those terrible women. . . . *If you wanted us poor mortals to have offspring,* he moaned, *why didn't you simply arrange for us to buy them . . . ?* Hippolytus longed for a world populated only by men. . . .

"His arguments raised a number of interesting issues. . . . The reason for sex, for example, the sense behind sexual reproduction, the need for sexes to differ. . . . These are questions we have been dealing with for a long time, and we now believe we can provide an answer . . . an answer that has played an essential role in the DIANA program now being carried out with undeniable success . . . an answer that will be explained in this series. . . .

"The firmest proof that sexual reproduction is not the one true way is found in looking at bacteria. . . . Bacteria thrive everywhere. . . . A single gram of soil or a human intestine contains ten billion microbes, twice as many microbes as Earth's human population has ever numbered. . . . The human body contains more microbes than cells. . . . One could claim that humans exist only by the grace of bacteria, because we form such an attractive biotope. . . .

"Bacteria are not only omnipresent, they are also timeless. . . . Long before life as we choose to define it was possible on Earth, bacteria flourished. . . . Before the sun shone so brightly, back when the days and nights passed more quickly than they do now, back before a quarter of the atmosphere was oxygen and when the earth's surface was scourged by ultraviolet rays—even then, bacteria flourished. . . . They divided and divided, each one sacrificing itself and splitting in two, at a furious tempo that finally conquered the world, every world, from a planet without oxygen to the human intestine. . . .

"By means of simple fission, bacteria reproduce at a rate that makes one wonder why nature never abandoned the drive for sexual contact. . . . Simple cellular fission involves no waste of resources on a sex that bears no offspring, like the human male. . . . There are any number of examples of higher organisms that reproduce asexually with great success: the strawberry with its tendrils, the tomato with its buds, the duckweed on ponds. . . . Drones are the product of asexual reproduction among bees, sons without fathers, born of an unfertilized egg cell, created for one chance in a great many to fertilize a queen, once and upon pain of death, to allow her to bring forth masses of females. . . .

"Many different types of insects thrive and reproduce freely without sex. . . . Like the tiny wasp fortunate enough to reproduce asexually and see only daughters crawl from her unfertilized eggs. . . . But after eating honey treated with penicillin, males reappear among these wasps, males with sperm. . . . The wasp had once snuck a bacterium into its egg cells that kept it from having to reproduce sexually, but that bacterium was killed by the penicillin. . . . The female wasps entered a symbiotic relationship with a bacterium, so they wouldn't have to tolerate males. . . . It was in the bacterium's own best interests to see to it that no males were produced, for it could thrive only in the rich nutritional environment of the egg cell. . . . If males were to make up half the wasp population, the bacteria's lebensraum would also be halved. . . .

"Sexual reproduction is not self-evident. . . . Single-celled diatoms die once they have reproduced sexually. . . . They continue to bloom as long as they don't become involved with another cell. . . . Occasionally a pair of these unicellular aquatic organisms is overcome by the irresistible urge to bond, to flow together, to become one and exchange genes. . . . A fatal error . . . a few days after the diatoms consummate their romance, comes their irrevocable doom. . . . Sex drives them to their death. . . . Sex introduces mortality. . . . Species that reproduce asexually do not die, they divide. . . . Species that use sex, however, must die. . . . The parents must make room for their offspring. . . . God took immortality from Adam and Eve after they had tasted of sexual sin. . . . Sex is deadly. . . .

"Yet the fact remains that sexual reproduction is widespread. . . . Sex seems to be useful. . . . Everywhere around us, organisms are on a spree of sexual fusion, despite the slow rate of reproduction this entails, despite the amount of energy wasted, despite the death inherent to it. . . .

"Sexual reproduction obviously offers great advantages. . . . Grass in a well-tended garden can go on reproducing asexually for centuries, but as soon as one forgets to mow it, disaster strikes, the urge for sexual contact arises. . . .

"Aphids, who prefer to reproduce asexually, switch to sex when their surroundings become harsh and hostile. . . . They can no longer afford to put the genetic eggs of their future in one and the same basket. . . . They must court variation in order to protect themselves from that which is to come. . . .

"Even the oldest bacteria on earth realized that. . . . Their genetic material must have taken an enormous beating when struck by particularly strong doses of ultraviolet radiation. . . . Recovery was needed, but recovery could not take place from within, for nature had not provided mechanisms that could actively repair genetic material. . . . That's why nature took refuge in what seemed a makeshift solution: the introduction of external genetic material to replace the defective parts. . . .

"That makeshift solution became sexual reproduction. . . . Cells fused, bringing together copies of their genetic material. . . . This allowed them to guarantee vitality under a wide range of conditions, and introduced the variety so advantageous to survival. . . . Cells exchanged genetic information and rearranged their contents to form new constellations, new combinations of characteristics sometimes disadvantageous, and then quickly eliminated, sometimes advantageous and preserved. . . . Cell fusion ensured a continuous blend of characteristics, from which the best combinations were selected. . . .

"At first, sexual contact had nothing to do with reproduction, only with the exchange of characteristics needed to promote survival and asexual fission. . . . But the two functions became interwoven. . . . Nature found the price of transition too high. . . .

"Yet it was up to nature to ensure that the conditions justified the price paid for sexual reproduction. . . . In comparison with binary cell fission, sex is incredibly expensive. . . . All the energy that has to be invested in locating and winning over a reproductive partner, all the foolish rituals of seduction and stupid infatuations, the whole fuss during the act itself, all of this with no guarantee of success, without the certainty that the child produced will be what one wants. . . .

"The genetic investment is staggering as well. . . . With sexual reproduction, one-half of the genetic material passed on to the offspring comes from someone else, from the indispensable partner. One has no control over that fifty percent of the material not necessarily visible in the partner: his image does not reflect all the information he contains. . . . The price paid for sexual reproduction is high. . . .

"After extensive research, however, we have come to the conclusion that this price is more than justified by the way sex ensures effective resistance to illness and decay. . . . Sex is needed to combat parasites. . . . Parasites form the major threat to the human species. . . . They are lurking around every corner, waiting to attach themselves to a cell, penetrate it and deplete it to their own ends. . . . Sex allows a limitless rearrangement of genetic characteristics, so that parasites must continually adapt themselves in their struggle for optimal reproduction. . . . Sex prevents parasites from being able to operate routinely, from easily breaching the defenses the cell throws up. . . . Sex guarantees better chances of survival. . . ."

A long pause, the classic pause before the end of every sermon.

"That's why we have decided to keep sex in the program," Diana concluded. "The disadvantages simply did not outweigh the advantages."

Ellen turned off the TV. She shivered, not only because what she'd heard gave her the willies—that woman just never learned—but also because the room was cold. Spring was on its way. The sun shone warmly on occasion, but she had become spoiled, she had always lived in heated houses and felt uncomfortable wearing layer after layer of sweaters. She liked being able to feel her own skin, she was used to walking around most of the time in long, loose T-shirts.

But the heating was on the blink. She had been on a waiting list to have it repaired for a long time, but no one had come by and no one could tell her how long it would take before it was her turn.

She couldn't get used to the idea that things would never be the same. She was a real city mouse. Village life didn't appeal to her at all. She couldn't reconcile herself to the trivial existence imposed on her. Only a few memories remained of her childhood in the village where she was born, disconnected flashes, a quarrel between fishermen and nature lovers about the stress anglers caused for the bird life around a municipal pond, a speech her parents made her give at a parish celebration, which had turned into a minor disaster when she forgot her text, the commotion surrounding the biannual, second-rate soccer match between the team from the village center and the one from an outlying hamlet, men who dressed like bicycle racers to go out for a spin with their wives, church bells that rang every time someone died, starting with a loud bell for a dead man and a muted one for a woman.

She had been glad to be able to leave for the city. The visits to her parents, which had become increasingly rare as the years went by, had confirmed her feeling that a village was a place life had passed by. She could never understand how her father, a man whose job allowed him to travel and therefore make comparisons, could appreciate the local restaurants, praise the local artists, involve himself in what he so coyly referred to as "municipal administrative affairs." City life had so much more flavor, but even during their rare visits to her world, her parents had never seemed to taste the difference.

Never in her wildest dreams had she thought she would end up in a village again. She hated it more than she had when she was young. She even missed the blaring burglar alarms that had irritated her in the city, and the demonstrators who blocked major arterials at the drop of a hat, trying to involve others in their discontent.

The silence was particularly hard to take. Silence that amplified the village sounds so loudly it made her jump. Without the bustle of tens of thousands of people on the go, even the chirping of the tiniest sparrow became unpleasantly shrill. And she slept badly. When she finally nodded off, the least little noise would shake her wide awake. Nature was not people-friendly. She was paralyzed with fear one morning when she opened her eyes to find the body of a bird dangling in front of her face. The cat had jumped up onto the bed with a dead chickadee in its mouth. She hadn't been able to sleep for days afterwards. Julie called it shell shock, from the war, and said it would be over soon. But death was something she thought she would never get over.

Things kept getting more difficult for Bert, too. He was plagued by loneliness, not accepted in the little community of which he had also become a part through no choice of his own. His eighth birthday was next week. Ellen had toyed with the idea of giving a party, the way they used to, but Julie and her other friends didn't think it was such a good idea. It could be seen as provocation. Circumstances were against him. Ellen had argued that he was only a child, that he bothered no one and was simply trying to make the best of things, but her plea fell on deaf ears. As far as her son was concerned, there was little tolerance to be found. But she refused to give him up. She would fight for him to the bitter end.

She heaved a deep sigh. Julie put her arm around her. Fingers glided through her curls. It calmed her a bit.

"Don't get so wound up about it," Julie said. "You know there's no going back."

Ellen knew that, but the changes had been so drastic: different surroundings, a village no less, and no work, except around the house or on the little plot of land the authorities had allocated to them. Boredom was the order of the day.

Her social contacts were extremely limited. There was still no phone book, for example, which meant she couldn't locate her old girlfriends. She had no idea what had happened to them. The women she met in the village, most of them in the round-the-clock bar on the main square, were all new to her. She had been forced to start from scratch. Contacts were hard to make. Strained, because there were no common ties. And the suspicion stirred up by DIANA settled only slowly.

"They say there's a man wandering around in the neighborhood," Julie said. "Someone down at the bar saw him close to a chicken coop at the edge of the village. When he saw that she'd spotted him, he disappeared. She notified DIANA, but the patrol they sent out after him couldn't find a trace. Maybe it was another false alarm."

It wasn't a false alarm. Ellen had seen him too, from far away, too far to be absolutely sure it was a man, but she'd sensed it. She hadn't told anyone, not even Julie, because she would only have become angry and notified the authorities.

Ellen wasn't frightened by the idea of a man in the neighborhood. It gave her a warm feeling, a feeling she hadn't come across often in her new life. Julie did her best, she was sweet and entertaining, but that was it. Ellen had occasionally had intimate contacts with girls in the past. Contacts that stemmed naturally from her work. She had become a doctor, a breast-cancer specialist, after she had had her own breasts removed at the age of twenty-five.

She'd had such a nice body. She still felt that her own breasts had been among the most beautiful she'd ever felt. But after her sister and one of her aunts died of breast cancer, she had decided to undergo preventive surgery. The risk that she also had the genetic form of breast cancer was too great. When they finally came up with a test to isolate the faulty gene responsible for the disorder, she found out that her breasts had been removed for no reason. Her gene didn't have the defect. Yet she hadn't been shocked by the discovery. She was still convinced that she had made the right choice.

The dilemma had aroused her fascination with breast cancer and bosoms. The investigative probing during her work had often softened to a sensuous caress, which was how she had met most of her girlfriends. But that superficial homosexuality had been so free and easy; now that it had become more or less obligatory, it didn't work for her.

She hadn't gotten far with her scientific work. Events had caught up with her career. The value of an individual human life had become so relative that the fight against cancer was reduced to a senseless and marginal scuffle. Her own experiences had caused her to rebel more strongly than most other women against the death which had become so omnipresent. But she'd had no more grip on the situation than any of the others. Like everyone else, she had been caught up by the course of events and had finally ended up, more or less by accident, in this big house with Julie. She was pragmatic enough to realize that she had little choice but to play along. One life more or less didn't matter to anyone these days.

Her train of thought was brusquely interrupted.

"Have you given any thought to having a baby?" Julie asked.

Ellen was startled, even though she had known the question would come up again. It was hard for her. She didn't want to have a child with Julie, but she wasn't really sure how to be clear about it and diplomatic at the same time. She had Bert, of course. It had been difficult to get him into the village with her. The head official in the village had asked a few pointed questions, but after enough pleading she'd finally shrugged and given him a residence permit. Julie was polite to him, but she kept her distance. For his own good, she said, but she also avoided mentioning the boy.

She had only recently begun to talk about having a child of her own. A subtle, seemingly offhand remark, but Ellen had caught the hint. Julie had no children, although she had tried to get pregnant before. Ellen hadn't responded that first time, and Julie had waited so long to bring it up again that Ellen had almost thought she wasn't serious.

But this was the real thing. Julie had already asked about waiting lists and the chances of success, and had even taken her medical file to the laboratory. The people at the lab had assured her that there was no problem as far as they could see. She and Ellen were both the right age, thirty-four. They led a normal life, and the service itself ran so efficiently that waiting lists were practically nonexistent. As soon as they made a final decision, she could call for an appointment. If all went well, she could be pregnant in another three or four months.

Ellen felt depressed. She wasn't sure she wanted to spend the rest of her life with Julie, and she was afraid a new baby would mean even less attention for Bert. Things were hard enough for the boy, and she was ready to do anything to make his little world as livable as possible. She knew Julie had trouble with that, and she was afraid the pressure would only increase. Julie wouldn't dare to lay a finger on Bert, even though the legal system had become so brittle that a murder would almost certainly go unpunished. Julie was in love with her, and would do nothing that would damage their relationship.

Love was a powerful weapon, Ellen knew that, and she made good use of that knowledge. This time, too. "You know how hard it is for me," she whispered. "If you really love me, give me some room. I'll come around." She kissed Julie lightly on the cheek.

"We don't have forever," Julie said.

Ellen pressed up against her. "The technology's been perfected," she countered. "Once we decide to start, we won't lose any time. There's no hurry."

Julie said nothing, but the fingers in Ellen's hair stopped moving. She was losing her patience.

The door opened and Ellen jumped up. Bert was standing in the doorway, sobbing, his mouth and pajamas covered in blood. Ellen screamed, ran to him and took him in her arms. The boy couldn't speak. Blood was gushing from his mouth. He held up his toothbrush.

Ellen took her handkerchief and pressed it against his bleeding gums. The handkerchief immediately turned a bright red. "What did you do?" she shrilled, but the child couldn't answer, he only wept and shook his head, clawing at her arms. She picked him up. "We have to get him to a doctor," she said firmly.

Julie stood up and looked at her. "He can't go to a doctor," she replied. "You know that as well as I do."

Ellen knew. At wits' end, she pushed the handkerchief into her weeping child's mouth.

I was almost sure it was Ellen. The yellow bodysuit she wore when working in her garden plot had attracted my attention one day. She used to wear it all the time, with jeans, very casual, as well as with a dress skirt. Even after her operation and the plastic surgery, it made her look very sexy. Going against my better instincts, I crawled up for a closer look. It was Ellen all right. She was out working in a field, imagine that, Ellen with her delicate hands.

I'd never understood why she married a pharmacist. Pharmacists were the acme of tedium and asexuality, bony men with big glasses who got nervous when they had to sell condoms, and women who wore white lab coats over a blouse buttoned to the chin. How the hell could she ever have fallen for a man like that? She had so much fire in her body.

She'd been reluctant about my advances at first. She'd resisted, kept putting off a date. When she made the foolish mistake of asking her husband if she could go out with me, she immediately realized how unwise that had been.

After a lot of hesitation and a few setbacks, it all began over coffee in some out-of-the-way place where friends and family wouldn't see her. I was dangerous company. At first she kept playing games, putting off the inevitable, until I became so desperate that I suggested tossing for it, fully prepared to reconcile myself to the outcome. She got to make the toss, and to choose whether heads or tails would mean the beginning of an affair. I had a 50 percent chance, but also a boundless faith in providence. And, indeed, she flipped the coin and tossed herself into an affair.

She had been so fiery, with a passion that was new to her and that reinforced my rather low opinion of pharmacists. We made love in the strangest places, amid the dry manure on the floor of an abandoned stall, where she kept jumping up at the sound of two pigeons building their nest up in the rafters, on a terrace by the sea, where she wound her arms so tightly in an iron trellis that you could see the welts for weeks, and in a garage where her synthetic breasts had left their imprints all over the dusty hoods. The slight embarrassment she felt about her bosom was completely forgotten when she was making love.

But she never forgot it at other times. She always insisted that we take a bath together only by candlelight. She hated brightly lit bathrooms—they revealed too many details. She couldn't understand why people wanted candles to lend everything a *flou artistique* during an intimate dinner, when they looked their best anyway, but had no problem with bright lights when they took a bath together.

The first few evenings she was cautious, wary, until she started letting herself go. Our relationship was so passionate that we could no longer keep things in perspective—the ability to drown our personal problems and desires in contemplation of the billions of years the Earth had turned on its axis, the endless diversity of life and the insignificance of the individual was lost, all to no avail. I spent hours swaying to the CD I associated with her, *Blue Hotel* by Chris Isaak, wallowing in fantasies about what we would do together without the constraints that had plagued our relationship from the beginning. Sometimes I purposely made love to her so long and so hard that she complained about how her mouth hurt from all the kissing, or about how her labia had been rubbed raw with fucking; that made me feel good, knowing she would have to keep her pharmacist at bay for a while.

She could come on pretty strong herself. Sometimes, when she'd had enough of hours of kissing and caressing, she would roll me on my back, ride me up and down and come like a man. Lovelessly. And she almost always fell asleep right away afterwards; she had to be home on time, which always presented me with the dilemma of not wanting to wake her, of wanting to keep her with me all night, right up until breakfast. But that would have been the end of our relationship.

The one thing she refused to do was make love when she was having her period. She thought menstrual blood was disgusting. It nauseated her when I once pulled a bloody finger from between her legs and stuck it in my mouth. She refused to kiss me the rest of the night. She didn't know why she found it so horrible. But sometimes, in her dreams, she was plagued by visions of being swept along in a swirling stream of blood. Was it a premonition? Her pharmacist died, too, just like the others.

I watched her from the bushes for months. If there was anyone I could trust, it was Ellen. We'd remained close friends, even after the affair had cooled. I didn't recognize any of the other women in the villages I observed. The thing was to find out whether Ellen was open for contact. How could I be sure she wouldn't betray me? Months passed before I'd convinced myself that this was one thing I could never be certain of. I had absolutely no contact with women, so I had no idea how they had dealt with the facts and adapted to the new situation. Gradually, it dawned on me: I had nothing to lose. Why try to stay alive as long as possible? The least I could do was try to find out what had happened. Maybe there was some way to turn back the clock.

Ellen didn't come out to the garden all that often. She only went outside when the weather was good. Hoeing and weeding were things she must have hated with a passion. Most of the time she spent sitting on a chair in between the rows of vegetables, staring at the sky with her hands locked behind her head. She must have really hated foraging too—she never walked out of the village to look for berries or pick cherries. And whenever she did go out in the field, her girlfriend was with her. Another complication was her son; he went with her everywhere. He didn't seem to go to school, he usually sat playing in the sand.

I'd had the chance to approach her on two occasions. Both times I'd let the chance go by at the last moment. Not so much because I was afraid of being caught, but because I was afraid she wouldn't want to have anything to do with me; that would mean the most obvious road to contact with the new world had been rigorously cut off.

Now she was back again, wearing that same yellow bodysuit and a broad-brimmed sun hat. She was carrying Bert, and she put him down only when they reached the garden plot. He sank to the ground and began grubbing in the sand at her feet. She stood looking at him for a while, hands on her hips, then went to get her chair from the little ramshackle shed in one corner of the garden. She carried it over and sat down next to the boy as he played. Her mind was obviously on anything but hoeing and weeding.

I watched her for an hour and a half, an hour and a half during which she didn't take a step into the garden, only looked at her child and finally seemed to doze off. The moment had arrived. There was no one else in sight as I scrambled upright from under the bushes where I'd spent most of my days for the last few weeks. I walked out to her garden, moving in a crouch until I realized how absurd that was; anyone looking in my direction would see me anyway. It was a good thing the villages weren't guarded. If anyone did spot me, I'd have plenty of time to make the woods before they sounded the general alarm.

Ellen didn't see me until I'd reached her own plot. She remained sitting in her chair, frozen in amazement, then put her hands to her mouth and stared at me until I stopped in front of her, panting. I must have looked even wilder than I used to, although I never had been a textbook example of fine grooming. But that wouldn't have bothered her. She'd always talked about how attracted she was to my wild side.

"What are you doing here?" she asked once she found her voice. People ask the silliest questions when they're amazed.

"I have to talk to you," I said, sounding more agitated than I'd planned—it's hard to fake composure when you're really wound up. "Come to the woods with me. It's safer there."

She just stayed in her chair, staring at me in disbelief. Now that I was standing right in front of her, I could see how tired she looked. Her hands were covered with a fine maze of cracks, some gray had crept into her curls. She never would have let that happen in the old days.

"Ellen, please," I begged her.

That was a mistake. She shook off her amazement and stood up. She picked up the boy, who had been watching the whole scene without a word, and started walking away.

I stood there, petrified. I couldn't believe this was happening. "Ellen, don't leave me," I called after her, forgetting my own safety. "You're the only one I can trust." She kept walking. "Ellen, what about the boy?" I screamed at her. "He's going to die if you don't do something."

She stopped suddenly and bowed her head. Bert started crying. She turned around and I could see the tears in her eyes. She rocked the weeping child in her arms and looked at me, her head tilted slightly to one side. Then she walked back in my direction.

Bedbugs are wriggly little animals with faintly rustling antennae, which they use to feel at each other all the time. Even in situations like this one, where there is nowhere for them to go, they wander around restlessly; their instinct is stronger than they are, stronger than the little bit of experience they can retain but that can't stop them from roaming about, even in the most desperate surroundings. Bedbugs aren't built to make logical decisions.

"But they are fun to watch. Bedbugs are living proof that nature doesn't necessarily treat its mothers with respect. The male bedbug is a real go-getter, and he's exceptionally equipped for the job. His organ is a spear; not figuratively, like in bad erotic writing, but literally: a large and serrated protuberance that he drives forcefully into the belly of the female, and really into her belly, not through some canal provided by nature. Such canals have the disadvantage of an orifice to be sought and found, no simple task when confronted with a restless and resistant female.

"The male bedbug doesn't tinker around, either. When he meets an appealing female he simply sticks his spear into her soft underbelly and ejaculates through that vaginal wound into the fluid surrounding her organs. The sperm cells thread their way between the female's intestines until they reach a gland with a chemistry in which they can survive for a long time: a sort of deep freeze from which the female can draw when her eggs need fertilizing.

"Very few sperm cells actually reach that gland, but the bedbug method offers the advantage of freeing the males from the need to wait until the egg cells are ripe and can be fertilized. All they have to do is open their own private vagina in a female, which closes up again after intercourse in a healing process that doesn't take all that long. This drastic form of penetration must have cost the lives of a great many females before nature provided them with an efficient means of dealing with this deep abdominal wound. Nature gave them the Berlese gland, a minuscule organ named after the proud scientist whose advanced dyeing techniques isolated it from other cells and allowed him, by means of ingenious experimentation, to determine its function. Work the world must have waited for with bated breath. The gland secretes a substance which speeds up the healing of the wounds inflicted by rambunctious bedbug lovers.

"In their urge to penetrate, male bedbugs don't worry much about whether the abdomen they pierce is that of a female. A male bedbug unfortunate enough to wind up between the sheets with a riled member of the same sex also runs the risk of being skewered. Should he survive the attack—Berlese wasn't able to discover a repair gland among male bedbugs—he then lives with rival sperm cells floating in his bodily fluids. That might seem wasteful. But a shot in the abdomen of another male is no fruitless effort. The injected sperm cells mingle with the cells made by the host, and can survive for years. If the victim of such homosexual rape pounces on a female, he then runs the risk of having his attacker's sperm cells squirted into her body as well. With a bit of tough luck, those cells will be the ones to nestle in her storage organ, awaiting an egg cell to lure them into fertilization. Among bedbugs, an act of homosexual rape can result in offspring for the attacker."

"They're fun to watch," the woman in the white lab coat concluded her explanation of the biology of the bedbugs in the terrarium.

Ellen thought they were horrid. Shivers ran up and down her spine at the thought that there were male insects crawling around in her bed, armed with a spear to pierce the abdomen of the first of their kind that happened to come along. She had an aversion to insects, even butterflies and ladybugs. Butterflies made her think of caterpillars, not of papery wings, and she found the dried carcasses of ladybugs everywhere around the house.

The insect population had grown forcefully in the last few years. Reports occasionally filtered through about plagues that were on their way, termite invasions for example. Cockroaches and ants had become bigger pests than ever before, and they had free run of the house because there were almost no pesticides. The vermin seemed to know that.

"This is a millipede," the guide began cheerfully once they'd reached the next terrarium. "Sometimes, in his attempt to get close to the sex organ—which is located at the base of the female's neck—the male embraces his mate so intently that he wrings her head off. Nature didn't make reproduction any easier by splitting things up into two sexes."

Dumb bitch, Ellen swore to herself, keep your stupid stories to yourself. "Do you think perhaps we could get down to the reason we've come here?" she asked politely. "I'm not very fond of creepy crawlers."

The dumb bitch never blinked an eye. "Of course, this is only a bit of entertainment before we get to the explanatory remarks. Most people seem to enjoy it."

Julie laid a hand on Ellen's arm. She looked even more cheerful than the lady guide, and listened attentively to the stories about the insects, even though she wasn't at all interested in nature. She had spent a lot of time on her makeup this morning, and she'd been so wound up all night that she'd kept Ellen awake with her tossing and turning.

Since encountering her friend, Ellen slept worse than ever. It had taken her days to get over the shock. But she'd finally realized that he was right. She had to do something to save Bert. Doing nothing meant giving him up. She had to find out if he could be cured. That meant talking to the scientists. And they were in the laboratory in town.

Julie was surprised when she started talking about a child of her own accord, even though she still showed a certain hesitation about the idea—giving in too quickly would have looked suspicious. But she had promised to give some serious thought to it, and she'd insisted they make an appointment to find out about the procedures they would have to follow. Julie didn't waste any time contacting the laboratory. It was one of the few places in the area you could always reach. The woman at the lab said they could come by the next morning.

They took the bus into town. There was, of course, a bus stop close to the laboratory. Although the lab had been built in an old barracks complex, everything reminiscent of military life had been removed. The walls were freshly whitewashed, there were plants and flowers everywhere and the women they met smiled with forced amiability.

A guide was assigned to them at the reception desk, another of those exaggeratedly friendly people. They walked through a long corridor, down which generations of recruits had trotted on their way to drill practice, where they had learned to defend themselves against an enemy busy preparing itself for the same war, only in different barracks. But they had been prepared for the wrong war. The attack that had finally taken the world by surprise had met with no resistance worth mentioning.

When they reached a large green door, the guide turned to them. "This is one of our research laboratories," she said. They stepped inside.

The laboratory looked just like the one where Ellen had worked. A jumble of tubes, jars and petri dishes, and boxes of pipettes, filmy plastic gloves and filter paper clustered around keyboards and computer monitors. Research methods seemed to have changed little in the meantime. A few researchers were walking around in the room, paying no attention to the visitors. When Ellen asked one of them a question, her only reply was a wan smile.

"This is where we're refining our fertility techniques," the guide explained. "We want to reach the point where we can store unripe egg cells for years, and then let them ripen at the moment they're needed. We can isolate the egg cells from an aborted fetus or from the mother, by means of a simple, one-off procedure like the ones being carried out here.

"A fetus is a rich source of unripe egg cells. You could almost go so far as to say that a woman is lucky when her body rejects a fetus, because that allows us to save her daughter's egg cells. A three-month-old fetus contains something like seven million germ cells, primitive sex cells with the potential to become eggs. Unfortunately, only a few of these cells are available at the moment of ovulation. Most of them haven't developed into ripe egg cells by that time.

"One of the spearhead areas of our research is the attempt to find a biochemical substance that will help us to determine whether a ripe egg cell is also viable. There's no use in investing in nascent life if it contains a lethal defect.

"Furthermore, we hope to be able to simulate the conditions under which germ cells thrive, and bring them to full development. That's proving hard to do. It's funny how quickly germ cells, which are actually bearers of new life, die off when they're removed from their familiar surroundings. They just bunch together into metastatic lumps and plunge into a collective suicide.

"The ripening of an egg cell can easily take six months, so we're looking for a technique to speed things up without affecting the viability of the cells. That's going quite well. We've put together a combination of three growth factors that seem to form the perfect medium for cultivating germ cells. Within two years we hope to be able to do everything, up to and including conception, outside the mother's body. That will free us of our dependence on biological rhythms and unpleasant hormonal treatments."

"But does that mean the mother still has to bear the child herself?" Ellen asked ingenuously.

"Of course," the woman said without batting an eye. "We are carrying out exploratory research to see how far we can develop a fertilized egg cell under controlled conditions, but that's still in a preliminary phase. The environment of the womb is so complex that it is very hard to simulate. Artificially grown fetuses will be science fiction for a long time. But we're keeping the option open."

She paused for a moment to see if they had any further questions, then led them back out into a long hallway with rows of numbered doors.

Halfway down the hall she opened another door, and showed Ellen and Julie a sparsely furnished room with two neat metal cots and two small army-issue nightstands, the crooked metal doors of which were rusting around the edges. "We're still getting organized," she said apologetically. "We didn't expect the applications for pregnancy to start coming in so quickly. We'll be replacing the furniture soon with something a little more appropriate, a little more like the rest of the room."

"The rest of the room" consisted of pastel pink walls and green curtains with a bright tropical print of bananas and oranges—two kinds of fruit Ellen hadn't seen in what seemed like an eternity.

The woman closed the door again and opened the one next to it. There were the same sparse furnishings, but this time the walls were light blue, the curtains yellow. There were no decorations anywhere.

"These rooms are for the couples who come in for fertilization, to rest and relax," the woman explained. "They're all decorated differently. We don't want it to look like a hospital here, more like a special hotel. We have hundreds of rooms, so we'll never need a waiting list. The births themselves take place at home, unless there's too much risk of complications. And we have a team of midwives to help the couples at home during the delivery, and for the first few days afterwards."

Midwives had survived in the face of progress, Ellen reflected; some professions never went out of style.

"Now we'll go to the laboratory where your fondest wish will be coming true," the guide said, dragging out the old cliché that apparently still appealed to a lot of mothers, even modern ones.

The woman never stopped talking, not even during the short walk to the sex lab. "Some people wonder why we don't make a few clones from every fertilized egg cell, just separate them during the eight- or sixteen-cell stage. The truth is, we do have the technology; we can already restore the protective layer around the embryo after fission, and we know how to store the early embryos for later development. We could also simply remove the chromosomal set from an egg cell and replace it with one from a normal human cell, the classic cloning maneuver, to produce offspring identical to the parent, but we don't want to stray so far from natural processes. The decision has been made not to take advantage of these possibilities. DIANA doesn't allow for asexual reproduction, and cell cloning can't be seen any other way. Our ethicists and philosophers agreed on this point too, but they added a nuance of their own. They felt that after a failed implant, couples should be free—by way of exception—to choose a cloned embryo. After all, the original hadn't survived, so in principle the clone wouldn't be a copy of an existing creature. But our own biologists rejected that option. They felt that quite a few pregnancies fail because the implanted embryo isn't viable, which would also apply to the embryo's clones. They recommended that couples start all over again after a miscarriage."

The room where the fondest of wishes came true was the biggest one in the entire complex. Ellen figured it had once been the recruits' mess hall. Women in white coats were sitting at long, narrow tables, staring at computer monitors connected to microscopes in front of them. Each screen showed a highly magnified image of the object under the eyepiece. Each of the women had a metal locker at her feet that looked something like a safe, but which was in fact a freezer unit. The screen was split into two frames: one window to view the fertilization process itself, the other for data registration. The microscopes were equipped with a metal attachment for manipulating the contents of the dish under the objective without taking one's eyes off the screen. Mass production.

"You may be wondering how you'll know that the child implanted is really your own," the guide began her pitch. "There's no need to worry. At the start of the procedure, you'll be assigned a personal assistant who will look after you, and you alone, until the pregnancy is complete and you leave the laboratory. The girls carefully note everything they do with the specimens they deal with at any given moment. There's no chance of anyone making a mistake."

Ellen stared at one of the monitors in fascination. On the screen she could see two tubes with heavy black edges: the pipettes, left and right. At the tip of each pipette dangled a translucent bubble with a rather confusing-looking internal structure. Those were the eggs. The lab assistant carefully maneuvered a much thinner pipette towards one of the cells, pricked the wall right where it was attached to a tangled, spool-shaped mass of threads—obviously the nucleus with its genetic material—and sucked this up into the pipette. Then she moved it to the other egg and injected the contents into the mass of threads in that cell. A slight movement could be seen in the fusing nuclei, then all was still.

"There we go," the woman said. "A fertilization. That's how simple it is. If you like, you can be one of the next couples in line."

Ellen could hardly believe her eyes. They could fuse the nuclei of two egg cells to achieve fertilization. The sperm cell was simply replaced by the nucleus of another egg. That had been unthinkable back when she was still doing scientific work. Amazing.

"In the early years of this century," spoke Diana, "the writer Rupert Brooke stated that man was the sole hope of the world, the source of all progress, expansion, imperialism and entrepreneurship. He was embroidering upon the edifying insights of his illustrious seventeenth-century predecessor, Francis Bacon, who wrote in *The Masculine Birth of Time* that *'By art and the hand of Man, Nature is to be forced out of her natural state, and squeezed and molded to yield her many secrets of excellent use.'* No mention at all was made of the hand of woman, except that she was to be seen as a part of that nature that would reveal her many secrets of excellent use to man.

"Philosophers never were able to understand fundamental science. Their opinions were of little interest, except as an illustration of how difficult it could be for people to correctly interpret the exact sciences.

"Even in the days of Aristotle and Plato, the assembled male philosophers drew a distinction between the rationality of men and the chaos of women. A polarity fed by two sources: the unproven claim for sexual differences in the workings of the human brain, and an obscure argument linking chaos and sexuality. Women were chaotic, unpredictable, easily influenced by dark forces and susceptible to dangerous sexual desires. Witches, in other words. Even after being locked into the chastity belt of virginity and virtue, women remained responsible for the uncontrollable lusts which sometimes arose in thinking men and unleashed a raging mental conflict between rationality and chaos.

"Most of these dogged thinkers didn't realize that rationality would never triumph over chaos. They tried for centuries to impose restraints on the chaos of nature, and to hedge it in with laws. They refused to see that the world is fundamentally chaotic, something we proved a few years ago with the help of that very science of which they were so proud. That is why they were doomed to lose the war.

"Men of science gave women no credit either, not even after their so-called 'emancipation' in the second half of the twentieth century. In a study of the effects of aspirin on heart problems, twenty-two thousand men were tested, but not a single woman; the first tests for the treatment of AIDS involved men only; scientific budgets reserved almost no funding for research into chlamydia, or other sexually transmittable diseases found primarily among women.

"And what was the gentlemen scientists' primary defense against accusations of scientific discrimination? The claim that the female body was too complex, that it was chock full of strange hormones that would complicate the normal process of scientific observation and render it impossible to make binding conclusions.

"Yet, in other areas, the more complicated the observations the better. Men drew up econometric models intended to reflect the entire field of finance; they charted the genetic material of the human with its billion information units; they assembled a virtual world they could enter from their computers. But a woman's body was too complicated for them. The most obvious solution, letting women do their own work on the female body, never occurred to them.

"But we beat them at their own game. They should have known better. They thought women were unfit for fundamental scientific research. They were wrong. The first pioneer in the study of ecology was not the German Ernst Haeckel, as everyone thought, but the American Ellen Swallow. In 1871, she was the first woman to be admitted to the prestigious Massachusetts Institute of Technology, on condition, however, that she was not to take her doctorate and that she would continue to work as a volunteer assistant. She studied the pollution in the streets and waterways of Boston, and drew up the first ecological models. She corresponded about those models with other scientists . . . including Haeckel. He recognized the value of her ideas, and later came to be regarded as the father of ecological science.

"In the nineteenth century, the French mathematician Sophie Germain was the first to publicly offer a solution to the famous last theorem of Fermat, which has never been conclusively proven. She distributed her calculations under a male pseudonym, to be sure they would be taken seriously.

"Marie Curie, one of the few women ever to win a Nobel Prize in the sciences, was at first accused of taking unfair advantage of the work of her husband, Pierre. When that argument proved untenable, they claimed that a combination of luck and dogged footwork, and not careful thought, had allowed her to explain a random observation.

"Even in the 1960s, Nobel Prize–winner James Watson, one of the discoverers of the structure of DNA, the molecule that bears all genetic information, bent over backwards in his book *The Double Helix* to play down the pioneering work of Rosalind Franklin, even though she had provided the scientific proof for the hypotheses of Watson and his two cronies."

Ellen thought Diana looked more impressive in person than she did on TV, despite her rather mousy appearance. She radiated authority, and something else that was hard to describe. Her thoughts ground to a halt when she realized what was running through her mind. Diana had something witchy about her.

She glanced around quickly. The other couples in the room were listening breathlessly to the woman who was responsible for the world in which they now lived. Ellen found this speech more interesting than the DIANA series she hammered out on TV. She herself knew how difficult it had been to start a career as a woman in science.

"Jasmine is now going to tell you a bit about the services we offer," Diana concluded in a startlingly practical vein, then sat down.

Jasmine was much more down-to-earth. "The technique we've developed offers a number of possibilities you will need to consider. You have already seen that we can achieve fertilization by fusing the nuclei of two egg cells, and I hope that your individual tours have convinced you that there is no risk of becoming the mother of a child that doesn't bear your own genetic material. We know how important genetic agreement is for an optimal relationship between parent and child. That's why we've taken all possible precautions to preserve that link. But there are two important decisions that you will all have to make for yourselves."

Jasmine paused for a moment to be sure she had the undivided attention of all of the women in the room. Ellen looked at Julie. She really looked happy, Ellen realized, and that made her sad. Julie was going to get hurt.

"The first decision," Jasmine said loudly, "has to do with which of you will become pregnant. There are couples in which one of the partners has no desire to become pregnant, or whose health precludes it. They will have no trouble making this decision. Other couples may choose to take turns and, for example, draw lots to see who will bear the first child. Finally, both partners may choose to become pregnant at the same time. We can heartily recommend this option for those whose family situation allows it; being pregnant together is a truly unique experience. Frictions may arise within some couples when one of the women feels inferior because she hasn't borne a child. In addition, raising two children of the same age can have its advantages. By the way, we're working on a system to provide home care for families who choose this option."

Ellen turned, feeling Julie's eyes on her. Julie mouthed the words: *What about us?* "I don't want to have a child yet," Ellen whispered in her ear, and Julie nodded understandingly. That was at least one problem out of the way.

"The second decision," Jasmine continued, "flows from the fact that we have to treat one of the two nuclei in a way which, and I use the word advisedly, 'masculinizes' it. One of the nuclei is injected into the other egg cell. We've come up with a procedure in which the nucleus to be injected is isolated from an egg cell grown in a culture of testicular tissue. This procedure can lead to delays in some cases, because egg cells ripen at different rates. The procedure itself is necessary, however, to avoid a genetic problem that we do not yet have under control. Without this treatment, the children conceived cannot achieve perfect development.

"It usually does not matter which gene is activated in the embryo.

A random choice is made between the gene inherited from the father and that from the mother. For a limited number of characteristics, however, only those genes received from the father must be allowed to express themselves. This problem is known as 'genetic imprinting,' and has its origins in the conflict between males and females concerning the size of the embryo. Men, of course, wanted their child to be as large as possible at birth, to give it the best chance of survival. For a woman, however, a large child could be a problem, as it tended to use more energy and resulted in a more difficult birth.

"Embryos that aren't genetically imprinted by a surrogate father usually fail to grow, then die off. Fortunately, embryonic development is largely determined by the mother's genes. We've learned this by observing fertilizations that went wrong. Egg cells sometimes accidentally receive a double set of chromosomes from the mother, and none at all from the father. Chromosomes are the bearers of genetic material, half of which comes from the father or his surrogate, the other half from the mother. Egg cells with two mother sets develop all sorts of tissue, such as nerves, bones, teeth and connective tissue, but no tissue for the placenta. The embryo can then receive no nourishment. Embryos receiving a double set of chromosomes from the father, on the other hand, develop almost nothing *but* placental tissue, and die off before they have really even been conceived. It's interesting to note, of course, that male genes contribute primarily to a system that allowed the embryos to live off their mothers.

"We have now identified the mechanism behind this genetic imprinting. During the ripening of the sex cells, special molecules attach themselves to some genes. These allow the embryo to recognize the genes as those to be expressed and translated into physical characteristics.

"We also know where the solution lies, but we haven't yet been able to consistently apply that knowledge. What we must do is identify those few genes that are never expressed in females and, by means of genetic engineering, activate them in one of the two egg cells. We have the technology to do that. All we have to do is locate the genes, and that takes time. But we will succeed.

"Before and after fertilization, of course, all egg cells are checked for genetic quality. And even during the course of the pregnancy itself, you can always come in for a checkup on the fetus. We do everything in our power to see to it that the children conceived here will be as healthy as possible.

"But I repeat: it's up to you to decide which of you will become pregnant, and which egg will be treated to receive the genetic imprint. I recommend that you give that some careful thought."

It was quiet in the hall. Julie looked less enthusiastic. "I'll do the treatment," Ellen whispered, but that didn't seem to improve Julie's mood.

Diana sensed the tension and stood up. "During the last few years, we've put a great deal of effort into providing women with the exclusive right to reproduction," she said calmly. "Women deserve that, in light of the energy they invest in pregnancy and the raising of children. I guarantee all of you that in less than two years we will be able to eliminate all vestiges of the role men once played in reproduction. Not a single trace will be left."

"There's a man wandering around our village," Julie blurted out; the remark rocked the assembly like a mortar shell in a crowded market.

Ellen was startled, but even more shocked when she saw Diana's reaction. In one furious movement, the woman threw the table she had been standing at off the podium, wheeled on Jasmine and screamed hysterically: "Go get Kristina. Immediately."

The manhunt was well organized. This time Kristina had left nothing to chance. That night, eight combat vehicles sealed off all the roads around the village—not only the two main ones, but also the paths leading to the fields. The Warriors maintained radio contact, and a heavily armed patrol was posted at places where the distance between vehicles was too great. During the day she had taken a couple of Warriors out to comb the woods and fields in the general vicinity. The non-inactivables she had hunted down during the last year had usually hung around a village, like tigers no longer able to hunt anything but easy prey, cattle or people, until the villagers became furious enough to corner and slaughter them.

Those non-inactivables usually left trails. And the frightened villagers usually had a fairly good idea where they were hiding. In the toughest cases, there were only subtle indications of their presence: blackened spots from campfires, vague paths, bits of cloth, and occasionally something striking: a scorched pot, a wool cap left behind in a hurry.

But in this case Kristina couldn't find a single useful clue. She began to fear for the worst: someone in the village was hiding a non-inactivable. It was something she'd been confronted with regularly at the start of the war. What would Diana do if she caught someone helping a non-inactivable? Even serious violations like that had never been dealt with harshly in the past. Diana preferred not to take a repressive approach.

The need to report the presence of clandestine non-inactivables, for reasons of health and safety, was constantly stressed on TV. The system had proven its worth. As soon as people realized there was no danger involved, the reports had come in quickly. The fugitives had become a negligible minority, too small ever to regain power. Working along with the DIANA program was not tantamount to classic collaboration. That was always stressed as well. It wasn't like providing active support for a foreign repressor, it was simply one's contribution to the completion of a program advantageous to every individual in society.

Non-inactivables could usually be overpowered without a hitch. If they offered even a smidgin of resistance, Kristina dealt decisively: anyone who put up a struggle was shot dead on the spot. There were almost no weapons circulating in this new world. That's why her unit was so effective, even though no huge stockpiles of arms had been put at her disposal. Diana didn't want her followers to gain too firm a grip on society.

Kristina's unit acted as both police force and regional army, but she'd never really had to fight. War was something inherent to male culture, a factor driven by the sex hormone testosterone, and by the struggle for absolute power that had terrorized the world for millennia. Women dealt with each other differently, even these days. Someone who knew how to use weapons and where to find them would have little problem filling the vacancy left by the removal of male power—many of the men's killing machines still existed.

Yet no such attempted coup had ever taken place. On the contrary: Kristina noted an alarming growth of apathy, a deadly lethargy that dominated the village communities. The forceful verbal abuse to which she'd been subjected in the early days of the program had lost its punch. She seldom ran into any resistance during a hunt these days. The women seemed to have accepted the situation, they seemed to realize that they were better off making the best of things, in the conviction that their generation may have been sacrificed, but that their daughters would reap full recompense for their mothers' traumas. It was an argument bandied about by DIANA's propaganda machinery, loudly and without pause. Today's discomforts were an investment in the future. Following generations would thrive as never before. The memories would fade, as always when the past was less rosy than the future.

History was not a part of people's lives. Most of them could come up with little more than a few anecdotes about their grandparents. Family went back no further than that.

Besides, DIANA had opened up a great genetic frontier to explore and develop. With the elimination of a sex that never bore or raised children, women could achieve a higher yield on their reproductive investment. The program promoted the maximum transferral of genes to the next generation, which was the goal of every living thing. There was room for new life. The discomforts suffered by this generation were partly compensated for by the added genetic value they would receive. The elimination of a runaway culture made for unlimited biological opportunity.

Television projected the dream imagery of that society of the future with ready-made images. But most women did anything but dream of the society of the future; they had enough trouble forgetting the one they'd left behind.

Kristina had encountered no resistance this time either, but also no cooperation. As soon as it was light she had the Warriors driven in to comb out the village. The women pulled the local authorities, who had not been informed about the manhunt, from their beds and gave them a short briefing. The search was to take place as efficiently as possible, working in from the periphery, like a lasso thrown around the village and pulled tight. They had to be sure the non-inactivable wouldn't slip into a house that had already been searched. If he was in the village, he wouldn't escape.

It was quiet in most of the houses. No children crying or playing, little music, almost no conversation. Here and there someone had a pet, usually a cat or a bird, almost never a dog—the greed with which they had devoured the corpses had given dogs a bad name.

Many of the houses were unimaginatively furnished: there were surprisingly few flowers when one considered that beautiful wild bouquets could be picked in these rural surroundings. A few people lived among collections of religious symbols, crucifixes and rosaries, as well as candles and icons of both Mary and the male members of the godhead. A room in one little farmhouse was fully equipped for the veneration of saints, with large statues of shepherds, sheep and a king, no doubt stolen from a church. There was no manger.

The walls in other homes were hung with dozens of photos of men, family of the women who lived there. Kristina knew that Diana didn't like this, but she said nothing. Diana saw the cult of former family as a danger, because it kept people from forgetting the past, but she didn't know how to deal with it. Banning such mementos would be a form of repression. So, for the time being, she went no further than to warn women who wanted to have children that they shouldn't needlessly burden their offspring with stories of a life they would never know. Educational material was being developed to teach the children what society had once been like, and why it had been molded into a more livable form.

No one knew exactly how to deal with the children who had lived through the revolution itself. They too had to be convinced, through special programs at school, that a carefree future was theirs for the taking. But a great deal of work remained to be done. A lot of children suffered from psychological traumas, and systematic treatment had been hindered in part by a number of psychologists' opinion that such scars could not be treated, because the lesions had been too deep.

Many of the children reacted fearfully when Kristina and her crew came in. The adults had no objections to their rooms being searched. The notion of privacy had paled enormously in recent years; everyone's life had been breached too forcefully. People usually didn't even go along with Kristina and her crew when they searched the house. They had to find their own way.

Most of the villagers denied having seen a non-inactivable. Many of the women had heard the rumors, though; two of them even thought they had seen him, but never in the village; no one knew whether a woman was hiding a non-inactivable.

Until an irritated farmer grumpily told Kristina that she was searching the wrong house, that the man she was looking for was living in one of the big houses close to the village square. Kristina clenched her fists. Now she had him. She radioed for a few of the Warriors to be driven to the center of the village; the house was surrounded in no time. She took her weapon from its sling and clicked off the safety before knocking on the door. When it opened, she stood staring in amazement: the woman in the doorway was the same one who had reported the non-inactivable. Kristina didn't know what to think. "There's a man in this house," she said rather dumbly.

"No there's not," the woman answered in a voice that sounded almost cheery, then she stepped aside to let Kristina and her colleagues in. "Ellen, we have visitors," she called.

The other woman was sitting on the sofa in the living room. She had a worried look about her. The woman who had opened the door for them went and sat down next to her. "Imagine that," she giggled. "These ladies seem to think we have a man in the house." She laughed loudly.

"Where is he?" Kristina demanded. "If you two don't cooperate, we'll have to take you with us."

The woman who had laughed was quiet now. The other woman still looked concerned. "Maybe they mean Bert," she said.

"Who's that?" Kristina asked.

The woman stood up tiredly. "He's upstairs. I'll go with you."

At the top of the stairs, the woman turned around and put a finger to her lips. "Please be quiet," she said. "He's pretty sick."

When she opened the door, Kristina pushed past her, then stopped in her tracks. A little boy, not even ten years old, was sleeping on the bed. She sighed and relaxed her grip on the rifle, stepped up to the bed and looked at him. He was covering his mouth with one hand, and clutching a stuffed polar bear to his chest with the other. She saw the label hanging from the toy; it said "Cuddle Club." She turned around and walked out of the room. The child must have been one of the last ones left. She felt queasy, the way she always did when confronted with things like this.

They hadn't found me. After Julie's outburst at the lab, Ellen had warned me about a search. I'd found a safe enough hiding place, that much was clear by now. Seldom had I seen such a tour de force, all those Mad Maxes and armed women. It all looked so absurd; unfortunately, however, this was real.

It was exciting somehow, kind of erotic, even after a few years without women. The big blonde who carried her weapon so casually and ordered her troops around so tersely reminded me of one of my old girlfriends. She'd had legs that went on forever, too, and a thick golden mane she could just twist into a knot and lay across her shoulders, or down her back, without it falling back across her face. Her hair was so sensitive, I could still see the way she trembled whenever I ran my fingers through her locks. Her breasts were small, but she had the most sensitive nipples I'd ever come across. I could tell how she felt just by looking at them; by touching them with the tip of one finger I could induce a reaction that coursed through her body and made her lazily stretch those long legs of hers.

The night after the hunt I lay half asleep, tossing and turning, caught up in wild dreams in which I tussled with armed blondes modeled after my ex-girlfriend. Dreams were the only place I was sexually active anymore, but I'd learned to live with it. Women had become too dangerous, and I could never start another affair with Ellen. Too much had changed for that.

The weather was nice the morning after the hunt, and the countryside was as deserted as ever. I stayed in my hiding place for hours. I saw a fox and a marten, which meant the coast was clear down below; they would never have come out in the open otherwise. Wildlife had prospered under all the changes. I had even seen a shrike, a bird that—to the dismay of every right-minded nature lover—had disappeared from the area long ago. Nature seemed to be recovering from the blows it had received from urbanization and intensive agriculture. The war had been good for animals.

There were pheasants and dozens of rabbits at the edge of the forest. It was becoming increasingly difficult for me to withstand the temptation to set snares for the rabbits—I'd done it so often when I was young, I probably hadn't lost the touch. But I was afraid some woman would find a snare and draw the conclusion that someone was trying to stay alive in the woods by trapping.

I'd been racking my brains about it for weeks; what was the biggest risk, stealing the occasional chicken from a coop in the village, or setting snares in the woods? For the time being, I'd decided that there must be someone in the village who knew there were foxes around and would blame the disappearing chickens on them. But I could tell that it wouldn't be long before I started experimenting with snares. It was about time to try something new.

My first encounter with Ellen had been tense. She'd become so timid, nothing but a shadow of the Ellen who had run through my life like quicksilver. She hadn't even dared to look me in the eye, and she'd avoided all physical contact as though it would kill her. She spoke in short, jerky sentences, and she refused to bring up old memories or talk about her life now.

It was strange to see how badly organized the new system was. The only people who seemed to be on the ball were the manhunters in their Mad Max Landcruisers. There were no more than four women in the whole village with any authority. You couldn't really call them officials, though; they received almost no instructions from on high, and their activities seemed limited to passing along complaints and suggestions, which usually got a reaction only after a great delay. The complaints almost always had to do with practical things: the electricity that had gone out again and had to be repaired, the need to replenish the village's diminishing supply of canned food, the demand for fumigation teams to deal with an insect plague.

Some of the things I simply couldn't understand were probably the result of a faulty division of labor, of putting the wrong people in the wrong place. The cherries, for example, were never picked. The starlings had a heyday. Ellen wasted her time hoeing her little plot of ground, while half a mile away the fruit was rotting on the trees. I'd pointed that out to her, but she didn't seem to want to talk about it, she just said the garden work was necessary because the distribution network had collapsed and they had to grow their own produce. Unaccustomed as she was to village life, she just didn't seem to get the point. And she'd become so impassive, she had no desire to spice up her life. She was only dragging herself from day to day.

Further up the ladder of authority, the lack of organization seemed complete. The telephone network was a shambles. What was left of it was strictly monitored and controlled; there was no more directory assistance, no telephone books. Gas had become prohibitively expensive, which ruled out long-distance transport. Money was almost worthless and the banks had never reopened, despite repeated promises. Black-market operations were severely punished, so almost no one dared to buy anything outside the official channels. Anyone caught black-marketeering could be exiled to another community, where her supplies would be cut off. And, unlike during a normal war, people weren't mentally tough enough to go on organizing such "parallel enterprises." People saw to their own needs as best they could: when that didn't work, they could count on the authorities for a little help; a bit of canned food, some fabric, basic furniture and other necessities, the supplies of which were shaky even years after the war had ended.

The information services and propaganda machinery were run locally as well, from towns located at the heart of each conglomerate of villages. Under the new system, small-scale operations were the order of the day. The sharp contrast with the abundance of the late consumption-oriented society took some getting used to.

The only way to escape this misery was through the laboratory Ellen had talked about. She would have no trouble getting in there, but it took me a long time to convince her that doing so might help her child.

And now here I was, dying of curiosity. I knew she'd been to the lab, she'd told me as much when she came to warn me about the roundup, but she'd been too frightened to say any more.

After the Mad Maxes had combed the area, days went by before she showed up in her garden again. It was driving me crazy. I'd been lying behind those damned bushes for days, staring at the deserted field and suffering the attentions of mosquitoes and ants. Before, I'd sometimes spent hours watching one of those ants in its jungle of grass and dead leaves beneath the bushes, but that didn't work when I was excited. I had to force myself not to dash across the open field to the houses, sneak into the village and find her. But I was pushing my luck as it was.

When she finally did show up, without the boy this time, she was even more skittish and sad than before. Her replies were almost mechanical. Yes, she had been to the laboratory. No, she had discovered nothing special. She had let herself be dragged along on a tour, and she sat in on an information session. I barely recognized her like this, she used to be so dynamic. I swore at her, insisting that she go back with a specific request, a question that didn't fit the mold, a question that would force them to tell her more about what they were doing. If they had carried out such a drastic program of elimination without anyone being able to do a thing about it, they had to be able to help her son as well. They could save her child if they wanted to—I was sure of that.

But she hesitated. She was always hesitating. She didn't want to believe that her Bert would fall victim too. The patrol had found him, but they'd done nothing to help. I had to make her see how important it was for her to gain the confidence of the people in charge at the laboratory.

"You're a scientist, Ellen," I shouted at her. "And you're a doctor. They must have use for someone like you. There weren't that many competent female doctors and scientists before the war."

She looked at me with something almost like pity. "What can you do on your own against these odds?" she sneered. "It's you against the world. Do you really think you can bring back the past? Sooner or later they're going to find you."

I grabbed her by the shoulders and shook her hard. "They're never going to find me, Ellen, and I'm not on my own. There are a lot of us, we have an army, we're getting organized. We've gone underground, literally, and we're getting ready for a guerrilla war. We have nothing to lose, and that means we'll take every chance we can get. That's why we have to find the weak spots in their defense. You can help us do that, and the sooner the better. Please, Ellen, get a job as a doctor and infiltrate that lab."

Ellen didn't react to my outburst. "They'd never take me," she said coolly. "Those women aren't interested in doctors. They don't want to heal people. They want as many sick people as possible. Sick people cause less trouble."

It took a while before Ellen managed to talk to Jasmine, the head of the laboratory. She'd taken the bus into town three times before she was able to make a personal appointment. But now that she was sitting across from the woman, she didn't really know what to say.

"I was here not too long ago with my partner, for a pregnancy," she began hesitantly.

The woman cut in. "I know."

"But I'm not sure it's such a good idea," Ellen continued.

"Why not?" the woman asked.

"Because I'm not in love with her, not at all," Ellen admitted rather shamefacedly.

Jasmine laughed and leaned back. "What does that have to do with it?"

Ellen looked at her in amazement. It seemed perfectly obvious to her.

Jasmine leaned over toward her. "Look," she said. "We're going through a series of very drastic changes, which means we have to distance ourselves as quickly as possible from a number of the principles we grew up with. One of those is that love is essential to a good relationship. That's a fundamental misconception. Millions of years ago, love came forth out of the need for men and women, who wandered across the savanna together in a prehistoric family setting, to stay together long enough to give the child they'd produced the best possible chance of survival. A child that was well taken care of by both parents had a better chance of surviving than a child who could only count on the attention of one parent. That discrepancy reinforced the factors that served to keep parents together, because genes coded for solicitude and cooperation guaranteed more children than the others. Those genes became increasingly frequent among the nomadic groups, and resulted in the development of the chemistry which later came to be referred to as 'love.' When a child reached the age of about four, it was able to become part of the group and move along with them under its own power. The loving ties between its parents were no longer necessary, so they dissolved, allowing the adults to start a new relationship. That's why an infatuation is programmed to last about four years.

"Meanwhile, however, people have become aware of the importance of transferring their genes to the next generation. The logistical and other means at our disposal make us no longer dependent on a loving partner to ensure successful child care. Romance and love are hopelessly obsolete. Worse than that. Because the energy lost to the stupid process called 'passion' can now be put to more useful ends, those who are liberated from their own passion can achieve a higher yield on genetic investment than those who remain stuck in their infatuation.

"I predict that love and passion will be selected out of the classic spectrum of survival strategies. Attention is essential, but that's not the same as love. Love has caused an incredible amount of suffering. As far as we know, however, lovelessness has no adverse effect on the successful transferral of an optimal number of genes to the next generation. Love is a mental defect that has never been recognized and studied as such. We've now set up a research program, the first of its kind, to deal with that very issue."

Ellen's mind reeled. She remembered the hours of passion, the daydreaming, the fruitless attempts to keep up one's concentration at work, the physical urge for the other, the surrender, the hours of ecstasy, the perfect satisfaction, the heavenly relaxation afterwards. How could someone give that up without running into major problems?

"I think everyone has the right to be in love," she objected curtly. "The couple as cornerstone of the family is something even you people have chosen to preserve. With the fertilization technology at your disposal, it would be easy enough to propagate the single-parent family. But you don't."

It was a good point, Jasmine had to admit that. She had talked to Diana about this very argument for hours, but they hadn't been able to reach an agreement. However broad-minded Diana was, however innovative the technologies she had used to change the course of history, she had a conservative streak and was too stubborn to admit it. She had rightly decided not to switch to a system of asexual reproduction, but at the same time she kept hammering on the fact that a woman had to bear responsibility for every child she helped to conceive. For her, the merging of egg cells meant the merging of interests and, therefore, of responsibilities.

"You're right," Jasmine admitted coolly. "That's the right vein of thought, but we can't expect everyone to replace four million years of evolution with a more rational approach, not within the space of a single generation. Love is etched in our brains with the force of four million years. Unfortunately, that part of the brain that makes us aware of what we do has too little grasp on our genetic clockwork to actively steer it towards increased efficiency. We've taken that into account by starting a dual research program, a program with a genetic and a chemical track, to allow us to make good use, for the time being, of the need for love.

"The genetic part of the program involves the search for the genes that stimulate homosexuality. A section of the X sex chromosome was once identified as being linked to homosexuality. Unfortunately, that study—like almost all studies at the time—focused exclusively on men, and our initial experiments with women have been unsuccessful. We suspect that homosexuality in women is stimulated by a different means. If we ever succeed in locating the gene responsible for it, we can selectively stimulate it in the course of an individual's development, or perhaps even use genetic engineering techniques to implant it in embryos, in order to provide new baby girls with the potential for homosexual love. But I'm afraid that the genetics of homosexuality is so complex that it will take a great many years before we reach that point.

"In the chemical part of the program, we are trying to develop a cocktail of chemical substances that will elicit feelings of love for those who believe they need it for a fruitful family life. We prefer not to use those passion-inducing substances that are physiologically comparable to those of stress, a link that illustrates the negative effect of passion on the human body. The neurotransmitters in the brain that broadcast the message that the bearer is passionately in love are the same ones that sound the alarm for stress. Natural amphetamines. No wonder infatuated couples can stay up all night making love. They're high on natural drugs.

"We all know how physically and mentally damaging addiction can be. Fortunately, the human brain has enough sense to see to it that the overwrought state of romantic addiction does not go on forever. The brain has provided its own brake: its nerves become immune to the effects of natural amphetamines, insensitive to the stimuli of love. The body will not allow itself to be exhausted by addiction."

Ellen's passionate affairs had never made her feel bad; on the contrary, she had never felt more gregarious and full of life than during those tempestuous periods. But she couldn't deny that it was exhausting.

"What we are in fact thinking of," Jasmine continued, "is stimulating what we have come to call 'tender loving care.' A much less taxing, much more pleasant feeling of calm and safety, elicited by natural painkillers produced in the brain: the morphine-related endorphines, which produce calm and inhibit fear. Those are the substances we would like to activate. There's also the hormone oxytocin, which is released during orgasm and makes people want to lie in each other's arms and enjoy each other's company after sex. We are looking for a way to encapsulate and distribute that substance, to meet people's need for affection. But we're not very far with that study either. We have other priorities."

Ellen saw her chance. "Maybe I can help," she suggested. "I studied medicine, I'm a researcher, and I have experience in what's probably the prime female-related disease: breast cancer."

"Breast cancer was a problem for the last generation," Jasmine said. "With the elimination of the need for hormonal contraceptives, and the environment's recovery from the effects of pollution, the two main factors that induced breast cancer have been removed. The next generation won't be bothered by it. And we can't do any more for women with the genetic form of breast cancer than they could in the past. We just hope they're aware of the risks, and we'll soon be starting adequate programs for genetic screening, so that women with a high risk factor can have themselves tested to see whether their gene bears the defect."

"What I meant," Ellen said patiently, "is that I have enough experience to be useful to you in your scientific programs. I don't have much to do anyway, and village life doesn't really suit me."

Jasmine countered immediately: "We don't need you."

Ellen was astounded. "What do you people have against me?" she asked angrily.

"It's the boy," Jasmine said quietly. "We know about your child. We don't want you using our facilities to try to save him."

"What have you got against my child?" Ellen shouted with a catch in her voice.

Jasmine stood up. "It wouldn't be fair to the others," she said dryly. "I hope you can understand that. Now, would you please excuse me? They're broadcasting Part Two of DIANA."

Diana looked exactly as she had in the first installment. The same way of staring into the camera, the same little gestures, the same slow, regular blink. Same picture, but a different story.

"One might wonder why evolution had to burden nature with different sexes for reproduction. . . . A heterosexual form of reproduction that plunges an individual into a demanding quest for members of the other sex, into an energy-guzzling ritual for attention, into the development of biologically expensive tail feathers, clumsy antlers and complicated little organs that emit light, into the need to take risks, behave conspicuously, leave hiding places and pick fights . . . The instinctive desire for members of the other sex is so strong that normal behavior is relinquished to the background. . . . Even the most reasonable creatures lose their heads. . . .

"Yet there is no valid reason why things have to be this way. . . . In some species, such as earthworms, the two sexes are combined. . . . But the need for genetic transfer has resulted in the hermetic separation of the two systems, even in many hermaphroditic organisms. . . . Hermaphrodites usually reproduce sexually as well. . . . One of them will play the role of mother, the other that of the father. . . . Even hermaphrodites cling to a gender, are unable to both impregnate and be impregnated. . . . People suspect that this is because a prohibitive amount of energy would be needed to keep two genders operational at the same time. . . . The fact that hermaphrodites are not common in nature supports the theory that, for most species, this is not a viable form. . . .

"Bacteria, the rulers of this planet, have access to both asexual reproduction and to a system of sexual reproduction that is extremely simple, extremely old, and therefore without a doubt extremely efficient. . . . Bacteria have hundreds of sexes. . . . Hundreds of strains that can exchange genes with any other cell, as long as it's of a different sex. . . . A mechanism to prevent inbreeding in a community which, at the moment that conditions demand sexual reproduction, must be able to obtain maximum yield from the exchange of genetic information . . . Bacteria of varying sexes resemble each other perfectly and have exactly the same behavior. . . . No fuss to improve appearance and so seduce another individual . . . They swarm around each other in a chaos of genders, and wallow at will in the genetic material of another, or simply exchange a few genes. . . . The pinnacle of social equality . . .

"Bacteria have even succeeded in developing a mechanism to guarantee such social equality. . . . Biologists used to refer to some of these strains as 'male,' because they possess a genetic detail that serves as a fertilization factor. . . . They transfer their genetic information to a partner, just as human males did. . . . You could say that the so-called 'female' strains were fertilized by these bacteria, because they received genetic material. . . . But in bacterial fertilization, the sex of both organisms changes; the fertilization factor is transferred as well, rendering the female male and the male female. . . .

"Bacteria are genetic transsexuals, capable of switching sex endlessly. . . . They are also so advanced that they can exchange genes with individuals of another species. . . . Another species in lieu of another sex . . . We know that some bacteria in our intestines take advantage of the resistance to antibiotics acquired elsewhere by newly arrived species. . . . The genetic material that provides resistance is exchanged through sexual contact for genes that can in turn help the new species to survive in its newly colonized environment. . . .

"Unfortunately, this transsexual flexibility is not available to all species that reproduce sexually. . . . Most of them are bound to a system of two sexes, one of which produces eggs, the other of which supplies sperm. . . . Eggs are relatively large cells that are almost incapable of movement, and which contain an energy supply for the developing embryo. . . . Sperm cells are small, having been reduced at some point to a temporary vehicle for the genetic material of the fertilizer. . . . It was once believed that this unfortunate system was the result of a chance selection in the cellular soup, from the early days of multicellular life on earth. . . . Cells varying in shape and mobility swarmed around each other in that protein sea. . . . It's been suggested that the combination of a large cell full of reserves with a small cell full of movement provided the best assurance for successful reproduction. . . . Inherent to this argument, however, was the assumption that the fusion of two sperm cells or two egg cells ruled out normal development. . . . The former, it was believed, were too small, the latter too heavy. . . .

"I've never put much stock in that hypothesis. . . . A theory so dependent on chance takes too little account of the uninterrupted warfare raging at the cellular level, with its origins in the conflicting interests of individual genes. . . . Genes fight for maximum transferral to the next generation, for reproduction. . . . A hypothesis that takes no account of the precondition of genetic advantage for heterosexual division at the level of the individual cell is itself inviable. . . .

"One hypothesis, however, does take this into account. . . . It says that the sexes arose to combat the deadly effects of the presence of parasites in the cells. . . . There are strong, albeit indirect, indications of the accuracy of this theory. . . . The point of departure is the observation that chromosomes in the cell nucleus do not transfer all of their genetic material to the next generation. . . . Located next to the cell nucleus are organelles, which not only provide energy, but also contain genes that are translated into proteins. . . . These genes are crucial, for defects in the information they bear can result in diabetes and deafness. . . . The genes of the male organelles are lost, because fertilization is carried out solely by the nucleus of the sperm cell. . . . We inherit only our mother's organelles, which should provide some indication of the female's added genetic value. . . .

"Originally, these organelles were bacteria that, because of their biochemical capacities, were used by the cell for its energy supply. . . . Because they were unable to divide as regularly as the nucleus itself, the cells threatened to become swamped with organelles during reproduction. . . . Algae, which simply combine—rather than selectively exchange—their organelles during sexual contact, are faced with an internal war that wipes out almost all the organelles, leaving the cell significantly weakened. . . . A mechanism was therefore needed to prevent the organelles of both parents from ending up in the fertilized egg cell. . . . The development of two sexes with two different types of reproductive cells, one of which offered up its own organelles, prevented such massacres potentially fatal to the embryo. . . .

"In addition, the viruses and bacteria present in every cell may fight when combined, thereby creating a needlessly exhausting situation for a recently fertilized egg cell, which needs all its energy for the onset of development. . . . A system that minimized the combination of mutually hostile viruses must have provided enormous genetic advantages. . . . That's why the sperm cell was reduced to a mobile bag of chromosomes, in which the presence of female-unfriendly viruses and other parasites was reduced to a minimum. . . . This hypothesis seems scientifically sound to me, yet provides no argument for the indispensability of the sperm cell. . . .

"A somewhat older variation on this theory appeals to my intuition even more. . . . It says that sperm cells themselves arose from viral sections that infected the larger female cells, and smuggled in their own genetic material to have it reproduced. . . . This is a mechanism viruses apply quite successfully in order to reproduce. . . . The hypothesis itself jibes perfectly with the detachment towards their offspring displayed by men and many animals. . . .

"Once fertilization had been achieved, the fertilized party had to apply herself to the development of embryos that bore only half her genes. . . . Men parasitized the female cells like viruses. . . . Evolution offered them the chance to obtain maximum yield from the obligatory exchange of genetic material. . . . They enjoyed the advantages of sexual reproduction, and shared in the benefits of the cell reserves stored by the farsighted female. . . . But they were spared the disadvantages; the male parasites could reproduce without restraint, while the burden of pregnancy and the biological duty to nurture placed constraints on the number of children a woman could bear. . . . This discrepancy laid the foundations for a great deal of female suffering. . . . Women had the misfortune of drawing from the bottom of the deck, and of being unable to play out their hand. . . ."

Diana paused for a moment. It was time for her conclusion.

"I see absolutely no reason why this system should be maintained. . . . We continue to opt for the advantages associated with sexual reproduction, so we also continue with the fusion of genetic material from two parents. . . . Yet we have discovered no incontrovertible scientific argument to prove the need for sexual reproduction by parents of different sexes. . . . The facts show that the sperm cell is intended only to transport genetic material, and to prevent a war between organelles and parasites within the fertilized egg cell. . . . If the task of fertilization can be carried out under the same conditions, and brought to a successful end, by another mechanism, then the sperm cell is no longer necessary. . . . We have developed just such an alternative. . . . As a consequence, males have become reproductively obsolete."

STRUGGLE

IN PYGMY CHIMPANZEE COMMUNITIES THERE are no fathers, only sons. Throughout their lives, the sons maintain an intimate relationship with their mothers, who dictate everything they do, who decide where, when and with whom they copulate. The sons provide the sperm with which the mothers have their girlfriends inseminated. In the world of the pygmy chimpanzee, the role of the male is reduced to the essence of his sex: supplier of sperm, and of a means by which that sperm reaches the egg it is to fertilize.

Pygmy chimpanzee society is run by females. The animals live in small groups, bound together by a matriarchal hierarchy. The females lead a dissolute life and paw each other everywhere, all in accordance with the rules of the hierarchy: the oldest female decides who is allowed to de-flea her, a form of behavior which quickly turns into homosexual contact, into group sex characterized by games of titillation in which the females fondle each other—particularly each other's genitals. They stretch and twist brazenly to make their sex organs more accessible, all under the interested gaze of the other animals in the group, including their sons; the sons watch uncomfortably, for they have nowhere to vent the excitement roused in them so quickly by the loaded atmosphere of this homosexual group sex. The females do not invite them to take part in their games until the end, when they decide that enough is enough, that it is time to relieve the physical discomfort of the ruttish sons and allow them to mate with their girlfriends. The higher the mother's rank, the more females her sons are allowed to inseminate.

Exclusivity plays no role within the pygmy chimpanzee group. Incompatibility does, of course, exist. Some animals can't stand each other, and make that clear. But, in principle, everyone is available to everyone else. A tolerant and frivolous female may be covered within a brief period by the entire band of sons, one after the other, her body the site of a merciless struggle for fertilization by hordes of cells from any number of potential fathers. It is a struggle only the best will win, the most powerful and best organized, who succeed in driving the fastest cells towards the egg and in keeping the competitors' cells at a safe distance.

No male in the group knows whether it was his cell which achieved fertilization. So none of the males know which of the young they have sired or, indeed, if they have sired any at all. There are no fathers in the pygmy chimpanzee community, only sons who must share their mothers with other children and are programmed to act solely at her command. Jealousy is kept under wraps; open rebellion does not exist. All mutual animosity is fought out in the womb.

Throughout their lives, the sons are lovingly cherished by their mothers and protected by them from other females in the group. A son who has lost his mother loses his rights, including the right to copulate. Without his mother, his life is barren.

Daughters, on the other hand, are tolerated only briefly. There are no daughters in the pygmy chimpanzee group, only mothers and sons. Females loathe their female kin, for the offspring of sons who mated with their sisters would not be viable. Female kinship does not exist in the world of the pygmy chimpanzee, only friendship.

Three years after they are born, the daughters reach adulthood and are ostracized, forced to undertake a difficult journey to make contact with another group. For only in a group can they survive and reproduce. The best way for them to establish such contact is along the lines of the hierarchy. The higher the rank of the female whose friendship they can win by grooming and entering into her sexual games, the greater the chance that they will be accepted, that the sons will be allowed to mate with them and that they themselves will bear sons in turn—a mother's success is determined by the number of sons she produces. The son as status symbol and supplier of sperm. That, and nothing more.

Ellen wasn't interested in the apes; they looked and acted like the ones no longer on display, the ones she used to see at the zoo. She read the plaque explaining the animals' behavior. She took the information at face value, it raised no further questions in her mind.

Bert was fascinated by the apes. He kept staring into the big cage, his hands pressed against the glass, giving a running commentary on the behavior of the baby chimps as they rolled through the straw on the cage floor, lay on their backs and submitted to the teasing of the other animals, and occasionally took refuge with a squeal at the safety of their mother's breast. One threatening glance from her was enough to temporarily rid the little ape of its persecutors.

Ellen was glad she had taken Bert to the zoo. It was a relief from the tedium of village life. She had gone to see a play recently, for the first time since she'd moved there. The phenomenon of the traveling theater company was making its reappearance; just as in the Middle Ages, culture had come looking for the consumer instead of vice versa, the way it went up until a few years ago. She had hesitated a long time before going, afraid of being disillusioned, and indeed the play had been tasteless, a vaudeville show revolving around sweet little angels who swayed their scythes and cut off the heads of cardboard men, loudly shrieking the biggest nonsense, largely in praise of lesbian love, into the former parish hall. The acting was bad as well, apparently with no director involved.

Ellen had always been a committed consumer of the arts. She'd helped organize literary events, but it saddened her deeply to see that—when all was said and done—artists had had almost no impact on the world when it really mattered. Rock Against Racism, Screenwriters for Sarajevo, Dancers Against DIANA, it had all seemed so intriguing and important. The people involved had truly thought they could influence the course of events, introduce a human element, but it quickly became clear that the artists were not the ones running the show. Outside the circle of the initiated, almost no sleep was lost over these initiatives to heighten public awareness. The world went on, impervious. Culture had been nothing but a footnote, and the new social order would do nothing to change that.

Ellen was still not used to traveling exclusively by public transport. In the past she had only rarely taken a train or bus. At one time she had driven thousands of miles a month, but now she found herself hesitating for weeks about whether to take her child to the zoo. Public transport made it quite a chore.

It reminded her of the cleaning lady her parents had when she was a child, who fretted for weeks beforehand about taking a trip to the zoo, a journey of less than thirty miles, with no need even to change trains. She hadn't been accustomed to leaving the security of the village. It was the only outing she had made that year.

The zoo looked neglected and many of the cages stood empty. The pygmy chimps were the main attraction. There were still lions as well, four lionesses and a male. The huge plaque next to the cage bore a long story about a mistake made by Charles Darwin, who had deduced from the male lion's majestic appearance that he was the relentless hunter whose power enabled him to supply his lionesses with food, while in reality the lionesses were the ones who went out hunting: Mr. Lion lay lolling about in the shade until his better halves had met with success, and he could belly up to dinner.

The zoo was no longer child-centered, Ellen felt; the information on the plaques consisted largely of official announcements for mothers.

As their visit wore on, she began to realize that the zoo had been converted into a piece of propaganda for DIANA. The rather heavy-handed message was that life without men, or at least life dominated by women, was no exception in nature.

The reptile house contained race runner lizards and Indian geckos, both species with exclusively female populations that reproduced asexually. In small print at the bottom of the plaque one could read that, although the visitor might witness a copulation, this was not to be interpreted as an error in the information. Instead, this was an instance of pseudo-copulation, a futile relic from when the ancestors of the animals in question still reproduced sexually.

Visitors to the aquarium were informed about varieties of fish in which the males clung parasitically to the females, or settled down communally in the vagina and fertilized the stream of eggs as it flowed by.

The terrarium was well populated, mostly with animals that could be kept inexpensively. Bees of course, a writhing mass of workers behind plate glass, praying mantises—the females of which bit off the heads of the males during copulation—and gruesome female spiders who blithely devoured their males after mating.

Ellen found them all equally ghastly, but Bert stared with eyes bulging in amazement. She let him do as he pleased. It was up to him to decide where they went and how long they stayed. His life was uneventful, and there was much she could teach him about the natural world. She eyed him briefly. He was plucky; although constantly weak and short of breath, Bert seldom complained.

In the nocturnal house, only one cage was lighted, that of the Australian marsupial mouse. The gist of the litany on the adjacent plaque was that the disposable male of this species was struck by such an extreme overdose of hormones during mating that he soon became a wreck and died of internal bleeding and infections.

Ellen was becoming nauseated by this constant flow of disinformation. Outside she was happy to see sparrows playing in the dust, chirping, their wings aflutter with excitement, the males with their brown-and-gray heads and the drabness of the females. Perched on a rafter just below the eaves she saw a pair of jackdaws that occasionally preened each other tenderly.

In the empty cages being overrun by greenery—it was incredible how swiftly nature filled the vacant spaces—pigeons cooed and butterflies darted around each other in a whirling dance of color. This was the real world, not the collection of freaks officially on display. She was starting to appreciate nature more and more, she noticed. It paid no heed to selective programs of elimination, it simply went about its business.

She showed the butterflies to Bert, who watched them wide-eyed. "Why are they all gray this year?" he asked.

Ellen looked at him intently. The butterflies weren't gray, they were white and yellow and reddish-brown. She pointed out different ones, described the colors of the flowers they landed on, but the feeling that she was confusing the child made her uneasy. "Are they all gray?" she asked, squatting down in front of him and brushing a lock of hair from his forehead.

"I don't know," he replied after a moment's pause, then scrambled down the path to another cage full of real nature.

There were only a few people in the zoo. Couples with children. Most of the children weren't interested in the cages. They played on the paths and patches of grass. Here and there were couples pushing baby carriages, no doubt containing the beginning of the newest generation.

Ellen felt the eyes boring into her back every time they passed a couple. The other visitors avoided Bert and her like the plague. Anything apart from the norm was dangerous. Bert stood at the edge of one of the playgrounds for a moment, watching the little girls shouting around a sandbox, but made no move to join them. When the little girls' parents called them away he grabbed Ellen's hand and pulled her along, further into the park.

Ellen seethed with rage, cursing the fact that she had to put up with this evasive behavior again; she felt like scratching the women's eyes out. It annoyed her sometimes, the way Bert consistently avoided confrontations. He didn't know much about DIANA; he was only a baby when the plan came into effect, but he could still sense that he was being ignored.

When she sat down on a bench in the sun, Bert let go of her hand and walked over to a big stone mushroom on the lawn. He leaned up against the statue, ran his hands over the red cap, then looked at his fingers. But as he was climbing up onto the mushroom, he banged his knee against the rough edge of the cap and fell to the ground.

Ellen jumped up and went over to him. Waves of panic rolled over her when she saw that his knee was bleeding. The blood wasn't merely dripping from the wound, it was gushing from his already weakened body. She grabbed the edges of the cut and pinched them together, but the blood kept coming, pouring from the wound, trickling through her fingers and dripping down to turn a dirty brown color in the grass. She pinched harder and Bert began crying. She knew she was hurting him, but it was all she could do to stop the bleeding.

It didn't help. She called out to the couples nearby, but no one came. She took a handkerchief from her handbag, wrapped it around the boy's leg just above the knee and twisted it tightly. Bert was still crying, but he kept his sobs under control. The wound was just below the knee, making it difficult to cut off the flow of blood.

She heaved a sigh. Why did this have to happen when they were miles from home, with no one to turn to? "You have to help me," she told the child firmly. "Hold on tight to the handkerchief and grit your teeth."

The little sewing kit with heavy thread had been in her bag constantly for the last few weeks. She took it out and removed the thin needle, already threaded and ready for use. "This is going to hurt," she said, wiping the blood from the wound. Then she stuck the needle through the edges of the cut, and roughly stitched it closed.

Ellen was getting cold. She sat, huddled up, on the bench at the bus stop near the laboratory. Bert was lying on her lap, asleep. She had covered him with her coat and was waiting for the night to end. It was too dark to see a thing. There was almost no moon, no lights on anywhere. Most of the houses had no generator, and natural gas was scarce. The laboratory, just a few hundred yards down the road, was blocked from view by the high walls that protected it.

After only a few hours, it became too much for her. She was frightened, all alone in that bus shelter. The streets were deserted, and she started imagining things about people who knew she was in the shelter and wanted to harm her child, about dogs that were going to attack her—in the city, the larger dogs in particular had banded together to hunt in packs.

The cold and her fear made her feel even more defiant than Bert's accident that afternoon. She had taken the bus again, not home, but to the laboratory, where she demanded that they treat her child. Unfortunately she had arrived after closing time and even under the new system the bureaucrats refused to show any flexibility. No one wanted to help her; they hadn't even offered her a room for the night so she could be helped in the morning, because the problems she came for couldn't be solved anyway. She had spent so much time begging, threatening, pleading with them to help her child that she missed the last bus home—that damned public transport again. Finally, exhausted from the struggle and without another word, she had gone outside, where she now sat propped up miserably, waiting for morning to come, waiting for the ladies who apparently didn't find their fertility program important enough to keep the clinic open around the clock.

She had kept it up for three hours, three hours filled with jumbled thoughts, images flashing by, Bert and his dead father, cruel women in white coats, beaming couples—like in the old TV commercials for life insurance and washing machines, couples with their new babies, sweetly dressed little girls dancing in slow motion around her Bert, her Bert who wasn't allowed to go to school, who wasn't even allowed to be cured.

Ellen's rage resurfaced. She really was becoming unstable lately, switching within a matter of seconds from total apathy to extreme defiance. She took the child in her arms and walked to the laboratory with long, determined strides. No one stopped her at the entrance. She walked past the main desk. The night matron was startled from her sleep but too drowsy to react when Ellen pushed through the broad swinging doors, past the sign AUTHORIZED PERSONNEL ONLY, and into a long white corridor with dozens of doors facing onto it, white doors bearing no sign of who or what was behind them.

She strode on, following the corridor around a corner until she came to a heavy door marked ABSOLUTELY NO TRESPASSING, and beneath that, in smaller print: PUNISHABLE BY RELOCATION.

Ellen walked up to the door without the slightest hesitation. But even before she had reached it, an alarm went off. The deafening wail of a siren echoed through the corridors. The child, who had only looked around in a daze until then, began crying with a sound that tore at her heart, and Ellen sank to the floor, put her hands over his ears, covered his body with her own and began weeping uncontrollably. Something in her broke. She didn't respond when hands dragged her authoritatively to her feet, only screamed when someone tried to help with the child, clutched him to her and meekly let herself be herded along, back where she came from, along the endless corridor to the main desk where a big woman with mussed blond hair was waiting for her. The woman spoke to her calmly, asked no questions, but gently pushed her down onto a chair and then picked up a phone.

"Come with me," she said after a brief exchange. "Diana wants to see you."

Diana received them in a sparsely furnished room with a few chairs and a bare little table—it looked like the waiting room of a doctor of little means and insufficient commercial insight to cover up that lack with old outdated magazines. She was wearing a floor-length silk bathrobe with lace trim, and her graying hair, which reached far down her back, was bunched together at the neck with a clip. It made her look more feminine and human than the bun she wore on television.

A much younger woman, wearing a bathrobe tied tight around her waist in a way that emphasized her breasts, came in with a trayful of cups and a pitcher. The scene had something of an old-fashioned tea party about it, ladies visiting each other on Sunday afternoon, sipping elegantly from their teacups and nibbling on cookies, discreetly spouting the most blatant gossip about other ladies who were spouting their gossip elsewhere.

But this was different. This was dangerous. Ellen realized she'd gone too far and was now at the mercy of the woman before her. She wondered what she was going to do with her, whether she would be relocated, whether Julie would be allowed to go along, whether they would take Bert. She was still clasping the child in her arms. He looked at the women in the little room with frightened eyes. Why didn't he ever say anything, why didn't he defend himself, play on their emotions? Sometimes he acted like he was already dead.

"Don't worry," Diana said—it was as though she had read Ellen's thoughts. "You can go home tomorrow and take your child with you. We know you're desperate, and that your desperation keeps you from realizing that you're acting senselessly. You can stay here for the rest of the night. I'd like to invite you to come to the studio tomorrow for the third DIANA broadcast. Kristina will take you home afterwards."

The heated room and the woman's calm dissolved the last of Ellen's resistance. All the energy had been wrung from her body by the hectic hours at the zoo, the cold in the bus shelter, the excitement of her raid on the laboratory and her relief that they weren't going to take her child away from her. Diana had not offered to help him, she realized that, but she didn't push things. She was too afraid of losing him.

Diana seemed to follow her train of thought. "I know you're concerned about your child," she said. "After all, nature never gave a mother the ability to discern between her feelings for a boy or a girl."

Ellen sat up straight. "He's so helpless," she objected rather weakly.

But Diana was unrelenting. "He is helpless," she agreed, "but he is also useless. You know that. You know the facts. Learn to accept them. Raising children is a great burden. It's an investment, both genetically and physiologically. A child like this demands an incredible amount of time and energy. It's in your own best interests to channel that time and energy into efforts you know to be useful, efforts which contribute to your genetic future. You yourself have felt what a heavy investment it is; a child takes everything you've got.

"But have you ever stopped to think that a child growing in your belly acts like a parasite, drawing the best your body has to offer to the womb, wallowing in your blood, in the nutrients you've absorbed, processed and carried through your body, a parasite that continues in its egocentricity even after it is born, demanding attention, bending a family to its will, manipulating adults on whom nature has imposed the most untenable of all emotions, parental love?

"You're a scientist. Take a look sometime at the literature describing the behavior of growing children. You'll see that children behave in a way that allows them to exploit their parents to the fullest degree, that they systematically simulate the love their parents expect, mislead their parents so cunningly that they themselves finally come to believe that the love they simulate is real, and self-deception is the best way to convincingly deceive others.

"Parents and children don't have the same interests at heart. Both are committed to their own survival and to transferring their genes to the next generation. Children unconsciously know that they carry half the genes of each parent, and use that knowledge to force their parents to clear the way for them to live as independent, reproductive beings. A difficult relationship, an unending haggle that nature has made acceptable by introducing that strange concept called parental love, and by giving it a concrete chemical form."

Diana sipped her tea, then carefully put the cup back down on the table. She looked Ellen straight in the eye. "A child acts as a parasite," she summarized. "Its presence can only be justified if it is also useful to you, for then it is no longer a parasite but a commensal, a creature that lives off of you like a lodger and which you need as a vehicle to carry your genes on to the following generation. A child becomes a commensal when it contributes to the reproduction of your genes. But that will never be the case with your child. Your child will never be of any biological use to you. He will remain a parasite, as long as he lives."

The TV studio was small, cramped really. A chair and a narrow table in front of a blank screen, with barely enough room to push back the chair and roll in a camera. The table was bare, no paper, no glass of water. Diana was looking dull and strict again, her hair in a bun, her clothing dark gray. Assistants pinned a microphone on her, but she needed no directions from the stage manager. She spoke without using the auto-cue, straight into the camera, her eyes fixed on the lens. They plopped Ellen into a chair in the corner and told her to keep quiet.

The third installment of DIANA began with yet another strongly worded statement to grab the viewers' attention.

"Women have paid a high price for nature's roundabout strategy of fusing sperm and egg cell for the purposes of reproduction. . . . Women had to tolerate the presence of the male, who thought of himself as the stronger sex from the moment he was able to think at all. . . .

"Yet nature never aimed at inequality between the sexes. . . . The only natural differences were those inherent in the reproductive task alloted to each sex: the male as fertilization machine, the female as the nurturer and bearer of new life . . . a difference which scores of evolutionary biologists used to persuade males of the validity of a frivolous life-style, of a dissipation and promiscuity perfectly explainable by biology. . . . Within that model, men could best promote their own reproduction by impregnating as many women as possible. . . . Women, on the other hand, were portrayed in this same male-hewn image as creatures who were to live faithfully at a man's side, and put claims on his attention so that he could help with the raising of their children. . . . A woman could produce relatively few children, so they had to provide maximum yield. . . .

"In this way, biologists introduced the concepts of the macho man and the faithful female. . . . But they were badly mistaken about the female. . . . Women could bring a powerful weapon to bear against the male and his pretensions: their ability to manipulate the fear that he was not the biological father of the children for whose welfare he worked. . . . Men came up with all kinds of tricks to guarantee their exclusive right to reproduce with their women, the least subtle of which were the chastity belt and infibulation. . . . They were terrified of bringing up someone else's children; a well-founded fear, for no one could know when a woman was fertile unless she chose to make it known herself. . . .

"Nature itself is fundamentally unfaithful. . . . So are humans. . . . Even in our own generation, ten percent of all children were sired by someone other than the man who thought he was their father. . . . Women reaped just as many benefits from unfaithfulness as men. . . . A woman who bore the children of different fathers bore children with varied genetic characteristics, offspring better prepared for survival in an unpredictable world. . . .

"Our distant female ancestors saw to it that the men they lived with did not know whose children they bore. . . . That's why they concealed the moment of their fertility, why they remained—unlike other animals—sexually active throughout the year, flirting even during their infertile periods and making eyes at all the attractive men in the group. . . . Their children were adopted and fed by the community, they received food from all the men, which increased their chances of survival. . . .

"When our ancestors began leading a nomadic life, when it became difficult for women to search for food and carry a child at the same time, a genetically driven parental bond developed, which lasted an average of four years and led to the rise of serial monogamy . . . a form of behavior prompted by the woman's goal of commanding the father's assistance in bringing up her child, and of ensuring a maximum of genetic variation in her offspring . . . a form of behavior that elevated the man to more than just a fertilization machine. . . . But as long as biology prevailed, as long as culture had no determinative grip, women remained at least equal to men. . . .

"Scientific research has also shown that women usually make the final decision when it comes to choosing a mate. . . . Partridge hens choose their males not for their excellent ability to show off their plumage, but for their ability to act as good guards, to keep an eye on the surroundings while the brooding hen goes looking for food. . . . They are attracted to inconspicuous behavior; males with a tendency to show off their plumage draw attention, dangerous attention, because the females they entice also stand a greater chance of being preyed on by a fox or a hawk. . . .

"Female guinea pigs unappreciative of the advances of a pushy male spray a stream of urine in his eyes, and escape before he can see a thing. . . .

"Sea elephant males are put through the humiliation of having the female—for whom they have fought themselves to tatters for days—start roaring during copulation, thereby attracting other males, who attempt to prevent the already problematic attempts at intercourse. . . . Only if they are strong enough can they ward off their attackers without losing the female in heat. . . . By means of her resistance, the female ensures that she will be impregnated only by a strong male. . . .

"Female animals of many species don't take things lying down. . . . The males display their capabilities and the females select the one to sire their offspring. . . . Studies have shown that modern women, despite male oppression, usually ran the show when it came to forming a couple . . . but in a very subtle way. . . . The best seductresses were those who made men think *they* were the ones making the decision. . . .

"Men should have considered themselves lucky. . . . Originally, nature didn't provide for males . . . not even among humans. . . . Embryological research has proven this. . . . It was always claimed that embryos were sexless, or neutral, during the earliest phase of their development. . . . That is not true. . . . A nascent embryo is female. . . . During the first month of their lives, all humans were girls. . . .

"Only after five weeks did the rudimentary sex organs develop into ovaries or testicles. . . . The choice was genetically determined. . . . An embryo that received a short Y chromosome from the sperm cell became a boy. . . . If it received X chromosomes from both father and mother, it remained a girl. . . . This means that, in a population without fathers, no sons will be born. . . . In the course of evolution, males gained control over their own sex. . . . They needed a gene to do that, a gene on their Y chromosome that would turn approximately half of all female embryos into boys. . . .

"The genetic route is not the only one nature followed to determine sex. . . . The sex of the offspring of some reptiles, such as crocodiles, is determined by the temperature at which eggs develop. . . . The eggs are laid in the sand and buried. . . . The eggs on the bottom develop at a lower temperature than those just below the surface. . . . Males hatch from the warmest eggs. . . . Higher temperatures are needed for males to develop. . . . Nature has to invest more heavily in males than it does in females. . . .

"Population density serves to determine sex among certain worms and fish. . . . When there are only a few of these animals, no males are born. . . . Only when the population grows do an increasing number of eggs produce males. . . . This gearing-down mechanism—males, after all, lay no eggs—prevents excessively rapid population growth. . . .

"Among certain coral fish, there is only one male in each group. . . .

When it dies, one of the females in the group becomes male, thereby ensuring the necessary fertilization of the eggs. . . . Nature has in this case provided for the transformation of females into males. . . .

"The same thing happened among humans. . . . Only in the early nineties did it become clear that probably a single gene was essential for creating males. . . . It may not have been the only gene involved in the process, but it played a key role in activating other genes. . . . This produced an avalanche of reactions, including the development of the sexless glands into minuscule testicles. . . .

"Comparable key genes were found in mice and flies, where a single gene also proved capable of prompting the reaction resulting in male development. . . .

"Men, therefore, had all the genes they needed to remain women. . . . The only difference was that their Y chromosome contained a section that made them male at an early stage in their development . . . a relatively small step in the course of evolution, no doubt, but one with dramatic consequences. . . .

"The mere presence of this key gene was not enough to turn an embryo into a male. . . . It also had to perform its task with inimitable perfection. . . . The important thing was for the rudimentary testicles to quickly begin producing hormones. . . . The sex hormone testosterone played a particularly female-repressive role—testosterone, that monstrosity of nature that made man run, that elicited war and violence, aggression and rape, that gave us such genetic monsters as the Tartar Tamerlane, perhaps the cruelest warlord the world has ever known, or Nero and Bluebeard, Al Capone, Mike Tyson, and the Serb Ratko Mladic, who advocated rape as a means of ethnic purification during the Bosnian war. . . . The list goes on forever. . . .

"The myth of Caenis contains a great deal of scientific truth. . . . Caenis, a lovely and vulnerable young girl, was raped on a beach by Poseidon. . . . To buy her off, the god of the seas allowed her to make a wish. . . . Her wish was to become Caenus, a man, an invulnerable warrior who soon became so arrogant that he defied the gods and had to be eliminated by the centaurs. . . .

"A simple act of intervention turned a girl into a reckless male. . . . It happened to half the human species. . . . Once an embryo received a shot of aggressive testosterone during the first month of its development, its sex organs became masculine. . . .

"That drive for masculinity exacted a heavy toll. . . . Some scientists claim that the relatively shorter life span of males was due at least in part to accelerated cell fission in the growing male embryo, which had to produce hormones as quickly as possible in order to keep from being overwhelmed by the maternal hormones with which it was bombarded. . . . Scientific research showed that, even as early as the bicellular stage, those clusters of cells whose genetic constellation ordained them to become male divided faster than those which were to remain female.

"Such heavy exertion caught up with them in the end. . . . The older humans became, the greater the difference in life expectancies between men and women. . . . The price men paid for their drive for masculinity was a heavy one: an early death. . . ."

Diana was silent for a moment. The third part of her series had almost come to an end.

"Men were an aberration that depended on a single gene, accepted by nature to solve the complicated problem of fertilization," she concluded. "Nature is fundamentally feminine."

"Do you believe in the philosophy behind DIANA?" Ellen asked Kristina, who was bringing her home in one of the Warriors.

"It's not a philosophy," Kristina said. "It's pure science." But she was quick to relativize her remark. The science Diana used to justify her program was correct, but other explanations existed for most of her theses.

Kristina had nothing more to say about it. She was no scientist, but she had spent enough time around the laboratory to realize that there was more to it than the arguments and experiments Diana used to promote her program. The fact that Diana had succeeded in carrying out her plan, however, was an accomplishment in itself; after all, what other scientific experiment had ever had such an impact? Only nature had ever been able to design and successfully carry out large-scale biological experiments; most of those, however, had been on a trial-and-error basis, random alterations in genetic information with a generally unwholesome effect on their bearer. But occasionally, when accompanied by drastic changes in the local environment, their effects could be favorable, and they would then filter down rapidly to following generations.

The biological experiment that was DIANA, however, was the product of a few human minds, based on solid brainwork and crystal-clear science. It had worked within just a few years. Nature usually needed generations to change things. So Kristina was prepared to assume that the scientific basis for DIANA was solid, in any event, and perhaps even more relevant than other interpretations.

Ellen wasn't so sure. Jasmine, the laboratory director, had voiced such a simplistic view of the facts about breast cancer, claiming that the incidence would decrease as a result of reduced exposure to pollution and hormonal birth control. No definitive scientific proof had ever been found for a connection between precisely those potential factors and breast cancer itself. An unhealthy diet and a modern life-style, in which women started menstruating earlier and having children later, were probably more decisive.

But those arguments didn't jibe with the doctrines of DIANA. Since the distribution channels had collapsed after the program's introduction, there was reason enough to complain about nutritional standards. And there was no way to predict the effect of promoting absolute freedom on the age a woman started menstruating or reached menopause. The new life-style and reproductive techniques were the subject of extensive study. The scientists certainly didn't know everything; that was obvious from their cautious references to the inconveniences of genetic imprinting when they presented their fertility program.

"What exactly are they studying at the laboratory?" Ellen asked. "Why's it so heavily guarded?"

Kristina's answer was once again evasive. She said she wasn't sure, most of the wings in the complex were off limits to her, too. A special detection system had been installed that set off an alarm whenever someone approached the classified zones, an alarm that automatically locked all doors, including those behind the intruder, so all escape routes were blocked. The alarm could only be turned off with a smart card that told the system its bearer had clearance to enter those areas. Only a few women had a card like that.

She volunteered nothing more, and Ellen didn't push her luck.

It was an exciting drive home over the badly maintained roads. A motorcade of four Warriors, with Kristina's up in front, all manned (as it were)—Ellen was aware of the absurdity of applying that term to an exclusively female unit—by six women loaded down with ammunition belts. There were crates of hand grenades and heavy-caliber ammo on the floor behind the front seat. The fighting machines were ready for battle.

"What do you do, actually?" Ellen asked as they drove through a dense patch of bushes that had grown up onto the road.

"We keep the peace," Kristina replied, half laughing, half irritated.

Ellen had heard stories about mandatory long-distance relocation, had felt the repressive fear that came at the thought of having to find your place again in strange surroundings. She had heard the increasingly persistent rumors about penal settlements—prison camps, some people said—where criminals or those who had opposed DIANA were confined without government support, forced to fight it out among themselves. No one knew whether those reports were true—there wasn't much reliable news coverage—or whether they were simply spread as a deterrent to keep the women in line.

The pangs that had accompanied DIANA had not been entirely soothed. The pain elicited by the program's implementation still raged in the minds of many. People had come to the mass realization that their former life of affluence was gone for good, while the doctrine of DIANA was pounded into their brains, beating them silly with a never-ending stream of propaganda about the need to invest in the next generation. The propaganda had spread from the laboratory where it was developed to all points around the globe, with the speed and impact of an epidemic.

All means of communication, including satellite TV and computer networks, were used to pound the joyful message into terrified minds. With the loss of global connections, the propaganda had become decentralized as well. Local women had taken charge of spreading the word.

And it had worked. The people had mastered biological thinking. They seemed to accept the logic behind DIANA. Few of them possessed enough insight into the basic principles of biology and genetics to come up with serious arguments against the program. Diana had played an almost unbeatable hand.

"What's that supposed to mean, keeping the peace?" Ellen pursued. "Hunting down men?"

For that was exactly what Kristina did. Keeping the peace was one of the responsibilities of the village authorities. But if the problems were too great for a local solution, they could call in the help of special tactical units.

Those units only rarely came into action. Everyone, including Diana, had been surprised at how quickly people had resigned themselves to the situation. Diana had, of course, counted on the fact that the concentration of testosterone in the female body was too low to provoke violence easily, but resistance even without its physical expression could be troublesome.

Yet most women had reacted complaisantly. Even those who rejected the program out of hand hadn't struggled too bitterly against it.

And the women from criminal circles, from whom Diana had expected problems, turned out to be so eager to shake off the yoke of their gangsters that they had never even thought to use their experience with violence against those of their own sex. On the contrary, most of the violence committed by women during the implementation of DIANA had been directed against men.

From the very start, the struggle to survive had been more important than the struggle against the program. The women who were assigned to villages—as most were, for the cities were uninhabitable as long as the channels of distribution and energy supply remained blocked—organized themselves well. Women from the country looked after the emigrés from the city, and taught them to provide for themselves.

A surprising, though awkward, form of solidarity arose within the small communities, reinforcing Diana's conviction that splitting up society into village units had been a smart move. In this she had also relied on biological information, on data indicating that humans had wandered over the savannas in small groups of a few dozen individuals for millions of years. This form of social behavior was deeply ingrained in the genes, much deeper than the recent culture-driven constructs that had led to the rise of cities with their epidemics, their famine and poverty, criminality, pollution and dependence on fragile technological devices that obstructed social contact and induced loneliness, that provoked stress and psychological problems—all of which showed that humans weren't made to live bunched together in large, complex groups. Cities were too artificial to be livable.

Kristina glanced at Ellen, who looked back at her with a trace of a smile on her lips. "That's right, I hunt men," she admitted rather hesitantly. "Men are a real danger. We're particularly out to prevent incidents like the one with the killer of Montreal, Marc Lepine, who stormed into a university auditorium on December sixth, nineteen eighty-nine with a semiautomatic rifle, gave the men there one minute to leave the room, and then began shooting the women. He killed fourteen women, wounded thirteen, then committed suicide on the spot. The police found a letter in his pocket, saying that his action was a political one: he was out to avenge himself on the women who had ruined his life, his world.

"Obviously, something like that could still happen. That's why we patrol conspicuously in areas where men have been sighted. It's a preventive approach, and it seems to work. There are very few actual incidents with men at large. Most of them surrender quickly. They know they have no future. And if they don't surrender, they die. They haven't adapted to living in the wild. And they have no organized structure like ours to fall back on when times get tough."

"What happens to them?" Ellen asked.

"They go to a special village," Kristina replied, "where they stay until they die." She hoped Ellen would believe that.

Ellen didn't pursue her questioning, even though this was the first time she had heard about a village of men. She was afraid someone would get the idea that her son might be better off spending the rest of his days in a village like that.

She looked tired, her clothing was wrinkled and dirty, and there were thick snarls in her otherwise so-neatly groomed hair.

Kristina knew Ellen was fighting a losing battle, and she felt sorry for her. She was the perfect embodiment of the traumas that had accompanied DIANA. She patted Ellen's hand consolingly. Ellen grasped her hand tightly and her lips began to tremble. She fought back the tears while she ran her fingers desperately through Bert's hair, the way she always did when she felt tense.

Bert sat on her lap, watching every move the driver made. Kristina acted indifferent, even though she must have noticed the boy's interest. Kristina said a few words to him, but Bert only smiled and laid his head shyly against his mother's breast. He clung to her like an adopted child to its favorite parent.

"What are your expectations for the boy?" Kristina wanted to know.

Ellen reacted cautiously: "He should be given a chance. He doesn't deserve this."

It was quiet in the car for a moment. The tension grew.

"No one's going to give him a chance," Kristina said. "You're only hurting yourself by fostering that illusion. Being naive won't get you anywhere."

Ellen bit her lower lip. "Well, I'm working on a solution," she snapped.

Kristina tried to make her see that there was no solution. Suddenly she had a hunch. "That man won't be able to help him," she blurted out.

Ellen looked at her aghast.

"We know you've been seeing him," Kristina bluffed, "but he can't do anything for your child. He's all alone."

Ellen was silent.

Kristina put an arm around her shoulders. "You're all alone too," she said. "I admire you for what you're trying to do for your son, but I can't help you either. You must realize, however, that it's dangerous to fix your hopes on that man. He's probably using you to get valuable information. Chances are you're his only contact with our world. You'd better be careful."

A tear ran down Ellen's cheek. She felt lonelier than ever. Her friend at least seemed willing to do something for the boy, however little that could be. But Kristina was probably right. He had plans of his own. Bert was just a child, he would only get in the way.

She leaned her head against Kristina's shoulder. Kristina laid a hand on her neck. Ellen felt warm, and suddenly sleepy—the tension of the last few days had worn her out.

"What makes you think he can help the boy?" Kristina asked after a while. "He's so powerless."

"He's not alone," Ellen answered without thinking. "He's part of an army. That gave me hope."

Kristina cursed silently. An organized group of men. She knew this would happen someday.

It was drizzling, which made me even more depressed. I hated the clammy feel of clothes sticking to my skin, especially when I knew it would be days before they could dry out again. I couldn't stop shivering. A forest can be chilly on a rainy day, even in late spring.

A few weeks earlier, having forgotten that not all trees are as dependable as oaks and pines, I'd fallen out of a cherry tree and wounded myself in the groin. The wound had become infected and itched. My impression had always been that wounds healed faster when you were out of doors and didn't treat them, but that obviously didn't apply to this one.

To make matters worse, I'd started in on the blueberries long before they were ripe and had come down with a bad case of diarrhea—fortunately I had the forest all to myself. You never saw Tarzan or John Rambo—or any of the other heroes of the silver screen who bent nature to their will before standing up to the rest of the world—fall out of a cherry tree or spend half an hour behind a bush with their pants around their ankles. They could fall hundred of yards into a deep ravine, land in the tops of sturdy pines and then sew up their wounds with great strapping stitches.

I spent some time observing the speed with which the creatures of the forest soil discovered a pile of runny shit and made off with it as a welcome alternative to the usual dry leaves, decaying pine needles and half-empty moth bodies. But my mind kept wandering back to the past.

My mind always did that when I was feeling bad. I could only think about the future, or at least how I'd get through next week or next winter, when I had my strength up. It had become impossible to make plans, which was why I took refuge in the past, sublimating the most banal memories into moments of boundless joy.

While I was picking blueberries, I'd suddenly started thinking about my mother. As a boy I'd once brought tears of tenderness to her eyes when, after a fight about picking strawberries, I surprised her with a whole bucketful of them. Her reaction had stuck with me. I wondered what had happened to her, whether she still lived in the village where I was born, and how she had arranged her life without my father. Would she still play golf, a sport she'd taken up only to keep my father company after his retirement?

She'd refused to adapt her life any further to that of a retired husband who had nurtured all kinds of plans, like writing a book, but who spent most of his time making a nuisance of himself for lack of anything better to do. He had finally ended up like my grandfather, something he had wanted to avoid at all costs, tinkering away his days in the big garden behind the house. Would my mother do the gardening these days, supposing she still lived there? The untended sections used to be the most interesting. I had discovered warblers there, mockingbirds and other fascinating creatures, and the loveliest wild plants. Those plants were probably having a heyday now.

How were the older women like my mother, who suddenly had to fend for themselves, reacting to life after DIANA? Would they be taking part in the fertility program? Controversial experiments before the war had shown that women over sixty, who no longer produced fertile egg cells themselves, were fully capable of carrying to term embryos that had been implanted in their wombs, and of giving birth. There was a certain degree of risk involved, of course: brittle bones posed a greater chance of fractures during delivery. The hormonal makeup also changed after menopause, which made it less than manifestly obvious that the baby would be born with all the necessary parts.

My mother would never do anything like that. She'd never been too crazy about modern reproductive techniques. What's more, she had three daughters after I was born, so she wouldn't have to worry about justifying her contribution to coming generations. But then again . . . Half her grandchildren had been boys. Maybe I should try to look her up. If she still lived at home, it was only a hundred miles away. But it would be a dangerous trip.

How would she react if she found out I was still alive? She'd probably be confused. Even Ellen, who was a lot younger and better acquainted with the more unpredictable side of my character, had found it difficult.

Not having seen Ellen for weeks made me even more depressed. Something must have happened. She was obviously leaving the little bit of gardening that had to be done to Julie. I lay waiting for her at the edge of the forest for days, a tactic that became increasingly dangerous as the weather improved and more and more people ventured from the safety of the village for a little walk. A few couples even crossed the fields to the edge of the woods.

It wouldn't be long before their misgivings about nature ebbed far enough for women to start coming into the forest to pick berries. If I didn't adapt, I'd be running a much greater risk of discovery. I hated the thought of having to adopt nocturnal habits, of having to hide all day. I could see pretty well in the dark, but I was appalled by the idea of spending the rest of my days as a pariah, begrudged even the light of day.

By keeping an eye on the women, and through my contact with Ellen, I'd almost felt like I belonged. The sporadic contact and occasional observations had lent a faint glow to the idea that I didn't have to live like an owl in the night, unseen and therefore nonexistent. A lot of people regarded their own sort, and themselves in particular, as the hub of existence, because they never noticed the rest. Most of them never even saw the diversity of nature.

Sometimes I asked myself whether keeping such a low profile was really so smart. Was staying alive as long as possible the best I could do? Choosing to do that implied passively accepting things as they were, and ruling out all possibility of change.

That question was bothering me again. The weeks without seeing Ellen had started weighing heavily. I needed to find out what had happened. Maybe she'd died, maybe something had happened to Bert, maybe I'd never see her again.

It was this horrible uncertainty that finally made me abandon the undeniably correct—yet intolerably frustrating—standpoint that passivity was the best policy. I was still afraid of death, even after the hell I had been through during the last few years, but I was even more afraid of a life without surprises. I had violated my intuition about safety before, taken steps that could easily have cost me my life. So why did I have so much trouble doing that now, now that I could actually put up some resistance? Was it because resistance—that elusive element that reared its head in every war—only became visible when it was all over? Only when the stories of opposition and heroism began to be told, stories that took on a life of their own once the threat of death was gone, stories that had nothing to do with the reality of war itself?

I eventually realized that my contact with Ellen had been prompted by the urge to break out of this rut, to show myself, at least, that I wasn't just abjectly giving up.

So, with this insight in mind, I snuck one moonless night into the center of the darkened village and found the big house where she lived. From the things she'd told me about its location and style, it wasn't hard to find. The streets were deserted at night, so I walked straight to the house, entered the garden and scouted out the situation. My old drive to offer resistance made me put my life on the line; I hid in a little toolshed that was rotting away in one moist corner of the garden. In the shed I found a piece of newspaper, and using the only pencil I had left after my escape, I wrote a little note to Ellen. I told her I absolutely had to see her, that she could pick the time and place, but that if she didn't respond to this message I would break into her house one night to talk to her. I rolled the note up into a wad and waited for hours, bunched up in front of a misty window. I could barely see a thing because of the rain, so I warded off boredom by trying to predict when a drop on the window would become big enough to pull loose from the sticky glass and roll down the pane.

95

When it stopped raining for a while around noon, Bert was the first person to come out of the house. I felt relieved. If the boy was at home, Ellen would be too. He walked into the garden, sat down in the grass and looked around. I waited. Ellen didn't come out. I had hoped I could throw the wad of paper at her without blowing my cover, but this was taking too long. I was getting nervous. I decided not to wait until Bert went back inside. I left the shed and walked over to him, pressed the wad of paper in his hand and made him promise to give it to his mother, only to her, and not to tell anyone that he'd seen me. He barely reacted. He didn't say a thing, but he didn't seem afraid either; he took the paper and followed me with his eyes as I walked back to the shed. If Julie found out about our meeting and heard where I was hiding, I was a goner. That was the gamble. But I had the impression Bert wouldn't do anything that silly. It was a gamble, but a calculated one.

Ten minutes after I'd handed him the wad of paper, Bert struggled to his feet and went back into the house.

"Hey, don't underestimate the power and importance of masturbation," I told Ellen. "I don't really miss making love anymore, it's something from another lifetime. When I do get excited, which is usually when I'm daydreaming, then I just masturbate until it goes away. It's fascinating, you know, masturbation. Scientists used to think so, too. Seems it's prompted by more than just the urge to have an orgasm.

"The thing that puzzled them was the paradox of the seemingly wasteful character of masturbation on the one hand—men lose so many cells and women so much energy in an apparently fruitless activity—and its more or less universal popularity on the other. It was hard for them to believe that a widespread biological commonplace could have no function.

"Besides, it seemed ridiculous for a man to compromise his chances of fertilization by shooting off hundreds of millions of his own reproductive cells. But studies showed that there was no connection between the quantity of semen that ended up in a woman—most of it ran out again anyway—and the chances of achieving fertilization. A masturbation session could even be useful to the male, because it allowed him to get rid of the older sperm cells and ejaculate only fresh cells during copulation, cells that would race up the fallopian tubes like college boys chasing their first coed. In that sense, masturbation could actually prove advantageous. But, of course, that's all history now."

"And what about when women masturbate?"

"Masturbation among women had to do with choosing the man she wanted to make her pregnant. A lot of married women had at least one lover, and they didn't always want to have a child by their legal spouse. Superficial behavioral studies suggested that such women preferred to make love with their boyfriends just before ovulation, at the moment they were reaching maximum fertility.

"Without necessarily being aware of it, they had a mechanism at their disposal to help influence the outcome of the spermatoid contest between the men who shared their bed. The muscular contractions during a female orgasm could act as a whip to drive the sperm cells towards the egg. The chance of fertilization was greatest when a woman had an orgasm anywhere between one minute before ejaculation to forty-five minutes afterwards.

"The same thing goes for masturbation. Sperm cells sometimes stayed alive for up to five days in a woman's body, and if she masturbated a few times she could actually propel the sperm swarming around inside her further up toward the ovaries. In principal, if she made love with different partners, she could influence the chance of being impregnated by the male of choice. In the days following a roll in the hay with her sweetheart, she only had to masturbate regularly to give his sperm a head start on the competition. And, by the same token, she could use orgasms to keep from being impregnated by her lawfully wedded husband. An orgasm before sex almost entirely ruled out the chance of immediate fertilization. The sperm that came along afterwards simply couldn't get up there far enough."

97

Ellen laughed. "Are you making this up?"

I laughed too. "It's all in the serious scientific literature. Most of the theories came from the same British research group. They also discovered that, on the average, men who suspected their wives of cheating on them produced more sperm per ejaculation than men who blindly trusted their spouses, and that men who made love with a woman who had all the physical traits of a good mother, such as broad hips and full breasts, ejaculated more sperm than men who made love to less maternal-looking women."

Ellen hadn't looked so relaxed in a long time. She really seemed to be enjoying herself. "How did they find out?" she wanted to know. "Or was it pure speculation?"

It wasn't. The hypotheses were based in part on sperm counts from condoms used by student volunteers, and partly on the number of sperm cells in the threads and clots of semen discharged by women after sex. It must have been a lovely project.

"Where do you get all this from?" Ellen asked.

From memory. I wrote about all this before the war. I used to be fascinated by the biological background of human behavior, but I'd never dreamed it would be used to deal such a massive blow.

"So how are things with you and Julie?" I asked her. "Do you two have sex?"

Ellen fell silent again. This was the sixth time we'd seen each other since I'd handed the message to Bert. It had taken ten days for her to respond, ten days during which I'd had to force myself not to sneak back into the village and go looking for her.

The first time she appeared in her garden—it was the first nice day since I'd gone to the village—I was so surprised that at first I didn't even dare to approach her. I stayed behind the bushes, fully aware that she knew I was there, but she showed no sign of wanting to contact me. She was alone, and she had gone on working rather distractedly, a chop of the hoe here, a bit of scratching there. She never even looked around. Finally I just walked over to her. She'd smiled, and apologized for keeping her distance, but said there'd been problems, with both Bert and her. She hadn't known what to do, hadn't known whether it was smart to risk these meetings.

But she seemed relieved too, and during our second meeting—Bert was with her again that time—they had walked with me into the woods to pick berries. It was a nice little outing. Bert was so excited, he kept looking forward to seeing me after that, reason enough for Ellen to make her visits more frequent. And those visits became just that, visits; we no longer made plans to change the situation. She was simply pleased to see me, pleased to see how Bert livened up when he was around me, and I was happy to have the feeling that I belonged a bit.

Now we were lying in a sunny spot at the edge of the woods, chattering away, relaxed.

"I can't seem to have a real relationship with Julie," she said after a long silence. "I tried as hard as I could for a while, but it's too forced. I just can't make myself love her. My whole life is forced. I have to spend so much of my time on Bert, no one else lifts a finger to help. I have nightmares. I go out and hoe even though I don't want to, because there's nothing else for me to do. I'm stuck in a relationship with a woman that I can't see as something lasting. And I'm sick of the propaganda machine that never stops rolling over us.

"When I do talk to other women from the village, I see how quickly they assimilate everything, how they erase all the details from the past that don't fit into the new framework, how they've come up with a new way of thinking that perfectly explains everything they want to hear. They're looking for another kind of truth, and they sweep reality under the carpet. It's terrifying. What's really terrifying is that it works, and that it works so fast."

She talked to me about the zoo with its selective menagerie. Zoos often come up in war stories, with animals being eaten and prisoners locked in cages.

She talked about her act of desperation in the laboratory, about the night she had spoken to Diana, the relief she'd felt when she realized that they weren't going to prosecute her, all elements that fit in the enforced brainwashing she had undergone. It was still strange that they had let her keep Bert. They must have known he didn't have long to live.

She never talked about the future. For her too, the future was a black hole full of hidden suffering and broken dreams.

We spent hours going over old memories, polishing up the image of a world we would never see again. We clung to the good moments we'd spent together, immersed ourselves in those few hours of happiness. It made us both wistful. Before long I would be kissing her the way I used to, making love to her, begging her not to undress too quickly, to linger over revealing her breasts, to postpone that *moment suprême,* that first caress I sometimes put off for hours because I was always so disappointed when it was over. I laid my hand at her throat and bent over her. She laughed and pushed me away playfully—just like she had the first time—but I grabbed her hands, folded her arms above her head and let my free hand glide down along her throat and over her breasts.

That's when the first bullet struck, hitting the ground nearby. I rolled over, flat on my back, and a second bullet whistled past. *Shit.*

Bert started crying, Ellen panicked. "They know we've been seeing each other," she shouted, a catch in her voice, and she pushed me away.

I kept rolling until I landed in a dry creekbed, then scrambled to my feet and walked into the woods in a crouch.

The shots had come from above us, from the woods. I tried to figure out how the creekbed wound through the forest with regard to the shooter's position. But it was no use. I crawled back down the culvert and peered over the edge. Ellen was stumbling down the slope with Bert in her arms.

They'd known we were seeing each other, they'd laid in ambush. I had to get back into the forest, back to my hiding place, but I forced myself to breathe calmly, knowing I could stay calm and make the right decisions under pressure. But my mind was a blank. I didn't act automatically or move off in a given direction, I just remained lying where I was.

Another shot rang out, further away now, not from up the hill but from the other side. I saw Ellen stand still out on her garden plot. A woman with a rifle in her hand was coming down the hill. It was Julie. I crawled out of the creekbed and ran, bent over, to the edge of the woods closest to Ellen's garden.

Julie was screaming at Ellen, screaming that she knew Ellen was seeing me, that she was sick and tired of it, that she could never love her as long as she was seeing me, that she'd put up with it long enough and that it was time Ellen started showing some responsibility.

Ellen said nothing.

Julie was raving. She kept shooting in the air to emphasize her words, but Ellen didn't move, she was quiet the whole time while Julie paced around her, cursing and shooting. No one came out of the village to help, not even to see what was happening. Fear still had the villagers tightly in its grasp.

When Julie stopped for a moment, panting for breath, Ellen said something I couldn't hear, then turned around and started walking toward the path to the village. To my horror, Julie pointed the rifle at her. I jumped up to yell but no sound came out, and Julie shot Ellen in the back. Ellen pitched forward, landing on top of Bert, who crawled out from under her, howling and trying to get to his feet, one hand on the ground and the other held up to ward off Julie.

She shot him dead on the spot. His body didn't move. Ellen's did, but Julie walked up to her and stuck the muzzle against her neck.

I ran down the hill, screaming loudly, but it was too late. Julie fired, then turned, calm at last.

I stopped, panting, looked at her, then turned around and ran for the forest, cursing my own stupidity. I glanced over my shoulder and saw Julie point the rifle at me, aiming from the hip.

A shot rang out immediately.

KRISTINA'S STORY

MURDER

LOVE CAN KILL. ON A LARGE SCALE. MILlions of people have died of internal bleeding due to the passionate embrace, the lifelong coitus, of two worms that nestle in the blood vessels of the intestinal wall. Once they are lucky enough to find each other—the blood vessels of the intestinal wall cover an enormous distance—they are so afraid of becoming separated that the female settles down for the rest of her days in a special groove in the body of the larger male. He pushes his penis, which is equipped with huge protrusions, so far into her narrow vagina that it can never be withdrawn. Both animals then subsist on love, and on the blood in which they live. Their excitement damages the walls of the blood vessel and causes the host to suffer internal hemorrhages, which worsen when the female lays her eggs, gooseberry-like orbs that use their quills to burrow a way to the intestines, where they are excreted in a stream of blood. With a bit of luck they will be ingested by another body, in which the worms that hatch will go looking for their lifetime partner. A passionate relationship, an extended orgy of blood and sex, till death do them part. The host is the first to pine away, but without his blood the loving couple cannot survive. Meanwhile, their offspring continue their amorous activities elsewhere.

Parasites rule the world. Parasites are the driving force behind evolution. Parasites lie at the root of the invention of sex, the best way for potential victims to remain a step ahead of the microbes. This is the theory of the Red Queen, named after that funny creature Alice met behind the looking glass, who ran as hard as she could without ever taking a step forward. The Red Queen needed to keep running just to stay her ground; genes have to keep rearranging themselves in order to ward off parasites successfully, to maintain the status quo. Sex is the best way to accomplish such a rearrangement. Sex allows them to ward off the parasites' attacks.

Parasites have had a huge impact on life. By the time of World War II, half of the historical population of the earth had died of malaria, the calling card of one of the world's smallest parasites, whose unerring choice of vector—a common mosquito capable of withstanding even the most virulent pesticides—unleashed a catastrophe at all levels, from the individual human body to the world economy.

Wars were not won by the best equipped armies, but by the armies best able to resist the parasites that attacked them. Until the twentieth century, soldiers died largely of disease, not of combat-related injuries. Alexander the Great held most of the world he knew in the palm of his hand, but died of malaria in his tent. The Crusaders were forced to bury the hatchet when malaria lent the heathens a hand. The Vandals were unable to conquer Rome because they were beleaguered by the parasite-ridden mosquitoes of the goddess Febris, fever personified by a hairless old hag with a paunch and veins that ran like cords across her body, who was lauded as powerful and just, but who killed on a large scale; a much larger scale than her colleague Mars, the man of war.

The plague was usually considered a woman too, a maiden who would crawl up onto a farmer's back and hitch a ride from village to village, killing people by fanning her skirts. Venereal diseases were named after the goddess Venus, beautiful and lusty but a real conniving bitch, who would have had no objection to being honored as the protectress of a series of nasty and fatal illnesses that struck more men than women.

The French thinker Voltaire wrote a fable about two sisters who held the world in their grasp: Smallpox and Syphilis. The eldest, Smallpox, had enjoyed the limelight for centuries and was out to mutilate people's appearance; Syphilis, a little younger but every bit as cruel, attacked all that made people lovely and valuable. Women as vectors of death, swaying the course of wars by poisoning armies; women, who had far more success with their biological weapons and won the war with ease from men, with their violence of muscle and steel.

People don't rule the world, parasites do.

In the fourth installment of her program, Diana evolved effortlessly away from biology, seasoning tough science with spicy bits of culture.

"The most striking product of male culture was war . . . war against members of one's own gender, and a never-ending, total war against the opposite sex. . . . War often had nothing to do with politics, it was a life-style, a form of cultural expression. . . . War departed from the principles of the struggle for survival in nature, where dominant individuals, the leaders of the pack, are the ones who do battle. . . . In a male war, the dominant individuals, most of them officers, kept well away from danger. . . . They drove the young men into the line of fire, into the arms of death, and stayed behind with the young women. . . . *The finest thing in life,* the Mongol conqueror Genghis Khan told his men, *is not hunting with the falcon, but hunting the enemy, seizing his possessions, leaving his married women behind wailing and weeping, riding his stallions and using his women's bodies as mats. . . .*

"War made heroes of men. . . . But woe betide the losers. . . . A heroic retreat or valiant behavior was wasted on soldiers heading for defeat. . . . Even the Huns, Cossacks, and Vandals scattered in panic when routed, undergoing the metamorphosis from cruel victors to cringing slobs who would do anything to stay alive. . . . A war between men always produced losers. . . .

"Those losses had to be vented and coped with. . . . The only war that men fought for millennia without suffering defeat was their war against women. . . . Yet men and women had long existed as each other's equals. . . . In the small communities that wandered the savannas, men did not rule over women. . . . Nothing points to a fundamental difference in the two sexes' capacity for emotions. . . .

"But male culture forced the woman into the subservient role of the gentle sex, blinding her to the less charming realities of life with the Prince. . . . Many women became a Reverse Sleeping Beauty, as the writer Bonnie Kreps put it in *Subversive Thoughts, Authentic Passions:* they kissed the Prince and promptly fell asleep. . . .

"The origins of modern woman's misery must be sought some three thousand years ago, with the development of the plough. . . . In *Anatomy of Love,* the anthropologist Helen Fisher stated that *'Probably no single tool in the history of mankind has created so much bad blood between men and women, prompted so many changes in human customs with regard to sexuality and love, as the plough.'* . . .

"This point of view is based on the notion that, throughout most of prehistory, both men and women played an essential role in survival. . . . The men went out hunting while the women remained close to camp and gathered fruit, dug up tubers and caught small animals, providing more than eighty percent of the group's food supply. . . .

"The men of the primitive tribes that still lived in the Amazon rain forest and the deserts of southern Africa during this century were no valiant hunters either. . . . They reacted fearfully when they cornered animals that weren't even that big, animals that clawed and roared in fear and that, if they only clawed and roared convincingly enough, were not attacked. . . . Men rarely attacked large animals, and when they did they made use of cowardly techniques, driving mammoths over cliffs. . . .

"Men were no heroes, and had no desire to be. . . . They regarded the females' contribution to be every bit as worthy as their own. . . . Even with the rise of agriculture, when hoes were still the tool commonly used to work the soil, the women—like their gatherer ancestors—did a great deal of the labor on the land, an arrangement that usually granted them a certain amount of power. . . . But the development of the plough changed all that. . . .

"The plough placed most of the work in the fields in the hands of men, because the equipment was too heavy to be handled efficiently by a woman. . . . As soon as the plough assumed an irrevocable role in production, a sexual double standard arose among the farming population. . . . Women became inferior, because they couldn't do the work. . . .

"This had consequences. . . . The general notion that men were more interested in sex than women, the conviction that men were more often unfaithful, the rule that a woman must remain chaste until marriage and the ineradicable belief that women were weak, stupid and dependent, all were redolent of the manure clinging to the farmer and his plough. . . .

"And what the economy imposed on the ploughmen was transformed as if by magic into rules and commandments by the ecclesiastical leaders, those most despicable of men, hypocrisy incarnate . . . rules and commandments backed up by punishments and rewards in a hereafter, and given the force of truth by the fear of death they instilled in the people. . . ."

Diana stopped to regain her composure. She obviously had a thing about the Church.

"The cultural repression of women lasted until very recently. . . . We were already in the process of shaking off the agrarian traditions and their role patterns so damaging to women. . . . The double-income household had made its reappearance. . . . Phenomena such as trial marriages, unwed mothers and small families had become normal. . . . We were digging our way back to the nomadic roots best suited to the archetypal human spirit, which guaranteed the equality of the sexes . . . but it all took such a painfully long time. . . . It was so frustrating. . . . Women could gain power only by fitting into the system. . . .

"Anna Walentynowicz, a Polish woman welder at the Gdansk shipyards, was the driving force behind the free Solidarity trade union, but it was the man Walesa who became president of Poland. . . .

"Indira Gandhi's greatest claim to power was that she came from the right family dynasty, and Margaret Thatcher got as far as she did by acting like a man. . . .

"When it came right down to it, even powerful women remained in the same role of puppet-on-a-string alloted to them in the course of history. . . . When the Turkish and Pakistani prime ministers, Tansu Ciller and Benazir Bhutto, went to Sarajevo during the war in Bosnia to show their support for the beleaguered Muslims, they came not as women with power over an army and the ability to exert diplomatic pressure, but as *mothers* who handed out chocolate and blankets to a population stricken by war. . . ."

Diana fell silent for the second time. She had kept herself fairly well in check until now; this last bit, however, was almost more than she could take. But she recovered quite quickly.

"With the rise of agriculture, humans lost their nomadic nature. . . . They settled in villages and invented the concept of property. . . . They soon found themselves obliged to defend that property. . . . Women were considered chattel. . . . Men invented constructs to bind women to them. . . . They thought up harems guarded by eunuchs, and tolerated minstrels who provided the women with the attention and romance their uncouth lords didn't give them, but who were not to lay a finger on the ladies whose praises they sang, upon pain of death. . . .

"Even in our own century, men saw to it that women knew their place. . . . *'Nature does not beat women,'* Marilyn French wrote in *The War Against Woman, 'men do. . . . By consistently viewing violence against women as an individual act, the foundations of that violence are hidden. . . . Men absolve themselves of all blame, and all social debate is nipped in the bud. . . .'*

"In the best of cases, men concealed their war against women behind a loving mask, in the worst of cases behind large bouquets of flowers. . . . They blamed their aggressive and lawless behavior on biology, on testosterone and the other hormones given them by nature, which forced them to act the way they did, which incited them to abuse and dominate women. . . . They used religion and moral values to impose their views. . . . And they let the media toy with women's bodies . . . the male media that portrayed women as open wounds that started bleeding at regular intervals, and that forced them to rearrange their bodies incessantly. . . .

"Breasts had to be bigger, and then smaller again. . . . Thousands of men earned their fortunes from the endless debate about the ideal female breast. . . . First they shot the breasts full of silicone, and the cash registers jingled; a few years later they drained it away, and counted their profits. . . . Female bodies had to be svelte, but after hordes of women had slaved away to achieve that male ideal, plump was suddenly okay too. . . . The media switched their images fast enough to keep women from living up to the ideal too long, from living too long in the realization that they were an example to the world. . . .

"No such norms were applied to men. . . . Men were never judged by their appearance. . . . Men were spared the shame of walking around feeling they had a body that didn't meet the prevailing fashion profile, a body constantly compared to the few figures that happened to be fashionable. . . .

"The columnist Julie Burchill had it all figured out. . . . In her *Sex and Sensibility,* she wrote about the penis and the importance of its size for women constantly judged by the size of their breasts. . . . *'Denying the importance of the size of the penis,'* she stated, *'is an argument advanced by the male medical classes to reinforce the male ego-armor, but it has done nothing at all for women's sex lives. . . . On the contrary, it has burdened women with yet more sexual guilt: if the size of the penis doesn't matter, then it must be my fault that I don't feel anything. . . .'*

"Unlike what Freud thought, it was not women who suffered from penis envy, but men. . . . *'The penis hangs above the male like a mighty sword of Damocles,'* Burchill continued, *'threatening to scuttle his self-esteem with every step towards bed he takes. . . . It's about time for women to roll up their sleeves and hit men where they're most vulnerable: below the belt. . . .'"*

A brief pause followed, then the conclusion.

"Burchill's suggestion was interesting, but not in the way she meant it. . . . A process of psychological warfare would have taken forever. . . . It's true, we decided to hit men below the belt, but not with psychology. . . . We opted for a hard, exact science that would burn all bridges behind it, once and for all."

Kristina hadn't been able to dig up much information about Diana. Soon after it became clear that the DIANA program was going to work, she'd carried out a discreet investigation of the woman's past. But she didn't discover anything dramatic. Only the fact that Diana had spent years working in a prestigious genetics laboratory, for a professor who had once had his eye on the Nobel Prize.

She had fallen into disfavor there after a colleague accused her of manipulating scientific data to provide new impetus—and so draw more grant money—for her marginally successful search for an unknown enzyme.

The enzyme was called "recombinase." It already had a name, because everyone was sure it existed. Its discovery, it was hoped, would facilitate the use of genetic therapies by allowing the insertion of new or healthy genes in exactly the right place to repair or replace the originals. Scientific honor and fame would come to the first researcher to isolate such an enzyme. Even the Nobel Prize wasn't out of the question.

But no such rewards were in store for Diana. She was accused of withholding all information that didn't jibe with her particular line of scientific thought—information for which she could find no convincing explanation at the time. She was forced to admit it, because she had jotted down the data in her scientific notebooks. It was a painful affair; two publications based on the doctored information had appeared in top scientific journals, and she was forced to rectify them. It was embarrassing, particularly for her boss, who had co-authored the articles and suffered the consequences of his credulity: his Nobel Prize ambitions were mothballed as well.

A few colleagues, who couldn't stand Diana's asocial and sometimes hateful behavior, went a step further and critically analyzed all the data in her notebooks. They claimed that, using special statistical techniques, they could prove that Diana had simply made up a large part of her data, instead of obtaining it from experimental research. Many of her colleagues had been overwhelmed by the speed with which she achieved her results, and their skepticism only fueled the rumors of fraud.

This latter accusation was never entirely borne out, and Diana defended herself tooth and nail. She had always worked hard. To the great amazement of many, her supervisor never turned on her, he never even fired her. Instead, he had assigned her a small laboratory and two assistants—one of whom was Jasmine—so she could continue her work.

There was the usual gossip about an affair. Diana wasn't attractive, but rumor had it that she was well-versed in sexual technique and an expert at oral gratification. The combination of this uplifting insight with the asexual character of the professor's wife did the rest.

No one knew what she was up to after her retreat from the world. She published no more articles, organized no more seminars about her work. She worked in her laboratory almost round the clock. But they all just let her go her own way, pleased to be rid of an ambitious competitor and a disagreeable colleague.

It was Diana herself who asked Kristina to set up the special unit to hunt what she had referred to from day one as "non-inactivables." Kristina had been involved in a shoot-out—a big word for something that had lasted perhaps thirty seconds—with two panicky men who had taken six girls hostage in a hospital. The men demanded treatment in return for the lives of their hostages. It was a rather unclear demand, and one that couldn't be met anyway: almost no one knew what was going on at that time, and no treatment existed for the program's symptoms.

The kidnappers had holed up in the pediatric ward of the hospital. They soon became nervous and, after only two days, started threatening to kill their hostages, one a day, starting with the oldest. They kept their word. On the third day they shot the oldest child and rolled its body out into the hall; the second victim followed the next day.

The men encountered no physical resistance and became reckless. Kristina found a vantage point in the neighborhood, and borrowed a rifle from a friend. She went to the hospital and convinced the head nurse, who was handling the negotiations, to lure the men out into the hall. Kristina then shot them both in the back, without batting an eye.

That very same day she was approached by Diana, who had one of the laboratories for her program in the hospital basement. Diana praised her for her courageous action, and offered her a job.

Kristina suspected that Diana had never realized why she had intervened in that hostage affair. Her daughter was one of the children in the pediatric ward, the youngest of the patients, so she'd had a few days' leeway. She was prepared to kill for her daughter. When she saw that her drastic intervention had not even generated a police report, she decided to join up with DIANA. For her, the incident was a sign that changes were really on their way. The police corps and justice department were no longer functioning, and death had become a part of daily life. Only a few months after the dawn of DIANA, no one even cared about what once would have been seen as a double slaying.

The program would work, that much was clear. The point had been to realize early enough that there was no going back, and not hesitate to throw fairness and principles overboard and work for one's own survival.

Kristina had always been able to see the big picture, even after the death of her son. No one had ever threatened him directly, and the consequences of DIANA had been so overwhelming, so many had fallen prey to it, that she had never even thought of avenging him. The sooner one realized that war devoured root and branch, the better one's chances of getting through it in relative comfort. She soon decided to play an active role in the program. It made sense to her to join forces with the people in power.

It didn't take her long to put together a unit. Weapons and military vehicles were easy to find. Everything society had produced was up for grabs amid the chaos. At first, most of her work was carried out in places where desperate and dying men were running amok; later, she began hunting the non-inactivables who had gone underground.

It never bothered her much. She had never been too wild about men anyway. Most of her life had been spent in a relationship with a man she was crazy about, the father of her two children. But right after their second child was born, the boy, he decided to move out. She'd done her best to accept that. As a modern woman, she felt she should be able to cope with it, especially since he continued to help with the children, who would spend one week with him, the next at Kristina's.

But before long she realized that this wasn't the kind of relationship she was after. She valued domestic life and a traditional relationship more than she had ever wished to admit. She missed the tenderness, the coziness at breakfast, the safe feeling of lying in his arms on the sofa in the evening and listening to him talk about his day.

That vanished, from one day to the next. She had trouble adjusting at first. During a ski vacation she had a one-night stand with a long-haired man who told her he was a property developer. When she got home she ran a check on him, and found out that he had gone into hiding after a deal fell through and left him deep in debt. She hadn't really minded, that one night had been all right, but nothing more than that.

Then she met the love of her life, a relationship that began romantically and soon turned passionate. Their first night together came after what she had insisted should be an evening without sex, an evening of kissing but no fucking. Things had gotten out of hand; for the next six months, the passion couldn't be checked, long absences were painful. The relationship ended the first time they spent a week at her apartment, rather than going to a hotel or a friend's house as before.

Suddenly he was walking around in rooms her husband had paced, suddenly she was lying in his arms on the sofa, listening to his wild stories and having breakfast with him on the balcony where she had so often sat with her husband. Once they'd made love on the kitchen table, the same table on which her youngest child had been conceived. That ended the relationship. She realized then that his presence in her life interfered with her struggle to get used to her status as a woman alone. She had been using him to keep from having to think about the way her life was going, from having to make clear what it was she really wanted. She was afraid of being seen as a woman unable to stand on her own two feet.

There had been almost no men in her life after that. She didn't need it anymore. Being alone never bothered her much; she could give herself whatever she needed, and it spared her all that macho stuff she was so sick of, the pounding away of men who were soothed only when someone acted as though they were fantastic lovers.

She was an expert at masturbation. She'd been masturbating since she was five—although it was only years later that she understood what was going on—and she'd perfected her finger technique to such an extent that the orgasms she gave herself were unsurpassable. She'd often masturbated after making love with her husband, once he'd fallen asleep. The first few years he hadn't even realized that she regularly completed their rolls in the hay all on her own. She still had to laugh whenever she thought of the dazed look on his face when she finally told him about it.

Men were strange. They'd landed on the moon, discovered bacteria in geysers at the bottom of oceanic troughs and used stunning machines to expose the most elementary particles of matter, but after tens of thousands of years of sexual diversion, most of them hadn't found out that women had a clitoris that could be stimulated to produce an orgasm.

Kristina didn't miss men. That's why she didn't mind hunting them down. She'd become opportunistic enough. Humanity and fairness had been overtaken by the facts.

Julie was the first woman she had ever killed. The jealous bitch had blown all her plans. She'd spent weeks lying in ambush on the top floor of a house that looked out over Ellen's garden plot, trying to gather information about the non-inactivable who was roaming around there. She'd had a solid strike, until that rabid harpy with the rifle had ruined the whole thing.

She had no qualms about killing the woman either. It just happened. She'd gotten used to death, the way most people had. Like in the Middle Ages, during the plague, when families would simply go out into the overflowing graveyards for a Sunday picnic, when fairy tales regularly featured Death in a completely acceptable role, when bandits hid themselves under corpses to hold up a coach. Or, more recently, during the period of genocide and the refugee crisis in Rwanda, when hundreds of thousands of corpses were tossed around a little country, when babies nursed at the breasts of their dead mothers, when fathers piled up the bodies of dead children like garbage, and Boy Scouts went out picking up corpses instead of litter.

Death had once again become so normal that no one in the village asked any questions about what had happened to Ellen and Julie. Murder and suicide, because of the boy, was the verdict passed by the village officials, and no one seemed to question it.

That was a good thing, too. Kristina was afraid this village might have the dubious honor of being the first to be attacked by a band of men. Ellen's casual remark about a guerrilla army had put her on her guard, forced her to work out a strategy she would definitely need some day, a strategy no longer exclusively focused on hunting down a lone non-inactivable, but on eliminating an entire group.

The non-inactivables seemed to be getting organized. She had to act fast. The man hiding close to the village was her lead. She couldn't afford to lose him. That's why she'd risked shooting Julie. He couldn't be killed. He had to lead her to his army.

Jasmine was bent in concentration over a graph one of her assistants was showing her, the results of last week's work. She seemed dissatisfied, kept shaking her head and staring at the paper. The girl started defending her work, saying she was sure she'd found the right substance.

"Where's the basal data?" Jasmine snapped. The assistant handed her a page full of statistics. She ran her eye down the column. "This doesn't add up," Jasmine ruled, and pushed the paper back at the assistant, who left the room without a word.

"What was all that about?" Kristina wanted to know.

Jasmine shrugged indifferently. "She's trying to find out whether sperm contains chemical weapons, substances used to eliminate rival cells at a distance. Sperm cells react to chemical stimuli in their environment. An egg sends out messengers to guide the sperm cells onto the one true way, chemical lights in the fallopian darkness. The sperm cells receive these messages through receptors that resemble the olfactory receptors in the human nose.

"I think sperm also had ways of surviving in an environment that was chemically hostile, packed with defense mechanisms against intruders such as microbes and parasites. Some women systematically killed all sperm that entered their bodies, simply because the cells weren't able to neutralize these defense mechanisms.

"Besides, it seems likely that cells molded by millions of years of evolution for success in a hostile chemical environment would have found ways to take at least partial advantage of that chemistry, and use it against their enemies. A substance like the one we're talking about need only slow down the rival stampede to achieve its purpose: preventing the egg cell from being fertilized by a competitor.

"The girl who was just in here made a synthetic product modeled after hyaluronidase, the substance sperm uses to bore through the hard wall of an egg cell. She thinks she's proven that her product is the same as that used in spermatoid rivalry to damage the walls of enemy cells. But I'm afraid she's mistaken. She hasn't proven that her substance has the kind of specificity needed to recognize foreign sperm cells, and keep it from liquidating allied cells as well."

Kristina said she couldn't figure out why Jasmine spent so much time studying sperm, now that there was a technique that made sperm cells obsolete for fertilization.

"Because we want to find out why nature chose such a roundabout way to ensure the survival of the species," Jasmine replied testily.

Kristina was startled by her snappishness. She'd always gotten along fairly well with Jasmine, but she was in a bad mood most of the time these days, sometimes even unapproachable. As her days at the laboratory kept getting longer, she also became increasingly sullen and uncommunicative about her results. The ironic distance she had once shown toward her scientific work and the unbelievable success of the program itself, back when DIANA had just started, had gone up in smoke.

Now all she did was complain about her working conditions and the quality of her assistants, even though she'd hired them herself. She was definitely a complainer. In one of their few intimate moments, she had told Kristina about her life before the war. She'd showed her a thick notebook she had kept, a sort of diary, but not with the usual anecdotes about her daily experiences and how she looked at things. This book was a register of her complaints, minutely detailed complaints—she was a scientist to the bone—about the men with whom she'd had affairs. Complaints about their appearance, about the way they covered up their many imperfections, how a neat pinstriped shirt opened to reveal a concave chest, rolls of flab and ugly, dirty-pink nipples in a wreath of matted black hair; how a pair of spindly legs, or knobby knees or a leg with a tumor behind the knee had stepped out of perfectly tailored trousers; about her systematic disillusionment with the penis that appeared, too skinny, too short, occasionally too long, too rough, too dirty, too much foreskin, too battered by the banging of other women or excessive masturbation—the diary was crammed with comments about the male organ. One thing was obvious: Jasmine had never found the perfect penis.

The book was also full of complaints about the men's performance, the speed with which they came and their lack of attention to her needs. She'd given each of them a double score for looks and performance, on a scale of one to ten, and she had circled the sum of the scores at the bottom of her report. None of the men scored higher than a five—a five, that is, for the sum of both parameters.

"The extinction of the male was no great loss to the world," Jasmine had told her. "They fucked like they had no brains, just jammed it in and squirted. They liked to talk about their cultural background and their education, always boring me with their so-called intellectual discussions, but when it came to fucking they threw all their fantastic achievements overboard and just started rooting. They could only do one thing you couldn't do with a woman, and they were lousy at it."

This morning Jasmine suddenly said she need to talk in private. Kristina frowned. "Nothing serious, I hope?"

Jasmine motioned for her to sit across from her at the desk. "How are things going with that non-inactivable they sighted a while ago?" she asked point-blank.

Kristina sighed. "We've got a tag on him," she began weakly, "but we have to be careful. We think he's part of a small army, so we're following him in the hope that he'll lead us to the others. But so far, no luck. He acts more like a lone wolf."

Jasmine eyed her critically. "Does Diana know about this small army?" she asked.

Kristina shook her head. She'd had enough of Diana's hysterical outbursts.

"She has to be informed," Jasmine said immediately.

That made Kristina angry. "What good would that do?" she snapped at Jasmine. "Are you afraid to take a little responsibility on your own? You were one of the cofounders of DIANA."

Jasmine began breathing heavily, her nostrils flared, a sure sign that she was upset. She exploded, called Kristina a bitch, a whore, with her long blond hair that she refused to have cut short. She shouted that she'd always thought it was a mistake for Kristina to be put in charge of the unit, knew for a fact that Kristina fucked the men she found in the woods before turning them over to the authorities, she wasn't the kind of woman who could break free of men, even a child could see that.

God, Kristina thought, she's really uptight. There's more going on here than meets the eye.

Jasmine's tirade ended as quickly as it had begun, but her chest continued to heave. She looked Kristina straight in the eye. "I want him in my office as fast as possible," she said—it sounded like an order, and that was something else that was new. "I want him, and as many of his buddies as you can find, here, alive." She slumped back in her chair.

"Why do you need them so badly?" Kristina demanded.

Jasmine rubbed her hands over her eyes. "Diana threw another tantrum," she explained almost listlessly. "In the laboratory." She heaved a sigh and clutched at her own closely cropped hair with both hands. "She destroyed the few experimental subjects we had left, just like last time. She went mad, threw herself at the cages, stood in front of the control panel, foaming at the mouth, making sure no one could stop the walls and slide them back." She looked at Kristina with tears in her eyes. "The screaming," she said. "The sound of bones being shattered. I can't take it anymore."

She shook her head and got hold of herself. "The worst of it is that she destroyed our sperm supply. It was all we had left. She really lashed out, raving like Medusa before her head was cut off. She cursed us up and down, she suspected us of inseminating women with the sperm we had. She took the racks with test tubes out of the freezer and threw them against the wall, one by one. Not a single one left. There won't be any sperm experiments for the time being, not unless we find new donors. That's why it's important that we get our hands on normal non-inactivables, and fast. We have to finish our experiments."

"But why?" Kristina insisted. "Why do you have to experiment with sperm?"

Jasmine straightened up in her chair. "A good scientist is always prepared," she said evasively. Then she showed Kristina the door.

Jasmine had something to hide, that much was obvious.

Even the herons had gone. The woods were empty without them, dead. My darling, the heron chick that had been pushed from its nest but survived the fall, had disappeared too. I'd found the little bird before the foxes or badgers had a chance to kill it, and I'd raised it on fish that the young herons in the treetops had vomited up in an unintentional display of solidarity. All I had to do was kick hard against a tree containing a freshly-fed nest and half-digested fish would come raining down around me, perfect for my precious little birdie.

He had stayed longer than the other herons. Even after he could fly he would return to the colony at night, although he slept in the safety of a tall tree from then on. But he finally deserted me as well. His visits to the colony became increasingly sporadic, then he stopped coming altogether.

Damn animals. How wonderful it must be to live by instinct. How convenient not to have to take into account the frustrating consequences of consciousness. People with Down's syndrome or some other mental handicap sometimes seemed like the luckiest people in the world.

I had never been able to understand how consciousness could be passed off as man's greatest attainment. Animals at least lived without worry. How simple it would be to live alone, with genes programmed for solitude. How liberating to be able to break a tie when nature felt it needed to be broken, with no emotions or other irrationality involved.

Consciousness drove man to more than just moral destruction. It was also the reason why his primacy on earth would last no more than a few million years; compared with other species, that was peanuts. Within little more than a dozen millennia, culture had pushed the human species into the abyss; other species hung in there for tens of millions of years. What had seemed to be a unique attainment proved a brilliant move on nature's part: a built-in self-destruct mechanism for a species that had looked down on others with too much disdain.

I couldn't cope with Ellen's death. It kept running through my mind, implying that my life had been reduced to the absolute emptiness and senselessness of pure survival. There was nothing left, except for an absurd struggle against a death that would come anyway. For a while, the world had seemed normal again, everything was the way it had been back when I could spend months clinging to experiences that made life special, and purposely lose my head in the intoxication of a lovely moment.

It was the same trait that got me through those first months of enforced loneliness. After the many traumas, it had been a relief to arrive in the woods, where the forest world went about its business without much interference, except for the occasional catastrophe, like a forest fire or a property developer. Fortunately, that last option had now been ruled out.

In the forest, killing had a clear purpose, a function: survival. Compared to that, the enormous scale of the killings committed in the most destructive war ever seemed absurd.

It took a long time before people came to grips with the idea that what was going on was mass murder. During the past few decades, especially after the debacle in Vietnam, society had become too anti-death, too obsessed with safety. People got hysterical about the death of a blue-helmeted countryman in a war zone where two hundred thousand people had died in two years' time. They were outraged by ten murdered peacekeepers in a country where half a million people had been professionally butchered within a few months. But no one shed a tear for the people of those countries; they weren't from around here, so it wasn't our problem.

Politicians had set up committees to investigate ways to reduce the number of fatal traffic accidents, which each year claimed no more than one person in every five thousand, for a total of a few thousand people in a small country. Absurd polemics were held about whether the number of lives saved by speed ramps to slow down traffic was balanced out by the number of lives lost by the fact that speed ramps also slowed down ambulances. An egg containing salmonella bacteria was whipped up to a health scandal of international proportions, forcing a handful of poultry farmers into bankruptcy. Houses were condemned and businesses closed because some government office felt they somehow constituted a fire hazard and might claim victims, in the statistically negligible event that fire ever broke out. No trouble or expense was too great in the struggle to extend the lives of the terminally ill by attaching them to machines or replacing costly organs. Billions of dollars were allocated to scientific institutions in a panic to combat AIDS, a disease that didn't even claim that many victims. Some of those victims, however, were definitely found close to home.

Death on the home front had become taboo. Men who murdered ten people became world news; the international community was shocked by two children who beat a toddler to death. Endless debates were held about euthanasia, life was sacred and had to be defended, even against those who no longer wanted to live.

Obviously, such hypocrisy could not go unpunished. Less than a year after the first reports came in about a serious public health problem, mortality rates had soared. A crash was looming, a dramatic and spectacular decrease in the world population. Nature didn't go in for logic; that was something for reasonable minds, and those were few and far between. Nature was full of surprises: genetic drift, random mutations, the coincidental confluence of hostile environmental conditions, evolution characterized by biological trauma, huge volcanic eruptions, meteorite impacts and the mass extinction of entire species. The world followed no preordained sequence of events; the world was fickle and would not be tamed.

The human crash would change the world again. The human species itself had been given its big break during an earlier crash, sixty-five million years ago. The rulers of the world at that time, the dinosaurs, had been wiped out in the geological wink of an eye, making way for new experiments in life.

It had all begun so innocently: AIDS-like infections among people who didn't test positively for HIV, and a slight but alarming increase in certain forms of cancer—back then, every increase in the incidence of a disease was termed "alarming." AIDS and cancer had caught the public eye because they were already a problem. Scientists weren't always resourceful enough to react properly to a new development. Many of them had been following the beaten path too long. Challenges weren't very popular—they called for more than an average amount of creativity and analytical capacity—and new developments were always a challenge.

The first consistent reports pointing in a different direction had come from ophthalmologists, who noted an accelerated degradation in the eyesight of a growing number of patients.

Epidemiologists, masters at drafting long lists of potential scapegoats, had rushed in to take part in the public debate prompted by these concerned physicians. They immediately provided the worried populace with the perfect alibi, and the relative reassurance that any responsibility would probably be shared among a great many others: they pointed an accusing finger at environmental pollution.

The hole in the ozone layer, for example, which continued to grow as the result of emissions of CFCs and other industrial products used on a large scale in aerosol cans and refrigeration equipment. This, they said, meant the ozone layer could no longer protect mankind against the harmful effects of the sun's ultraviolet rays. Among other things, these rays could damage eyesight and cause cataracts, as well as affect the structure of the genetic code and induce cancer. But measurements showed no increase in the amount of harmful ultraviolet radiation reaching the earth, except in the area around the South Pole.

There had been a scare about a "greenhouse effect" that would cause global climatological warming, because the sun's rays reflected off the earth's surface were imprisoned by a layer of carbon dioxide and other pollutants. The rise in temperature could promote the proliferation of viruses and other pathogens; scientific observers, however, were never able to register a substantial rise in the earth's temperature.

A debate had raged concerning acid rain and other aspects of an environment gone to pot: sulphur pollution, nitrate saturation, smog, dioxins, lead poisoning, they all had their day. One politician hungry for publicity even dragged in the unhealthiness of hormones used to raise cattle. Prophets of doom pointed to the innumerable illegal chemical dumps, the thousands of miles of high-tension wires, the nuclear power plants, the discarded atomic weapons and the nuclear waste dumps that had surely started leaking by then. In other words, the environment took the blame for everything. It took a long time before it began to dawn on people that there was more to it, that murder was being committed on a massive scale.

The fear only really hit home, however, when people realized that no one was safe, regardless of origin, sexual preference, education or class. The targets were not only those vulnerable in the eyes of society, the less able-bodied, the drug abusers, the artists, the homosexuals.

The victims came from all levels of society. It was this insight in particular that caused the initial panic. Leprosy and smallpox were for beggars, the plague and TB for fringe groups, AIDS for those of aberrant behavior; at least, that's what people chose to believe.

But this was different, this had far-reaching consequences for everybody. Science brought its full weight to bear on the problem. Suddenly there was no lack of money for research. Additional funds were allocated, torn away from budgetary items that became trivial from one day to the next: costly physics research was no longer so urgent, space became uninteresting, miniaturization programs in electronics could be scrapped; all available resources were pumped into saving mankind.

Researchers spoke resolutely, saying they would find a remedy, pool their efforts and coordinate their activities on a global scale—that was real news. They would succeed, because they had to. Only nitpickers were bothered by the fact that science had failed to eliminate cancer, or AIDS, or malaria, or that it had been powerless to keep TB from rearing its head again.

The first major breakthrough came when someone noticed that only men were becoming ill. The epidemic's seeming lack of effect on animals was noticed before it occurred to anyone that women, too, were spared. That's how narrowly science and health care focused on the male.

It was time for the epidemiologists to enter the limelight again. There was no longer any doubt about where the blame lay: chemical substances had entered the environment on a large scale, mimicking both the structure and effect of the female sex hormone estrogen. Hundreds of industrial substances, such as the PCBs commonly used in consumer electronics, the insecticide DDT with which the world had been heavily dusted, some of the phenols used in plastic products, substances that were almost entirely resistant to degradation and could accumulate in the environment for decades on end—hundreds of these substances had the same steroid structure as estrogen, and could release the cascade of reactions otherwise reserved for the body's own sex hormones.

It was discovered that alligators were unmanned by DDT, that there were more surrogate estrogens circulating in the blood of male pumas than natural hormones in that of their mates, that male predatory birds had become sterile biochemical hermaphrodites, because they'd developed too many female characteristics.

Humans weren't spared either. They took in these steroids at their mother's breast, then later in the food they ate and the water they drank. Someone recalled that men had suffered before from increased exposure to estrogenic substances. Hadn't the number of sperm cells per ejaculation been halved within fifty years' time? Wasn't this latter male generation only half the men their grandfathers had been?

But things turned out differently. Molecular biologists failed to find supportive evidence for this hypothesis. No abnormally high concentration of steroid chemicals were found in the bodies of those who had died. The feverish search continued for months, tests were carried out for the presence of a running series of potential causes. With no success. The hypothesis had to be rejected.

The world only truly began to understand the challenge it faced when, two days after the announcement of the first success in the struggle against the new threat, the laboratory in question was leveled by an explosion. All data were destroyed along with it.

Diana didn't seem impressed. She sat, stiff as a ramrod, in her chair amid the statues of black butlers in her room. Jasmine was acting nervous again, Kristina simply waited to see what would happen. Jasmine had insisted that Diana be informed of the possibility of an organized revolt.

Diana didn't even react to the news at first. The room was quiet for a long time.

"Not all thinking women are backed up by good common sense," she said at last. "Living proof of that was the writer Camille Paglia. In her *Sexual Personae: Art and Decadence from Nefertiti to Emily Dickin-*

son, she had the nerve to claim that, without men, women would never have gotten further than a banal farming existence, that civilization without men never would have progressed beyond the thatched hut.

"She never realized how close she was to the truth, albeit for all the wrong reasons. In their megalomania, men never saw that humans weren't made to operate on a large scale, that they weren't programmed to live in communities larger than a village.

"Paglia said that men had always crammed the world full of ingenuity in order to impress women, who—starting with the influential mother figure—played a dominant role in their lives. Her theory was based on historical and cultural studies, strictly in the social sciences, so her errors were flagrant. For why were men the ones who wrote operas, committed mass murders, the ones who wanted to pack space full of laser weapons, who wrote aggressive rap music, collected hunting trophies, ran marathons and took the challenge of completing double triathlons? Because men needed to have their egos soothed, because they wanted to prove to themselves that they could reach the top, that they had the power to leave the world speechless. This drive to prove themselves was specifically directed at the other men in the world, not the women. The women would follow of their own accord.

"Men were terrified of being thought of as victims. That's why poor Salome had to die, a woman who dared to court a man without being chosen first, a calculating seductress who dropped seven veils in a spectacular dance for her powerful stepfather, and was rewarded with a wish. She didn't wish for half his kingdom, nor for the most dazzling pearls; she wanted the head of the man who had rejected her, on a silver platter—an evil deed for which she paid with her own life.

"The figure of Salome remained firmly rooted in men's collective fear of falling victim to a woman. I gave a lot of thought to calling the program SALOME, but DIANA finally seemed better. The huntress implies an active struggle, more so than the calculating schemer."

She ended this speech abruptly as well, then gave Jasmine a penetrating look. "There's no reason to panic," she assured her. "Men won't be coming back. The blow we dealt them was final. They won't get back on their feet. Not even if they're able to raise an army. But that risk is quite limited. These men must be sterile, otherwise they would never have escaped DIANA. So there's definitely no danger of them reproducing. Of course, that doesn't mean they shouldn't be eliminated. Even if it's only to keep the peace in the area."

She turned to Kristina. "I want you to comb the whole area, use all the machines you can mobilize, until you've located the threat and wiped it out."

Kristina went to work more thoroughly than ever before. She detached eighty Warriors, each with a heavily armed crew of eight women. They were to cover every inch of the surroundings; every crack in the ground, every caved-in river bank, every barn and stable was to be searched.

The women were ready for a fight. They weren't specially trained for combat—discipline and organization were not the most striking characteristics of the new system—but they felt strong: they had the weapons and, more important, the moral fortitude that came from knowing they greatly outnumbered their opponents. It was inconceivable that men would have been able to contact each other over great distances without being detected. There could be no more than twenty of them. Even if they were armed and had enough ammunition, they were doomed to fail. There was no way they could defeat six hundred women, who could even call in reinforcements if necessary.

Kristina wasn't sure how her women would react if their lives were on the line. A single life wasn't worth much in a society that had watched millions die, but one's own life, even during that Armageddon, was always worth that of a hundred thousand others. Her women hadn't been given the kind of tough training that would weave their unit into a many-headed whole, an organism that could think abstractly about its constituent parts and drag them into the attack when ordered. They hadn't been trained to advance in the face of common sense, past parts of the unit that had been shot away and left behind to die without slowing down the rest. They were not trained in the conviction that not they, but the bodies next to them, would be the ones to catch a bullet.

Kristina wasn't even sure how she herself would react under heavy fire. She had become used to killing. Not indirectly, like Jasmine with the scientific program she'd unleashed on the world, but with bullets she fired herself.

She had shot down dozens of men, most of them non-inactivables she had tracked down after DIANA had already done most of its devastating work. Her strangest case had been the man who disguised himself as a woman. He lived hidden away in a group of elderly ladies who had been active before the war in an association for the promotion of breast-feeding. The group had somehow managed to stick together after the revolution. The man was a son of one of the members. As usual, it was the neighbors who reported him. But Kristina had trouble locating him; he was quite feminine-looking, even without his disguise.

The surprising thing had been the reaction of the women themselves. Kristina always thought that ladies who lobbied for breast-feeding were a bunch of Milquetoasts, but that was a serious misconception. The amiable-looking social club not only had a man hidden in its house, but also an entire arsenal. Fortunately, the weapons were all smaller-caliber handguns. The women hadn't been such great shots either, and no one from her unit was hit during the gun battle. The rest was child's play. Only the man was killed. A few days later, rumor had it, his mother committed suicide.

Women hadn't fought for their men all that often. On the contrary. As the DIANA program progressed, an increasing number of the male bodies piled up were found to have been stabbed repeatedly, riddled with bullets or had their throats slashed. Some women hadn't waited for DIANA to mow down the men in their lives.

A number of men had defended themselves to the bitter end. One of them had blown up a Warrior with a few hand grenades he had concealed on a belt under his sweater. That was the first time Kristina had lost members of her unit, and the last time she had taken a man into custody without searching him thoroughly. That was how she'd learned the tricks of the trade.

She'd wondered whether she could have learned to kill so easily back before the war. Probably not. For the first time in human memory, death had become more common than life. What's more, the lives of the men she killed had been rendered senseless by the successful implementation of DIANA. It didn't matter whether they lived or not; they had been reduced to tumors that had to be cut away, not only because they were dangerous, but for aesthetic reasons as well.

She'd spent most of the first two years working the edges of the cities in the region where she ended up. She had moved along with Diana when she chose her definitive quarters, at the point when the program had begun living a life of its own and decentralization became a fact. She had hunted down non-inactivables in the warehouse of a large department store, and in the disused freezers of a slaughterhouse; she caught men who had hidden themselves in the smokestack of an abandoned factory, amid the network of pipes under a swimming complex, in the ventilation shaft of an abandoned subway line, and beneath the garbage in an old landfill.

The man in the dump had buried a number of large crates and two containers under the rubbish, and connected them with tunnels like those in a rabbit warren. There were piles of pornography in one of the containers, magazines he'd found during his excavation work. It was his way of entertaining himself. He was able to subsist on what he found lying around the landfill, even though no fresh garbage was being dumped anymore. Kristina had taken him to the laboratory, but Jasmine found him so distasteful that she gave him a shot and had him cremated right away. Jasmine tolerated no evil odors. If one of her assistants had an unpleasant smell about her, because she was sick or overworked, or because she'd been eating too many fresh vegetables, Jasmine would always send her home for a few days.

Gradually, however, Kristina had been forced to shift her field of operations to the rural areas. Not only because the cities were slowly becoming purged, but also because the women had been distributed over the villages and the non-inactivables had followed, like parasites adapting to the changed habits of a host.

It had taken some getting used to at first. She was a real city person, and although she used to spend a few days each year at her parents' lakeside house, she had done nothing there but daydream or read a book on the sunny patio. To teach her units how to work in the countryside, she had recruited rural women. To her surprise, those women were no less hardened than the city women who formed the original core of her troops. She had even taken a few of them on permanently.

Yet she was always a bit uneasy when she had to hunt in the countryside. And now she was uneasy again. She stared distractedly into space. Images flashed through her mind, images of a tropical forest and a wide river, of screaming parrots and a wild night on the town that had begun with a seafood banquet, rolled on past a dance party with foreign legionnaires in some sleazy club, and then, after a long walk through a downpour in the company of some friendly stray, had ended with what was intended to be a no-sex session. But the sex had never been as good as it was that humid night in the jungle.

She still thought about the man she'd been going with then, but without remorse, without wondering how he'd met his end. They were just memories that popped up, the way memories of her youth popped up, of her college days and her children. Sometimes it made her sad, especially when she saw that this new life wasn't always an improvement. But that was the way things went.

She looked around, saw the Warriors spread out along a front that stretched across the fields for miles, then gave the order to start tracking. The women advanced in a long cordon, with no more than twenty yards between them. They advanced from the edge of the village, heading north across the garden plots, up the hills and through the woods, slowly and concentratedly, paying close attention to the ground.

They found almost nothing, only a few spots where a fire had recently been built, but no real tracks. In any case, nothing that showed there was more than one man wandering around in the vicinity. There was almost no doubt about it: Ellen had been mistaken.

It was an awesome sight, all those Mad Maxes advancing, badly maintained vehicles of every color and size, most of them with a machine gun mounted on the back, here and there a sling on which the barrel of a cannon rested, vehicles disgorging hundreds of lightly dressed and heavily armed women, female warriors who spread out over a long line, scrambled up the hill and walked into the woods, staring at the ground, their weapons at the ready.

I saw one of them walk by under the tree I was hiding in. She didn't look up, didn't see the abandoned herons' nests or the huge nest I was lying in, looking down through the thin branches at the goings-on on the ground. I let the long row pass, waited until they were long gone before I started climbing down. I didn't plan to get caught in a trap, like the hare that circles back but gets shot anyway by the clever hunter, who lags behind in the knowledge that a clever hare always circles back.

But there was no need to be so careful: these women didn't know the fine points of driving prey. Women just weren't hunters.

I'd thought about it, thought about it for a long time after Ellen's death. There was no sense in staying alive like I had the last few months, with my only hope that of being allowed to waste away in my soggy forest. I had to do something, something I could tell made a difference, even if it was only to myself. If my plan ended in disaster, then so be it, then this was The End, no quarter asked, no quarter given.

I slid down the tree, dove into a dry creekbed and crept toward the Mad Maxes, which were being guarded anything but alertly. I had no trouble following the network of familiar culverts until I had passed through their lines. The guards, who seemed bored to tears, were hanging around lazily on top of or next to their vehicles, keeping absolutely no eye on their surroundings.

I took a good look at the cars, concentrating on one that had its bed covered with a large tarp. I was taking a gamble by running for it, the last two hundred yards were out in the open, but the guards were looking the other way. I made it to the Mad Max in one piece, pressed up against the back of the vehicle and peered into the bed. The tarp was being used to cover up ammo cases, which were lashed to the sides of the truck bed. The women wouldn't be needing them, no shot would be fired, except maybe at a rabbit or a pheasant. No war was going to happen here.

I carefully eased myself up onto the bed of the truck and crawled under the tarp. The adventure could begin.

SURVIVAL IS A MATTER OF INGENUITY. THE larva of a certain parasitic flatworm related to the liver fluke nestles in an ant. Once it's had enough of its host, it advances to the ant's head and manipulates its brains in a way that makes the hardworking animal change its behavior. Instead of foraging discreetly among the blades of grass, the ant will climb to the top of one of those blades and remain there until it dies of starvation, or until it is eaten by a sheep. Once inside a sheep, the fluke reaches maturity and lays a mass of eggs, an endless rosary that drops from the animal's body into the grass. The eggs fortunate enough to be eaten by an ant are the start of the next generation.

A circuitous but impressive way of life, unparalleled in its inventiveness; except, perhaps, by those members of the flatworm family that also infest humans. These worms begin their lives inside freshwater snails—more than one hundred and fifty species of snail, for fastidiousness limits impact—and then move on to a fish, a crayfish or an aquatic plant before reaching their final destination: the cozy body of a mammal such as man, where the living is easy enough to allow the production of two thousand eggs a day. Once those eggs enter the water, the circle is complete. A complex strategy that rules out all preventive control, and renders the worms indestructible.

Compared to bacteria, though, flatworms are small-scale operators, conspiring in the wings to take a mere handful of lives for their boundless offspring.

Bacteria do things in a big way. The mouth of a healthy human houses more than forty species, not counting viruses and fungi. Hundreds of bacteria cling to every cell of the human tongue, a billion streptococci dart about in every drop of saliva. A sick person's mouth may spray herpes, gonorrhea, TB, and hepatitis B, species that laugh in the face of all natural defense mechanisms, that shake off the enzymes attacking their protective cell walls like pesky flies. Bacteria are totally in control.

In the course of billions of years of evolution, bacteria have achieved something very like perfection. For the last billion years, the thin film across the surface of fresh water has housed exclusively the same species, thousands of them, which no longer take part in evolutionary modification; they became optimally attuned to their environment long ago. Rapid evolution would only complicate things needlessly, would only threaten the security offered by millions of years of uninterrupted success. The goal can never be change for its own sake; the goal is optimal adaptation to one's environment.

Bacteria have had a stunning effect on the world. Without ever allowing their own survival to be endangered, they changed the earth's atmosphere in a way that allowed for multicellular life, for the introduction of complexity, complex life forms that formed new and suitable biotopes for billions of bacteria. The earth's true rulers live hidden inside those visible creatures who think the world is in their hands. But they are mistaken. Humans are not the masters of their fate, they evolve too quickly for that, they change for the sake of changing. Man races ahead with giant steps, yet stumbles over roots almost as old as the world itself.

And the bacteria blithely go along for the ride. For when the humans are gone, new biotopes will arise. Not even man the thinker has been able to defeat them. The most complex organism on earth is no match for the simplest, with its strategic advantage: greater control over the process of evolution. Humans and bacteria fought a war humans could only lose, because bacteria have been fighting long enough to become virtually invulnerable.

Sexual reproduction was one of the defenses thrown up, but even sex couldn't ward off the attackers.

Humans went a step further by making antibiotics to combat bacteria, but the bacteria survived the most ferocious onslaughts, learned from experience and girded themselves for the next battle with a resistance to antibiotics that hadn't even been developed yet. They formed pacts and exchanged genetically acquired immunities—armies trading cannons and munitions to render both allies invincible. Man clung far too long to the belief that antibiotics were an unbeatable weapon in the war against a microworld he could never keep tabs on anyway. He fought an incredibly aggressive war, realizing only too late that he was doomed to lose.

The ultimate attack on mankind, however, didn't come from bacteria. The ultimate attack was launched by even more ingenious organisms, organisms that understood the art of gaining maximum efficiency by delegating energy-guzzling processes—such as reproduction—to a subordinate, to a body charged with the mandatory production of a creature inimical to itself.

Such organisms exercise maximum control over the power of evolution. They know when and how fast to change in order to skirt the latest defenses. They continue to harass man with deadly cocktails of infection. The runaway evolution of mankind makes it vulnerable to attack from an army it can't see. An army of viruses that cannot lose the war, because it can afford to sacrifice billions of its troops without weakening its attack.

Faced with such an army, mankind can never win.

The shed was packed with cars. Jeeps and big station wagons of every color, DIANA painted in huge letters across their flanks, were parked at random, not in rows, let alone arranged according to size or firing power. Military discipline was secondary around here. Rust had eaten its way through most of the car bodies. Heavy artillery and other masculine products of an aggressive caliber poked through the busted-out windows of station wagons, shells were scattered over the back seats, nothing had been unloaded or stockpiled after the last foray.

The shed was filthy too, with waste paper tossed about, oil drums everywhere and tools left lying on the floor between the cars. Order and regime had become unimportant; the role patterns of the past had met their day of reckoning.

It had taken a while before DIANA's vehicles first hit the streets of those large Western cities where the program had started before it was copied and exported on a global scale. By the time I saw the first one, loaded down with heavily armed women, the battle had been fought and lost. That Mad Max—I called them that because they reminded me of the apocalyptic vehicles from the second part of the film trilogy of the same name—had been a clear signal: the women were going to carry on to the bitter end, hunt down the survivors and eliminate them with weapons that had never been able to win a war as absolute as the one these women had unleashed.

The women wanted to distinguish themselves as much as possible from male soldiers. Even after their victory, the tanks and other military vehicles remained behind closed doors. The Mad Maxes were more than improvised battle wagons, they were symbols of the fact that no organized military force was in power. This was no classic war for dominance, but a struggle for survival; no war guided by technological attainments, but by natural ingenuity. The fighting machines weren't an essential part of the struggle, either. They were applied merely to isolate hearths of resistance—local brush fires that would go out by themselves—and to protect crucial locations, like the laboratories. They were useful only to hunt down those unfortunate few who had survived.

The realization that I would survive had dawned on me only gradually. The uncertainty about whether I would be struck down had gnawed at me, especially when I was feeling bad—which was most of the time, even though I had had only a few friends whose deaths I regretted. My health had suffered more from stress than from the epidemic. Every ache and pain seemed a sign that my time had come, that I was the next in line. At first I had been panicky in my avoidance of all contact with dead bodies, but I stayed healthy even after I'd become lax about that. That was how I discovered I was immune to the plague.

Increasingly, though, even my closest female friends began avoiding me. They'd started acting aloof before the first year had passed. But they still had difficulty admitting their reticence to see me. It didn't take long, however, before they lost their scruples about my status as a potential health hazard. The mysterious virus claimed the occasional woman too, and that made me a possible source of infection. Just because I hadn't fallen ill, one of them confided in me, didn't mean I wasn't a carrier. That's why she didn't want to see me anymore.

Later on I started worrying that someone would kill me because I might be carrying the virus. That was when I fled the city, and went underground in the countryside.

At first it had been a relief to be alone, free of the burden of being avoided like a leper. Yet the macabre atmosphere still hung over me, even out in the woods. Death never went away. The day I arrived in the woods with the heronry, I found the first body. The stench alone showed me where it was, a rotting corpse half hidden beneath a briar patch, the body of a man being eaten away by the creatures of the forest soil. Even after his death, the microscopic world was profiting from the sluggish complex of cells that had dragged itself into the woods.

Later I discovered more bodies, and even an illegal dump containing about forty men, just tossed on a pile and barely covered with soil. This used to be called a "mass grave," an object of disgust. I'd never really understood the public outcry whenever a mass grave was discovered. Why were forty corpses in a grave so much worse than the notion that crowds of people had been murdered within only a few years' time? After all, we were all doomed to be forgotten. And if a dead body stayed put long enough, it was suddenly no longer a corpse but a scientific wonder whose last actions could be reconstructed, sperm cells isolated and foot fungi revived without anyone taking offense.

I recalled a scene from my youth: gravediggers working in an old cemetery next to an abbey who hit on the first bones only a few inches under the ground. The coffin had been allowed to drop down on top of a few skulls; everyone could hear the cracking sound they made when crushed. But none of the mourners seemed to mind. The owners of those skulls were long forgotten, the person in the coffin was still fresh in their memories.

At the start of the epidemic, in an attempt to curb the spread of the virus, strict orders had been given to cremate all male corpses. In principle, the cremation was to be paid for by the family of the deceased, but that obligation was soon dropped when the regulatory bodies themselves became decimated. Various government offices had issued directives, accompanied by official lists of diseases and infections associated with the plague and therefore subject to cremation tax. That was why I'd figured the pile of bodies in the woods was an illegal dump; cremation on the conveyor belt was every bit as anonymous as dumping bodies in a mass grave.

I tried to burn that first body myself, afraid that it would contaminate my part of the woods. It took a long time before I became convinced that I was immune to the disease. During that first half-year in the woods, still unadapted and shivering continuously from the cold, I developed the idée fixe that I was in for it anyway. But when I wasn't able to burn the corpse down to ash, I realized that it would be better to just leave it alone. I covered it with soil and let the animals do their work.

Living alone with a few bodies in a dark forest was much spookier than living among a crowd of talking, walking, warm people amid piles of corpses. It took me weeks to adjust to the idea that I'd be living with the dead from here on out, and that they were less dangerous than the virus that had killed them.

It took some getting used to, being back in a man-made environment, being inside again. The shed was huge, but it seemed completely deserted. Out in the woods I'd never been able to shake off the impression that the world had become empty after the epidemic. But I had to keep my eyes open. The women were still around.

A strange kind of excitement came over me. Here I was inside their complex, with no real idea where I was, what I had come to do or how I was ever going to get away. I toyed with the idea of arming myself, took a look at the weapons in the Mad Maxes, felt the heft of a Kalashnikov, examined its safety and trigger, but couldn't see how the thing worked. There was no way to try it out, so I left the rifles alone. They wouldn't have enough firing power to take on the rest of the world anyway.

I found a spot where I figured I could spend the rest of the day in safety—a disused grease pit—and, before going out on reconnaissance, I memorized the layout and structure of the shed and its adjoining garages. Outside, in the darkened courtyard, I decided first to search a nearby complex, a long L-shaped building with curtained windows at regular intervals that reminded me of a school.

The first door was locked, and so was the second. I looked at the building and had more or less decided to try my luck elsewhere when a pair of silvery metal flues caught my eye. They looked almost like giant extractor hoods protruding from the wall beneath the eaves. My curiosity was aroused.

I walked around to the back of the building and saw a little window that didn't match the rest. I found a piece of a plank in the grass and smashed the window. The sound of breaking glass startled me. I listened tensely, but didn't hear a thing. That didn't mean much, though: hearing wasn't exactly my sharpest sense. I opened the window anyway, crawled through and landed in a storage room full of cleaning products. Fortunately, the only door in the room wasn't locked.

It opened onto a dimly lit corridor that led to a room where, to my horror, a woman was sitting in a chair, reading a book. My heart pounded as I snuck back to the far end of the hall and tried the last door there. It was open too. I entered a little room, closed the door, then waited for minutes, maybe even half an hour—I lost all sense of time in the dark. Everything was still quiet, and after what seemed like an eternity, I worked up the courage to click on a little lamp I'd seen on the desk when I came in.

The room felt familiar; I'd spent years of my life in places like this: it was a researcher's office. White lab coats on a rack behind the door, books about physiology and biochemistry scattered around, papers piled on the table. There were graphs on the wall, pinned up between snapshots of a group of women in a rowboat, and a poster full of sharp, yellowish-pink needles and malachite-green blocks: a photograph taken with a polarization microscope. It was a picture of crystallized sex hormones, the female estrogen in blocks, the male testosterone in the form of sharp needles. The caption under the photo read: FEMALE REPRODUCTION IS A DIAMOND, MALE REPRODUCTION A WEAPON.

I sat down at the desk and pulled a blue dossier from the pile in front of me. VAN NULLE, J. was written on the cover in black Magic Marker—Van Nulle, Van Nulle, the name seemed familiar, but for the life of me I couldn't figure out why.

I opened the dossier and my eye fell on an experimental protocol: date, hour, product, dosage, observation period, readings, conclusions.

It was dated earlier that same week, as I could see from the calendar on the desk; I no longer had any sense of days or weeks, even though I'd resolved to keep track of passing time. But keeping track had soon become irrelevant. The only thing I cared about was how long the summer would last, how long it would be until winter came, and I could figure that out easily enough from what was happening in the forest.

The observations in the report had been made in the course of one late afternoon. Next to PRODUCT the researcher had written *nitrogen monoxide;* next to DOSAGE, *maximum,* and there was a zero next to READINGS. When I read the conclusion, I was horrified: *Even upon injection of the maximum nonlethal dosage, Van Nulle fails to achieve an erection.*

My hands felt clammy as I flipped through the rest of the dossier, through a series of results of an experiment recorded on a daily basis. The product was always the same, but the dosage had gradually been boosted. At the back of the dossier—the daily reports had been filed from back to front—was a graph indicating the course of the experiment: injected dosage as function of duration, two weeks' progressive increase and a leveling-out from the third week on. Behind that was another graph bearing almost no data. A zero had been entered for every date on the abscissa, the result for physiological response expressed on the ordinate as TIME TO FIFTY PERCENT ERECTION.

A photograph was stuck to the next-to-last page of the dossier, a picture of a dim-looking middle-aged man. He had been photographed naked, standing against a white wall. The following details were written in pen on the page beneath the photo: *Non-inactivable taken into custody on January 23, transferred February 7, sterile but with no demonstrable genetic defects, requisitioned for sperm experimentation on May 3.*

The last page bore a neatly typed report, under the heading GOAL OF THE EXPERIMENT. *Research has shown that male erection is controlled from the brain, and that nitrogen monoxide is the messenger bearing signals of lust from that organ along the spinal cord to the penis, where it prompts an erection. Nitrogen monoxide is an industrial waste product shown to contribute to environmental acidification. In the human body, this substance serves as an anti-bacterial and neural messenger to provoke, among other things, dilation of the blood vessels. In nonexcited state, the muscle cells of the penis are—paradoxically enough—at maximum contraction and allow little blood to flow through the vessels, thereby keeping the penis flaccid. Under influence of the slightly toxic nitrogen monoxide, however, the muscle cells draw together and allow more blood into the penis, resulting in erection. The goal of this experiment is to determine the amount of nitrogen monoxide that must be injected into the penis to elicit an erection.*

So good old Van Nulle couldn't get it up, not even with the maximum nonlethal dosage. But why were they interested in that?

I closed the dossier and leaned back. The real news wasn't that Van Nulle couldn't get an erection. The real news was that there were men in the complex.

"Biological warfare is not a modern invention." That was how Diana began the fifth installment of her program. "The Tartars tossed the bodies of their companions who died of the plague over the walls of besieged cities, to introduce the Black Death. . . . They brought the plague with them from the Mongolian steppes at a time when Europe was groaning under a population that had reproduced too quickly, without the facilities needed to deal with such growth. . . . The population was weakened, and the results of the plague were disastrous. . . .

"Yet for nature, the plague was a blessing . . . without it, Europe would now resemble the arid plains of the Horn of Africa. . . . The Black Death decimated the population, and saved nature from further assaults on her pristine virtue. . . .

"Under the centuries-old banner of Progress, man had savaged nature to ensure his own survival. . . . The scale on which he began farming finally severed the relationship altogether . . . but nature didn't surrender so easily. . . . The farmer bent to his plough and unearthed anthrax. . . . He cut down so many trees that rats, ticks and fleas were forced to live closer to humans. . . . Their parasites were free to infest a mass of almost defenseless bodies. . . . The farmer's animals also passed along their parasites: measles from the dog, diphtheria and tuberculosis from the cow. . . .

"Yet even then, agriculture could not fully provide for the needs of the growing population. . . . More and more people began retreating to the cities, where they lived amid their own waste water and garbage, breeding grounds for parasites that caused skin diseases and intestinal infections. . . . Cholera, dysentery and leprosy were the results of unhygienic living conditions for citified humans in their densely packed masses. . . . Agriculture, deforestation, migration, commerce and war—all man's undertakings contributed to the parasites' ability to escape isolation and move into a frantic world full of easy victims. . . .

"Man learned a few lessons from the biological holocausts he was confronted with during the Dark Ages . . . but they were not the right lessons. . . . From these traumas, he deduced that nature was an enemy to be vanquished, or tamed at the very least. . . . He developed a mechanistic view of nature, thought of her in terms of simple laws that could be explained and therefore controlled. . . . He shifted his trust from nature to technology, which had to be innocuous, because he'd designed it himself. . . . He used his technology to combat nature, discovered an arsenal of antibiotics, heavy artillery to repel the attacks of nature, weapons that failed miserably. . . .

"Technology was incapable of reconciling man with the natural world. . . . Man didn't understand the danger of self-inflicted vulnerability. . . . He continued to grow without limit, traveled from one corner of the globe to the other, engaged in the mass transport of products over long distances, crowded together in cities, polluted his surroundings and became obsessed with living as long as possible. . . . What he didn't realize was that he was creating the very conditions that would provoke a new biological attack on his position of power. . . .

"That attack did not come unannounced. . . . Familiar parasites reared their heads again, antibiotics had all the effect of a musket against a tank, the most powerful defenses were undermined by new threats for which no remedy existed. . . .

"Man, the farmer and technician, made the world uninhabitable with his ill-considered assault on nature's integrity. . . . Man used his power over the earth to prop the world full of superfluous individuals. . . . His mass breeding produced individuals he could control, but ruined the world for his species. . . .

"In his runaway conquest of the world, man clung to two fundamentally incorrect assumptions, the fruit of an arrogance that told him he was predestined to rule the earth. . . . Man misused the chance development of consciousness to establish himself as the pinnacle of creation and the goal of evolution. . . . Yet there is no indication that evolution stopped with the arrival of the human species. . . . A great many other species did, however, disappear in the intense competition for breathing space. . . .

"Only a few people realized this and warned of the disastrous consequences. . . . Most people saw it as the confirmation of their belief that the earth existed for man—and for man alone, if need be. . . . A handful of deluded minds hushed the collective conscience by fighting for the preservation of a few other species that appealed to the popular imagination. . . . No one seemed to care that yet other species were meanwhile disappearing at an unheard-of rate. . . . And they overlooked the fact that completely different species were beginning on an ascendancy, the likes of which had never been seen. . . . Rats, flies, and mosquitoes surpassed man's own expansion. . . . So-called 'harmful' bacteria and viruses survived the total war declared on them by man. . . .

"The world is no exclusive reserve for humans. . . . A few billion humans pose no insurmountable obstacle to creatures that have survived every atmospheric and evolutionary cataclysm. . . . Man is not the pinnacle of creation, man is a biotope, explored and settled by creatures that will compete him out of existence when the time is ripe. . . .

"The first misguided assumption with which man hoped to exert his will over the world was that consciousness, and the culture which sprang from it, had been a blessing to mankind. . . . No species, except man, has ever suffered the knowledge of its own existence. . . . Yet no other species has ever remained as blind to the limitations of its design. . . . Not a single species was arrogant enough to claim the world for its own, except man. . . . But then, no other species ever wasted as much energy on designing the wrong survival strategies. . . . Man assumed that, because they came from the brain of a thinking species, his strategies would be more successful than those custom-tailored tactics at which nature had arrived by trial and error. . . .

"This assumption was fundamentally flawed, because it took no account of the fact that nature's systems had been proving themselves for billions of years. . . . Consciousness, and the culture which sprang from it, were no blessing to mankind. . . . They were to blame for the accelerated extinction of our species. . . . Few species will ever have lived so briefly on earth as thinking man. . . . Few species will ever have left such a lackluster evolutionary record. . . . Man's primary distinction will be the speed with which he thought himself into oblivion. . . .

"The second misguided assumption, which ruled man's thinking for centuries, was that both biological and social evolution were processes of continuous progress. . . . Biological evolution is no such thing. . . . Increasing complexity does not equal increasing progress. . . . An organism that consists of more specialized cells is not necessarily more successful in terms of genetic survival. . . . In fact, there is more reason to believe that complexity increases vulnerability. . . . The simplest creatures, viruses and bacteria, are the ones that have survived longest. . . .

"Social evolution, despite the claims made for it by those who wished to be seen as eminent thinkers, follows no logical line either. . . . Changes were abundant, but if they failed to follow the path mapped out for them they were seen as incomprehensible, and therefore undesirable. . . . Sexual morality swung like a pendulum between extreme prudery and total lasciviousness. . . . The pinnacles of civilization were punctuated by the depths of barbarism. . . . When survival was threatened, culture turned out to be nothing but a thin veneer that cracked and chipped away. . . .

"The complexity of social organization did, however, increase in direct proportion to the exponential growth of the population. . . . Yet it was a complexity that ensured no success, a form of growth that dragged all thought and action in its wake and could only be maintained if all other factors grew along with it: the economy, the sciences, the social security system, the bureaucracy, the degree of political interference. . . . A growth that became compulsive, as illustrated by the disgust with which analysts mouthed the word 'recession'. . . . Recession, which butchered the golden calf of progress but was also its natural counterpart in the cyclical course of things. . . .

"Ultimately, a growing population was needed to keep up the rest. . . . Feedback had formed a vicious circle. . . . More and more people were needed to keep the economy running and avoid a crash. . . . Unemployment had to be solved by creating more jobs, yet unemployment wasn't a matter of excessively slow economic growth, but of excessive population growth. . . . Never before had so many people on earth been redundant. . . . Never before had so many people tried to make themselves useful by performing tasks that produced only annoyance. . . . Never before had there been so many useless products and initiatives, because so many people felt they had to provide proof of their existence. . . . Society became a sluggish colossus without the agility to react to sudden and coincidental change. . . .

"Man kept his shoulder to the wheel, over-organized himself, increased exponentially in number, but remained—despite all his cleverness—unable to see that he was digging his own grave. . . . He had hit the wall. . . . Conflicts became bloodier, civil wars more frequent, society more dangerous. . . . Marginality became increasingly important. . . . The gap between citizens widened. . . . Street violence, infanticide, gang rape, racism, homosexuality—all became more common, all mechanisms to gear down the unbridled growth of an increasingly vulnerable population. . . .

"And mankind's most dangerous enemies were rallying for the grand assault. . . . Viruses and bacteria readied themselves to storm a fortress that was already cracking under its own weight. . . . An assault force that would be no respecter of persons, that would spare no one. . . ."

Diana was silent for a moment, ready for her conclusion.

"So we decided to act. . . . We couldn't reconcile ourselves to being victimized again by the pursuit of male dominance, to being struck down by way of collateral damage, as the generals so nicely put it, in a settling of accounts with the ruling sex of a species that thought the rest of creation was in its service. . . . We decided to take the offensive . . . an offensive aimed primarily at rearranging society in a way that would no longer jeopardize the survival of the human species. . . .

"We decided to harness the force of nature to eliminate the male half of the world population. . . ."

The attack had come as a complete surprise. Its consequences were overwhelming, especially since no one knew who or what was behind it. It was so massive and all-embracing that no one could see it as the work of a power using a genetically manipulated superplague or anthrax bacteria in a cowardly biological war against the rest of the world.

In fact, it took months before it became clear that this was an epidemic. The symptoms and afflictions accompanying the offensive were so varied that no one thought they could be produced by a single organism. When it gradually became clear that a simple mechanism was behind the many causes of death, panic broke out. That amplified the impact of the epidemic even further, in a classic case of positive feedback.

Nature had summoned up all its fatal creativity, bundled its centuries of experience in the scorched-earth tactics of smallpox and plague in the form of untraceable cells, able to attack all bodily tissues. The cells had not been dormant for years, nor had they hidden innocuously in normally functioning tissue only to sneak out and pounce once their striking power had reached its zenith. No, the cells pounced the moment they were released, sweeping out across the world, killing as they went. Soon they had dominion, not only over death, but also over life itself, which was ruled now by the presence of the hidden enemy and the attempts to locate it.

Reason and logic were quickly devalued in the process. Sects and cults had the world in their grip, preachers of evil and those who fought against licentiousness competed to scream the truth most loudly, the Lord himself had unleashed the Fourth Horseman of the Apocalypse with unbridled power, the Horseman whose name was Death and rode a horse that was pale, for it was without blood, who killed on a huge scale and eschewed no means; the sword, starvation, disease or the creatures of the earth.

Flagellants, priests of Satan and brotherhoods of the Cross appeared from nowhere to proclaim their bloodthirsty messages. They sought and found scapegoats, the classic scapegoats: Jews, homosexuals, and whores were persecuted without mercy, publicly executed with virtual impunity, for the judicial system had fallen into ruin along with the rest of society.

Yet the flagellants, priests of Satan and brothers of the Cross were confounded, exterminated too before they could gain any real influence in the new and lawless society.

Scientists searched feverishly for the evildoer, especially in the early days of the epidemic, but the offensive had spread so quickly over such a tangle of fronts that no logic could be found in it. Without logic, science was lost.

Kristina realized only later how devilish the plan behind the offensive really was, how calculating Diana had been in her operations. She had seen the documents predicting the scientists' disoriented reactions, the speed with which chaos would overrule people's thinking, and how the battle and patients would be lost as hospitals and medical services became overrun and unable to anticipate the massive fatalities among their own personnel—yet another case of positive feedback, and one which gave the creatures free rein.

And the creatures struck without mercy. They unleashed a huge rise in known maladies such as Duchenne's dystrophy, a genetically controlled weakening of the muscles leading to respiratory disorders and cardiac arrest, and in hemophilia, a defect in which patients can no longer produce coagulants and may bleed to death if such clotting agents are not administered.

The supplies of coagulants in the hospitals lasted only a few weeks in the face of such huge demand. Public appeals for blood donors remained largely unanswered, because many people were afraid of being infected themselves, afraid of bleeding to death while giving blood to keep others from doing the same. Solidarity waned under people's fear for their own survival, and the destruction of that sentiment's major breeding ground: mutual altruism, helping in order to be helped in turn.

Rare diseases and cancers soon became common, like Pelizaeus-Merzbacher's syndrome, which attacks the nerve endings in the brain and causes the patient to lose all conscious contact with his surroundings, and Alport's disease, which for some reason attacks both the inner ear and the kidneys, leaving the patient both deaf and renally insufficient.

The creatures also produced entirely new disorders. They attacked the eyes and ears, paralyzed muscles, disrupted the metabolic energy system and caused exhaustion. Some patients suddenly no longer had the strength to carry their own weight, and collapsed as soon as they stepped out of bed. People were no longer able to move from one place to the next, to look for help, so they became dependent on the lucky few who had not been stricken, the healthy ones who were also bound to armchairs and hospital bedsides and therefore unable to contribute to daily life. The creatures induced one infection after the other, on the skin, in the liver, in the stomach and intestines. Digestive systems went awry and turned on their own cells. The enzymes responsible for removing dead cells went haywire and began breaking down vital tissues, nerves, blood and bone marrow, hindering the transfer of metabolites, blocking messengers, cutting off centers of reaction and coordination.

The creatures overpowered the body's immune system, which then ran riot, no longer concentrating on intruders but attacking its own cells. Bodies were digested from the inside out by their own virus-maddened cells, and rotted away like living corpses.

And the creatures didn't stop at that, they penetrated the brains, generating hellish pains at the slightest mental activity. The victims forgot who they were and what was happening to them; that was a blessing, for their brains were no longer in control, nerves fired off messages at an alarming rate in spastic bodies devoid of intelligence or instinct. It didn't take long for most attendants to put such patients out of their misery, before the creatures had completely devoured their way through the brain.

Science couldn't cope with the chaos. Many scientists were infected themselves or entangled in engineering their own survival. They had panicked, too, and lost the calm needed to search for hidden tracks.

Even now, Kristina was amazed at how long it had taken them to find the common factor behind the known diseases and syndromes: the link with genes on the X, the female sex chromosome. One of the world's largest leading genetics laboratories had put all its manpower and vast funding into the search for the unknown assailant. The lab had concentrated on finding deviations in the pattern of disease, a step science had used often enough before, and to good end; studying deviations sometimes led to the discovery of mechanisms that otherwise remained vague amid a complex uniformity.

Yet the researchers didn't look at the few men who had been spared. Healthy men could either be immune to the monster threatening their sex, or simply not yet infected, in which case there was little sense in studying them.

They turned their attention to women who had fallen victim to the epidemic. Hundreds of dead or dying females, struck down by a range of afflictions as broad as that seen among men, were brought in for examination. At first this research bore no fruit; the corpses apparently included women who hadn't been killed by the epidemic, but had died of normal causes. That made it hard to isolate a relevant factor.

But it wasn't long before the relevant factor was unearthed. Someone noticed that a few of the female corpses had strikingly small breasts. A number of the bodies could even be described as quite masculine. When these manlike corpses were dissected, the scientists discovered a series of relatively minor structural deviations, such as underdeveloped fallopian tubes and slight skeletal deformations.

A study of the chromosome chart confirmed their growing suspicion: these women all suffered from a special genetic defect. Strangely enough, their fathers had not given them an X chromosome, but a Y. These were, in other words, X-Y women: pseudo-hermaphrodites who looked like normal women only because the Y chromosome remained unexpressed. This discovery led to the insight that the Y chromosome, normally responsible for an embryo's development into a male, had to play a crucial role in the epidemic.

How so many different diseases could be linked to defects on the X chromosome—the Y itself bears few active genes—was the following subject for dogged research.

Unfortunately, the answer was never found. Diana had seen it all coming. Jasmine informed her of the discovery. The laboratory had hired her to assist in the struggle against the virus, as it had most of the women familiar with research into genetic defects; more proof that no one had any idea what was going on.

Jasmine had told Diana about the growing euphoria surrounding the discovery that X-Y women were also struck down by the epidemic, and Diana decided it was safer to intervene. It was only a precautionary measure; the epidemic had spread so widely by then that it could hardly have been curbed before most men were destroyed.

She had the laboratory blown up.

It was a man, for that matter, who carried out the assignment; a man who asked no questions, a mercenary with a lot of experience in blowing up mosques in former Yugoslavia. The only man who ever proved useful to the implementation of DIANA.

Just how firmly the world had been in the grasp of men became painfully clear once so many of them had died or fallen ill. Everything ground to a halt, at least temporarily. Companies with installations that needed maintenance couldn't resume operations. Many of them shut down permanently because there were too few managers and employees left. Production and distribution collapsed.

Agriculture was hit heavily as well, even though farmers' wives knew as much about work on the farm as their late husbands. But crops were still left to rot in the fields, and overripe fruit fell unpicked from the trees—yellow jackets waddled drunkenly from one splattered, fermenting piece of fruit to the next.

Even in places where farm women joined forces with others, harvests were complicated by the shortage of fuel. Produce could no longer be processed, because processing had become separated from production. And even if the processing plants had been running, there would still have been no way of getting the products there.

Male society had clearly become so over-organized that it was stuck in its own mold, too inflexible to react to a catastrophe. In its impenetrability, its sense of irrevocability, of evolution towards ever greater complexity, it had become too rigid to withstand a frontal attack on its population; and certainly not an attack on those who had designed it.

The dying men dragged the women partway down with them. The survivors were set back at least a century. Only knowledge remained, but knowledge was useless without the means to apply it. Without an infrastructure, knowledge could produce no large-scale yields. An inventive woman, a woman handier than most, could only make her own life a little easier by using the means at hand.

Nature took every chance it got, seized every opportunity to recover lost ground. Plants and animals, I was pleased to see, bounced back much more readily than humans. Animals that had been held captive on stock farms, especially pigs and chickens, were freed in huge numbers by distraught farmers' wives who had watched their husbands die, and could no longer summon the will to go on farming alone.

Enterprising women here and there joined forces to run breeding operations, but those efforts were frustrated by failing feed supplies—temporarily solved by feeding the animals from one stall to those in another—and the impossibility of bringing fattened stock and other products to market. They slaughtered as many animals as they could fit in their freezers or, in anticipation of the looming energy shortage, preserved the meat with the traditional salting and pickling methods from grandmother's day.

Neglected cows and sheep broke out of overgrazed pastureland and went in search of food. During the first few years after the epidemic, farmlands were overrun by hogs accustomed to the stall, pigs that survived by finding fields left unharvested or subsisted, like the dogs and other animals, on the huge quantity of easily available food that was temporarily there for the taking.

I was shocked the first time I saw dogs and pigs gorging on a rotting corpse, although later I wondered why. Dead is dead, and a corpse like that was a source of life for the animals. But you can get used to anything, even the idea that people can serve as food for animals, just as easily as the other way around.

The fresh supplies of partially decomposed flesh didn't last forever. The animals ran into problems too, particularly because they'd reproduced freely as long as they had access to an almost inexhaustible food supply. Dogs and pigs started fighting over the corpses they found, and later on the dogs formed packs to attack and kill the pigs.

It didn't take long for most farm animals—first the pigs, later both chickens and cows—to disappear from the wild, especially after the feral dogs began reverting to the behavior of their ancestors, the wolves. I wondered how they'd do if wolves themselves were able to make a comeback. Maybe I'd still be around to see that.

And how long would it be before the first vultures started colonizing the area? Would their arrival come at the expense of smaller birds of prey? Most predatory animals were doing exceptionally well. Buzzards and kites glutted themselves so heavily on the cadavers that they could barely fly away when startled. The sky was full of circling birds of prey, and the dismal cawing of ravens and crows was the perfect complement to the macabre atmosphere during the first years of the epidemic. Ellen once said she thought everyone should be given a gun to blow the nerve-racking caw of those opportunistic black monsters out of the air once and for all, but I didn't agree. I watched the crows, and thought they were fantastic. It struck me that they had abandoned their territorial behavior and started brooding in makeshift colonies, undoubtedly an adaption to the new, rich and randomly occurring source of food.

The herons didn't mind the occasional cadaver either. Sometimes they acted like well-groomed versions of the carrion-eating African marabou, walking around on their long stilts, necks cautiously extended toward the dead bodies. Like the ravens, they were primarily interested in the contents of the eye sockets. A young heron lying flat at the bottom of a deep nest had once pecked me right between the eyes with its rapier-like bill, leaving me with two shiners like a pair of spectacles. Herons are fond of eyes.

It was almost impossible to sleep away the days in that grease pit in the garage full of Mad Maxes. I was too restless, and too much on my guard. Images of the epidemic kept running through my mind, and food had started to become a problem. There was almost nothing to eat in the complex. I wouldn't be able to stay much longer. Besides, I kept wondering what I would do when I found the men.

For the time being, however, the problem was a hypothetical one. I'd been sneaking around in the laboratory for the past three nights, but I still had no idea where they were keeping the men. They could be carrying out the experiments somewhere else, but there was no indication of that in the protocols I'd seen.

On the fourth night I began searching a completely different wing of the complex. A wing that remained lit even at night, yet didn't seem guarded. It was easy for me to force my way in, but I found only empty rooms, or rooms filled with what at first seemed to be trash, but turned out to be disposable diapers, of varying brands and sizes. Strange.

I had the feeling I wouldn't find my men around here, but I still followed all the hallways until I came to a broad corridor, the only one in the wing, which ended at a heavy door with an iron wheel. I hurried over to the wheel, which spun easily, and opened the door.

Moving cautiously, I entered a room full of bubbling sounds, sparsely lit by a great many weak, bluish-white lamps from aquariums stacked up on metal racks against the walls. The tables were covered with lab equipment, pots of fish food and piles of paper, both handwritten documents and copies of scientific articles. The articles were about mollies, little Central American fish of the topminnow family, unusual in that they bore live young.

The handwritten texts were reports on reproductive experiments with the mollies. The laboratory seemed to be dedicated to biological behavior research. I was stumped. Why would they be carrying out fundamental research on fish? Was this someone's hobby? I ran my gaze over the aquariums and saw fish in groups of various sizes, gliding lazily through the water, apparently oblivious to each other.

Suddenly, through the water, I saw a slight movement on the other side of the glass boxes. The semitranslucent paper stuck to the back of the aquariums made it hard to tell what it was. I held my breath and pressed my forehead to the glass, but saw only faintly moving shadows. Were these the men I'd been looking for? I could hardly believe it. I looked around until I located a door, went through it and found myself in a room stocked with fish food and chemicals. There was another door in the far wall. The key was in the lock. I turned it and swung the door open carefully.

The first thing I heard was the sound of panting and smacking. I took one step forward, but the figures on the floor didn't react. The room was much bigger than I'd thought, a hall really, one small part of which was partitioned off from the rest by the aquariums. The figures lay on mattresses, covered with thin blankets. I bent down and pulled back the blanket closest to me. It was a child. The child rolled over and stared at me with big bulging eyes, then made a rattling sound deep in its throat. It frightened me. I took a look at the next body, and saw with a start that this was a child too. I couldn't believe it. I searched for the switch and flicked on the lights. The bodies began to groan and move, but it wasn't the kind of movement I'd expected. My God. My stomach flipped.

I switched off the lights and rushed back through the storeroom, out into the hall, but my body was no longer under control. When I tried to close the heavy door, my stomach seized up and I vomited, mostly bile.

Sirens began screeching immediately, all over the building. The door closed automatically. Before I could make it down the hall, a rifle was pointed at my head.

The woman kept me covered until three other guards came to back her up. None of them said a word. They took me outside, across an expanse of pavement, to another building where they hustled me into an office and pushed me down on a metal chair. I asked for water, to wash away the terrible taste of bile, but they acted like they hadn't heard me. A fifth woman, when she showed up, was clearly shaken. She had me handcuffed to the chair and frisked, then told the guards to leave the office.

This woman, a mousy type, sat down at the desk and eyed me in silence. Her lips were pulled back in a tense grimace and her eyes kept running over my body as she clenched and unclenched her hands convulsively. She was waiting.

It wasn't long before someone came in. I remembered her, with the obligatory Kalashnikov slung over her shoulder. She was the one from the Mad Maxes, the woman who had tried to hunt me down, then inadvertently smuggled me into the complex. She looked at me with intense blue eyes that radiated toughness, but not complete disinterest. There was something about her that inspired confidence; maybe it was the blond hair, or the naturally nonchalant way she stood there.

"Is this the non-inactivable you failed to catch?" the woman behind the desk demanded gruffly.

The blonde nodded.

"How did he get in here?"

The blonde turned to me and repeated the question: "How did you get in here?"

Images flashed through my mind, images from a TV documentary that had impressed me, an interview with the pilot and the navigator of a British Tornado bomber shot down over Iraq during the first days of the Gulf War. They had told about being interrogated by the Iraqi secret police, about how hard it was not to forget one of the most elementary lessons: keep your distance, tell them nothing but your name and serial number, keep them from getting in too close, from creating a feeling of togetherness, an atmosphere in which even the most banal confession is transformed into primitive camaraderie as it breaks the tension and stops the pain, a camaraderie that will help them find out everything they want to know.

I was already feeling the urge to talk; openness was fairly natural to me—and besides, knowing how I'd gotten into the complex wouldn't help the women a bit. But I kept my mouth shut, every bit as grimly as the woman behind the desk. I was determined to keep my secrets, and to keep living a little longer.

The blonde didn't seem too anxious to hear what I had to say. She didn't even repeat the question. But the mousey one shrieked hysterically: "Why didn't the alarm go off?"

The blonde shrugged. "Maybe he doesn't have any hair under his arms," she answered flippantly.

The drab one jumped up from her chair. "Goddamnit, Kristina, they found him in the secret wing! Don't you understand what that means?"

Kristina didn't understand, because she didn't know what was so secret about that particular wing. No one was allowed in, except for the scientists who worked there, and they were never allowed off the premises. It was a security measure, based on the old Soviet model, to keep information from leaking out. Even the actual guard duty around the critical wings was kept to a minimum, so as few women as possible would know what was going on there.

That's why they had installed a special alarm system, another of the new discoveries made as part of the DIANA program. The system was based on the observation that humans emit pheromones, and the discovery was Jasmine's.

Before Jasmine began her work on the subject, science didn't know much about human pheromones. Insects used them: to sound the alarm, to locate sexual partners and to transmit messages, sometimes over as much as a mile. The sex life of many higher vertebrates is controlled by pheromones with an effect similar to that of sex hormones. Even plants use pheromones, to warn each other of an invasion of aphids or to attract ladybugs, which attack aphids.

Jasmine's reasoning had been that anything so common in nature must have left its mark on humans as well. She'd focused her research on the apocrine glands in the armpit. These glands, found especially in men, and mainly under the arm used most, produced such substances as 3-alpha-androstenol—which is also found in high concentrations in

162

the saliva of boars, along with 5-alpha-androstenone, which produces sexual excitement in sows (and is also found in truffles, which is why pigs are so skilled at locating those delicacies).

The assumption was that these substances also exerted a sexual attraction on humans, partly because the apocrine gland only becomes active from puberty on. The maturity of these glands runs parallel to the growth of hair under the arms, which is intended to better spread the glands' secretions—a shaved armpit emits almost no such odor.

Tintoretto's *Vulcan Surprising Venus and Mars* was one of many works of art depicting a frivolous woman with the armpit fully exposed. Even in modern times, men had instinctively pinned their lover's arm above her head, presumably to better enjoy the arousing pheromones from her armpit.

The scientific literature contained experiments that supported this hypothesis. In a dentist's waiting room, chairs treated with androstenol were occupied almost exclusively by women, and avoided by men. An unidentified substance from the male armpit was used successfully to rectify excessively long or excessively short menstrual cycles. And everyone knew the classic experiments in which the menstrual periods of girls at a boarding school became synchronized under the influence of mysterious substances generated by glands under the arm.

Jasmine's plan had been to design machines that could detect androstenol, and so track down non-inactivables. The project had failed for a number of reasons, one of which was that the effective range of the substance was too short to serve as a tracking mechanism—in the course of evolution, humans had developed other mechanisms for transmitting sexual information over longer distances. Besides, women also produced such pheromones—albeit in much lower concentrations—so the machines' sensors could not react selectively to the presence of males.

As a spin-off, Jasmine had developed the androstenol-triggered alarm system for the laboratories. And, for the first time, that system had failed miserably: it had overlooked an individual of the very sex against which it had been developed.

"Have you told Diana?" Kristina asked.

Jasmine nodded and sank down limply in her chair, looking like she was about to collapse.

Jasmine was going downhill fast, Kristina thought. She had been so enthusiastic, she'd had so much faith in the program. Her ultimate satisfaction had always been the predictability resulting from a perfect mesh between theory and experimentation. And the program seemed to be running perfectly: most men had been eliminated, and the women were adapting even better than expected. But something was wrong, otherwise Jasmine wouldn't be acting so panicky.

Kristina looked at the man sitting in the chair. She figured he was in his late thirties, but he had something boyish about him. His wavy hair was long at the neck and he had a rather patchy beard. His jeans were spotted with mud and he wore a thick sweater with chalk-colored smudges on the shoulders and dirty Timberland shoes—indestructible, just like the old ads had said. He didn't look as derelict as most of the men she'd tracked down; this one had a special look in his eye, resigned, but belligerent at the same time. It was hard to tell what color his eyes were; one minute they looked green, the next a sort of steely gray. He watched the goings-on like a hawk.

Something about him interested Kristina. She felt like asking him a couple of questions, but didn't. It wouldn't be wise, not with Jasmine in the room. But she wanted to know why he'd come here, what he was looking for, and what had happened to that army of men she'd heard about from the woman he'd been meeting.

The door opened and Diana came in, wearing a heavy bathrobe.

Jasmine burst into a verbal deluge, saying they'd found the man in the secret wing, that the alarm hadn't gone off, that she had no idea how long he'd been in there or how he had gotten in, that he wasn't carrying any identification.

Oh my god, Jasmine, Kristina thought. Why would someone like him be carrying identification? She'd noticed that when Jasmine got nervous she fell back into the automatic assumptions of the society she'd helped to rub out.

Diana waited until Jasmine stopped babbling. "He must be sterile," she decided once Jasmine had finally fallen silent, still panting from the exertion of producing such a torrent of words. "We knew that was the weak spot in the alarm system, that a lot of non-inactivables were sterile and didn't produce the androstenol needed to trip the sensors. It's no big thing. What worries me is that he got into the complex. Do you have any information on him?"

"He's the one with the army," Kristina replied, "the one we couldn't locate earlier in the week."

Diana, of course, drew the obvious conclusion. She had a brilliance that was almost akin to genius, but, unlike Jasmine, she could also apply her ingenuity in areas outside her field of professional expertise. "You brought him in here," she snapped at Kristina. "Haven't you learned anything yet?"

Kristina was angered. "I didn't pick this job because I wanted to make it my life's work," she sneered. "A few years ago I was still making radio documentaries."

Diana didn't react to the reproach. "If you brought him in here," she asked, "then how long has he been in the complex?"

"Three days."

Jasmine began whining about the secret wing again, but Diana shut her up. "What finally made the alarm go off?" she wanted to know.

"He vomited," Jasmine replied. "I'm sure he was inside, that's why he vomited."

Diana shook her head. "Have you checked the computer to see whether the door was opened?"

Jasmine stuck to her guns. "He was in there," she repeated.

Kristina looked suspiciously at the bickering women. What could be horrifying enough about the secret wing to make a man—a man who must have seen a great deal in his life—come out vomiting?

Diana noticed her curiosity and turned to me. "Come on, honey," she said to Kristina. "Give me a hand with him." She unbuttoned my pants and pulled them—along with my underpants, which were absolutely filthy—down around my ankles. I slid back and forth nervously on the chair. Diana grabbed me between the legs and felt my balls. She looked at my crotch, and I could see her mind working.

"He's normally developed," she said, more to herself than to anyone else. "So why doesn't the alarm pick him up, not until he vomits?" She thought about it. "He must have some rare genetic defect," she decided, "something that allowed him to develop normal sex organs, but still messed up the hormonal control over his sperm production."

She turned to Jasmine. "Get the masturbator," she ordered.

I was becoming increasingly uneasy. I hadn't sorted out the mysteries of the secret wing, the bitter taste of bile was still in my mouth, and being studied by three women while my pants were down around my ankles made me feel rather uncomfortable. What's more, that "masturbator" sounded pretty ominous.

"There's nothing wrong with my sperm," I said, trying to save myself. "I have a daughter."

It didn't work. Jasmine came back with a little briefcase, put it on the desk and opened it. She pulled on a pair of thin surgical gloves, used a syringe to extract a tiny bit of some product from a little vial, then took hold of my penis and jammed the needle in at the base. I cursed with all my might, called the women the worst things I could think of, but they just went about their business. After a few minutes I felt myself getting hard, and I couldn't do a thing about it. The erection was huge and painful.

The little dish they slid under my balls next seemed to vibrate slightly, then warm up. They took a flexible sheath, attached to a tube,

166

and slid it over my member. As soon as they flipped a switch in the case on the desk, the sheath began to move and hum. I concentrated on the bitter taste in my mouth, on the terrible sight of the monsters in the secret wing, but the machine was relentless. It sucked the sperm out of my balls. A few minutes later the tube filled with white gobs, a release with no relief, because the erection never went away.

Jasmine couldn't believe her eyes when she saw the tube filling up. She burst into another hysterical tirade, shouting that the program was falling apart, that nature seemed to be doing its best to foul them up, that a normally fertile man had failed to trip the pheromone alarm, that an invisible army of non-inactivables was out there somewhere, that more and more women were clamoring for the men to come back, that sperm still hadn't revealed its deepest secrets and that, in the long run, DIANA might just exterminate the women as well.

Diana slapped her hard. "Now you've got a fertile man you don't have to manipulate," she said toughly. "Take him and use him for your experiments. He might just save the program."

ORLD WAR I WAS THE FIRST WAR IN
which fewer men were killed by disease
than by their fellow men. The consequences
were horrendous. During the first war to be
fought between healthy armies, no means of
destruction was left untried. The list of the
fallen was staggering.

The week before the Battle of the Somme,
the British army fired more than a million artillery shells at the enemy, more than twenty
thousand tons of metal and explosives. The first
day of the battle itself, the British lost twenty
thousand men, more than had been killed in
South Africa during the entire Boer War, including those killed by disease.

During that four-year war, the French army
amassed three million fatalities, a half million of
them at the Battle of Verdun alone. The com-
manders were confronted with a growing number of deserters, men who no longer wanted to
attack because they knew that all attacking
meant was being massacred.

Within a period of four years, a total of

twenty-five million healthy men from all over the world were led to the slaughter.

The world's last major fatal epidemic came shortly after the First World War. Within four months, an influenza epidemic claimed as many lives as the war had in four years. Within eighteen months, the epidemic killed more than fifty million people.

The shock waves which pounded against the human defenses owed their power to the ability of the virus to infect through simple contact with saliva, the virtual impossibility of eliminating it without killing the cell in which it was hidden, and the speed with which the virus could change its own genetic structure, rendering hopelessly obsolete all antibodies meant to repel it.

Nature's offensive weapons were much more effective than those produced by human technology, which could not even guarantee success against a seemingly inferior opponent; this had been seen repeatedly during civil wars in which the losing party had access to a much grander stock of heavy weapons.

Even the smallest war received a mention in the history books; whole chapters were devoted to World War I. But the influenza epidemic and the force with which it struck were soon forgotten.

The speed with which humans eradicated the memory of nature's attacks on their health was enough to make your head spin; man was afraid to face the fact that nature was so much more efficient than he in designing weapons of mass destruction. And those natural weapons worked selectively as well. Nature's biological weapons spared the species who designed them; man's atomic weapons did not.

The war against men could not be won by conventional means. That was why, in a sinister echo of the century-old claim that women were much more a part of untamed nature than the thinking, studious, tinkering male, Diana and her assistants developed a biological weapon that soon swept away all defenses.

After due consideration, they decided against influenza, that neat and modern virus which, unlike some of its illustrious predecessors, brought an easy death without trauma. Influenza did not drag its victims down a long road of suffering, it carved no deep craters in their faces, nor did it leave the testicles rotting from their bodies. But influenza was also too familiar, had been studied too closely in the context of the flu epidemics that circled the globe each year. The virus that was to offer the remedy for the human male had to be a good deal less conspicuous. Instead of influenza, Diana finally opted for one of its relations: smallpox, a virus that could lay claim to having caused the greatest demographic catastrophe in the history of mankind. During the conquest of the New World, sailors and soldiers from the Old World had barely needed their own weapons to exterminate the Indians: smallpox cleared the trail long before the conquistadors had to follow it.

The smallpox virus was extremely aggressive. It smuggled its genetic material into the cells it besieged with astonishing speed. Its contagious power was mind-boggling. It could spread through the air and by direct contact, and—an important point—it could not be passed along to animals. Moreover, a smallpox-related virus called vaccinia had often been used in experiments in which genes were spliced into the chromosomes of test subjects. That was essential to developing the weapon Diana had in mind.

It had long been claimed that smallpox no longer appeared in nature, although a few reprobates dared to suggest that the corpses of smallpox victims frozen in permafrost could release viable virus particles when thawed. The United Nations' World Health Organization, however, claimed a total victory over the virus; the last known case of natural infection had taken place in 1977.

At the time, it was agreed that several laboratories would preserve viral samples for the purposes of scientific research, until the genetic information on the smallpox virus had been fully decoded. This information was made public in the 1990s by the scientific journal *Nature*. Yet two of the laboratories that had assisted in developing the vaccines against smallpox continued to disregard the UN directives and refused to destroy their virus stocks. They claimed that they wanted to be prepared for any new attack by the virus, should it be lying dormant somewhere.

One of those laboratories was the Institute for Viral Preparations in Moscow, the other was located in the United States. Diana tried first to genetically modify the smallpox virus found in monkeys and make it contagious for humans, but the experiments took too long. After due consideration, she decided to steal a quantity of smallpox virus from the Russian laboratory; a risky and expensive business, for virus laboratories were known for their extremely tight security.

But Diana had taken good advantage of the growing malaise among Russian scientists in the post-Soviet, post-Communist era. She approached a man, a dedicated but deeply unhappy scientist, whose own research work had been scrapped for financial reasons. She offered him unlimited funding and carte blanche in her own laboratory, on condition that he bring a small quantity of smallpox virus along with him, for research purposes.

Her plan succeeded, but it literally cost her a few gray hairs. If her request had leaked out, she would have had to forget the whole thing, forever. But it wasn't leaked. The man who stole the virus was murdered, for safety's sake, to prevent any slips of the lip.

Once she had the virus, all went smoothly. The plan had been carefully thought out, all experimental protocols established in advance, and the results lived up to expectations.

She had inactivated the virus by suppressing its contagious elements, in analogy to the development of the vaccines originally used to defeat the disease. Then she used genetic engineering technology to add the information needed to attack males and mislead the vaccines. She unleashed the manipulated smallpox particles on the world with a steady hand, but gradually, for only a select group was in on her plan.

The virus did its work, reproducing wildly, spreading from person to person. As soon as the machinery of society itself began to crack, it was easy enough to get to places where rapid proliferation was guaranteed: the water supplies of hospitals and office complexes, the ventilation shafts of train stations and concert halls, warehouses filled with fabric for the textile industry.

Diana had traveled like a tourist, taking her virus cultures to the bastions of male power—stock exchanges, two houses of parliament, police headquarters in major cities—a quirk rooted in her drive to be physically involved in the extermination of the sex she hated so badly. But she soothed the consciences of her assistants by assuring them that they were not the ones killing the men—it was the virus.

The plan worked without a hitch. Before long, the modified smallpox virus had conquered the world for women.

Put a person in a cage and, like many animals, he'll turn into a beast. Before they locked me in the lab cage, I had to take off all my clothes and let myself be washed, clipped and shaven. It took some getting used to, no hair and no clothes.

The cage was a nightmare. Four white walls and five square yards of white floor. A rough concave silhouette of a human body had been molded in the walls at the front and back of the cage. They looked something like the forms my grandfather, a baker, had used to make gingerbread men. The door had no handle on the inside, only two barred hatches; one at eye level like a normal cell, the other at loin level. At the bottom was a slot through which they slid my meals. That was the only improvement over life in the forest; they apparently wanted to keep their test subjects healthy. Food arrived three times a day, but I only really enjoyed it the first time. It didn't take long to realize that I would go crazy if I didn't get out of there soon.

The noises the other prisoners made told me everything I needed to know. I'd finally found the men I had been looking for, but they wouldn't do me much good. They were insane, crazy as chimps locked in tiny cages in some private zoo.

My cage was the last in line. I could only catch a glimpse of one of the poor bastards—five toes sticking through the slot under the door—but the sounds they made spoke volumes: beastly growls, tenuous sing-song tones that would collapse into hysterical giggling, loud smacking and slurping sounds that went along with what I soon came to think of as feeding time.

The first day I tried to strike up a conversation with my neighbors, asking them their names and how long they'd been in the cage. But except for the growling, smacking and giggling noises, the only reaction was a desolate scream. My fellow prisoners were in a state of advanced mental decay.

But then, of course, I hadn't gone through the experiments yet. Without them, life in the cage would have been senseless but tolerable, a mere exercise in avoiding compulsive behavior and coping with imprisonment as a naked body in an empty cage. Without them, I could have tried to keep my mind alert by solving conundrums the way I had on lonely days in the woods, by immersing myself in the past or inventing an imaginary role in a more promising future. A future in a villa on the Tanzanian coast, where I could write about my encounters with the manta ray in the Indian Ocean, the orca off the coast of Argentina, the cheetah on the plains of the Serengeti, or about the first time I ever kissed Anita's lovely breasts, about lobster dinners during a visit to Mogadishu, or about the attempted suicide—for he had botched even that—of a frustrated critic who couldn't find a publisher for his *Banana Republic.* I could write for the sake of writing, without a message, just tell stories.

They ran experiments on us as though we were animals, with no explanations given, no details about how long they would last, what they were about or what would happen when they were over. The only thing the young woman assigned to me said was that, when the back wall began sliding, I'd do better to line myself up with the recesses in the walls. If I didn't, I'd be crushed, and broken bones would make me useless to science . . . and to the world. She treated me like an animal, especially after I answered a few of her questions with noncommittal little nuggets of irony—I wasn't going to help her any, even though I was terrified of what was about to happen.

But she didn't seem to need answers. She soon stopped the questioning and went through the rest of the formalities without a word, scrutinizing me with eyes half-closed, jotting down her impressions, taking a whole series of body measurements and what seemed like a quart of blood, much more than they'd ever tapped at the blood bank. She injected the blood into an array of little tubes and put them in a freezer. Then she took me to the room with the cages.

It wasn't until the day the experiments began that I realized what the hatch at loin level was all about. The hatch at eye level shot up, my tormentor announced gruffly that the experiment was about to begin, then shut the hatch again. When the back wall started sliding forward, my neighbor screamed. He must have been here long enough to develop an obsession about the humming of the walls. He let out a howl that seemed to go on forever, before subsiding into violent weeping.

The wall was approaching slowly. I turned to face the door and placed my feet and shoulders in the silhouette mold, feeling like I used to when I had my lungs X-rayed. But then there'd been no wall pushing against my back. Suddenly I felt a surge of panic; the wall didn't stop once it pressed my buttocks flat, it just kept coming, pushing against my back and thrusting my hips forward. I thought my ribs and vertebrae would crack, and just when I figured I was going to be squashed flat, the humming stopped. The wall stood still. I could move my hands, my feet and my head, which was too small for the concave recess made to accommodate it, but I was completely helpless. Hanging there, pinched between two walls, I could relax my leg muscles and still remain upright.

The hatch in front of my loins clicked open and nimble fingers in slightly sticky plastic gloves started manipulating my penis and balls through the bars. The hands held something up next to my member that must have been a ruler, then a tape measure was wrapped around it and my balls landed on a cold platter, where they were spanned one by one with what must have been the legs of a compass or a pair of forceps. Someone seemed to be surveying what would have been referred to in happier times as my "family jewels."

But my cynicism didn't help for long. That very first day they subjected me to the masturbator, the injection and the milking machine the women used to draw off sperm. The first time it happened, the synthetic erection gave me an uncomfortable feeling I'd known before only when some involuntary excitement overcame me in situations where rearranging the rebellious member was inconvenient. Like the time I sat across from a fairly unattractive lady in the train who kept eyeing me suspiciously, making it painfully but unintentionally clear that an erection can sometimes get out of hand.

That first experimental erection lasted for hours on end, and soon spoiled my sense of humor. Every time I'd go flaccid and start hoping that they would leave me alone, another hypodermic would be jammed into my member and the whole thing would start all over again: stiff penis, vibrating tube, burning ejaculation, hours of tumescence followed by a liberating, but brief, quiescence.

They put me through the paces four times that first day. They were milking me dry.

As soon as the wall withdrew and the pressure was off my back, I fell to the floor of the cage, shivering and tired. But this time there was no welcome black hole with its irresistible attraction to pull me down after an orgasm, not like in the old days.

I lay curled up on the floor like a fetus with a rock-hard erection, a blood-red penis like a pole between my legs. I wrapped both hands around it in the hope that a bit of warmth would make it go soft, but pharmaceutical science apparently had no intention of budging for a slight change in temperature. Less than half an hour later, someone slid my tray under the door. I looked at it, but there was nothing there to ease the pain. It was only food, and I kicked it away in a rage. I knew it wouldn't be long before they would have to shoot me full of something to keep me quiet. It was only the first day, and I'd already started losing control.

The next day was no better. I spent hours pressed between two walls with a huge erection, waiting for the next shot. Why did these women keep pumping me? I couldn't be spouting anything but semen, fluid with no cells, but they still kept sticking that horrible needle into my member. I could feel that the tip of the syringe had started hitting internal scar tissue, like in the arm of some junkie prostitute.

I couldn't have cared less about the other poor bastards in their cages; I even flew into a rage when I realized that their experimental regime was much lighter than mine. The world had turned against me, and me alone.

I spent most of that second day trying not to explode in rage and start screaming as loudly as the others. I was determined to postpone my degradation to the animal level for as long as possible. I wanted to stay human, even in a cage, to stay aware of what was going on, even if it meant I had to suffer physically *and* mentally.

On the third day, it took all my concentration not to react like a madman. I barely succeeded. I was just hanging there, producing sperm for some woman who was looking for Christ knows what, but I resisted the urge to scream. To my horror, though, I realized that my thinking had become limited to the confines of the cage, to surviving the experiment. All plans for the future had faded, the urge to escape was ebbing away.

I tried to imagine how the people held hostage by Muslim fundamentalists in Beirut must have felt during their years of imprisonment, blindfolded and chained to a bed, how they coped with the idea that every day could be the last: the last day of imprisonment, or the last day of their lives. I couldn't do it; my mind was slowly grinding to a halt, to passive submission to the treatment. I had to concentrate to keep myself under some kind of rudimentary control.

The suction experiments were only the beginning. On the fourth day someone stuck a needle deep into my balls. I screamed in pain, but the needle seemed to stay in there forever, probing around, until it was withdrawn just as suddenly and the loin hatch slammed shut. Goddamn women. I wept with pain, cursed and swore, but nothing could relieve my suffering.

The next day a needle came through the hatch and injected a cold substance into my leg. I felt myself staggering without being able to fall, then passed out.

Diana looked different, less aloof, almost approachable, like some baroness who had fallen on bad times but was doing her best to fit in. Her thin hair hung with forced casualness over one shoulder and she had changed her mouse-colored, formless dress for something a bit more upbeat, still dark of course, but with a pattern to it. She seemed to look into the camera a little less strictly and tried to put some feeling in her voice, although her presentation still consisted of monotone sentences punctuated by a brief silence.

"Someone once told me," she said, as though she were interested in anything outsiders had to say, "that it was impossible for a small group of people to change the world within a short period. . . . I'd like to point out the impact made by a person like Adolf Hitler. . . . If Hitler had not been one of the few survivors of the October 1914 slaughter of thirty-six thousand young Germans near the Belgian town of Ypres, the world would be a very different place. . . .

"Hitler's chance survival had an effect on the world comparable to that of the equally chance collision with the earth of the meteorite that eliminated the dinosaurs. . . . Hitler's survival can be seen as analogous to the cataclysmic shocks that regularly steer the course of biological evolution. . . .

"I'd also like to draw your attention to the Yalta agreements. . . . In the aftermath of the Second World War unleashed by Hitler, three old white men—Winston Churchill, Franklin Roosevelt and Joseph

Stalin—divided the world among themselves. . . . They drew the contours of a map meant to create order. . . .

"We know how that turned out. . . . The men plunged themselves and those who believed in them into a technological arms race that differed on one essential point from the biological arms race of evolution. . . . Their urge for preventive deterrence, but particularly their pride, caused them to develop nuclear mechanisms with no direct relation to man's survivability. . . . Those weapons had never been assessed by nature, never weighed against the price of development and maintenance, as had the deer's antlers, the peacock's tail feathers or the speed with which parasites adapted their genetic information to breach their victims' defenses. . . .

"Such incaution had disastrous results. . . . The Soviet Union took an economic nosedive, while the United States spent a sum of money on the Cold War equal to its total fixed assets, real estate not included. . . . And the wars of the 1990s were not fought with expensive high-tech weapons that could be fired at an invisible enemy from a safe distance, but with machetes, hand weapons and guns, wielded by armies and gangs who faced off directly. . . .

"Without a biological basis, culture has no survival value. . . . Deer whose antlers become too heavy must ultimately bow to their rivals. . . . Peacocks whose tails fan too broadly invest too much energy in an ornament that parasites may tarnish. . . . Parasites that are too lethal destroy their host population before they have a chance to reproduce. . . .

"At the end of their arms race, the world's superpowers fell into an economic oubliette from which they never reemerged. . . .

"Compared to communism, the West got off easy. . . . The West at least never underestimated the value of the individual. . . . An overorganized social structure, one in which the individual served the interests of a society comprised largely of people with whom he had nothing to do, was doomed to die a painful death. . . . Social organization fails when it conflicts with individual survival. . . .

"I don't know what historians will someday call the society we're building today. . . . What I do know is that the name they give it will apply to all those who are a part of it. . . . Not the way ancient Greece was termed the "cradle of democracy," ignoring the fact that this democracy did not apply to women . . . nor like the Renaissance, that intellectual and artistic rebirth which only benefited men. . . . And certainly not like the Enlightenment, which brought men out into the sunshine of basic rights regarding education, work and politics, but plunged women into darkness, into a curtailment of those very same rights, ruling out female ownership and higher education. . . .

"The Modern Age will have to be renamed. . . . I propose that the new name refer to the way men exhausted themselves and their still-powerless women with an unsuccessful arms race. . . .

"The facts show that women are better managers than men. . . . The history of the British monarchy shows that, generally speaking, the country was better off in the hands of queens than of kings. . . . The reigns of Elizabeth I and Victoria lasted longer and brought greater stability than those of many kings, who exhausted the realm with protracted wars and wasted their energy on such enterprises as the establishment of a new church that would give them the right to dispose of their wives. . . .

"The biology of the male sex hormone testosterone demonstrates that men had a greater lust for power, the use of force and the manipulation of sex as an element in their political games. . . .

"Men wanted more and more. . . . They wanted to go on expanding their spheres of influence. . . . But the Americans in Vietnam and the Soviets in Afghanistan found out that fighting on the home front was not the same as interfering with people who had different ideas and fewer weapons, but who fought for their own ideas, not against an enemy foisted on them by the powers that be. . . . It was a lesson that cost hundreds of thousands of lives. . . .

"Men always wanted to expand. . . . It was imperative that Europe become a single major power, even though small-scale operations had proven successful for millions of years. . . . Europe had to become an economic union, but the process served largely to unearth conflicts that stimulated a rise in nationalism and discord, because the superstructure clashed with the individual interests of a growing group of people. . . .

"Whatever this new era will be called, that name will denote its significance for everyone alive at this moment, not just for some ruling group of thinkers and combatants. . . . This does not mean, of course, that it will all be smooth sailing from here on out. . . . Enormous changes are taking place in society. . . . Society's evolution away from its biological foundations had accelerated to such a point, the deviation from genetic reality had become so striking, that it would be absurd to claim that the reforms now needed will guarantee heaven on earth for all of you. . . . Centuries of male domination, combined with obstinate male faith in the power of culture, led to a virtually irreconcilable breach with biology. . . .

"By evolutionary standards, culture was able to sear its ugly brand deep in the human frame within a relatively short period of time. . . . Culture had a more pronounced impact on awareness and human consciousness than biology. . . . It pounded its way into people's minds and stuck there. . . . It made people think they were creatures of culture—a grave underestimation of the power of nature. . . . But nature could not foresee the extent of the aberrations resulting from the chance rise and rapid evolution of culture. . . .

"As far as we know, there is no form of what we define as life that is not based on biology. . . . Culture is not essential to life. . . . We do not live longer because we know that we exist, or because we are aware of the infinite nature of the universe, or because we know why Cleopatra poisoned herself. . . . Humans, with their culture, surpassed all other species in maintaining the number of individuals unable or unwilling to reproduce. . . . No sexually reproducing species but man ever abandoned the dogma, needed to ensure sufficient resources for the new generation, that sex implied the timely death of parents. . . .

"I am starting to believe that the survival of a species can be compromised by the weight of a superfluous generation. . . . That was why we had to make room, why we had to take a load off the shoulders of the human species. . . . We eliminated what was no longer necessary. . . . We invested in a future that will significantly improve the quality of life. . . . Individual survival will become easier. . . .

"Yet adaptations are called for, and we must temporarily follow a hard road back. . . . Our minds are not programmed to feel at ease in strange surroundings. . . . Even minor social changes take time to sink in. . . . Between the establishment of the French nation and the time it actually achieved coherence lay a gap of more than one hundred years. . . . Yet that change was minuscule compared to the one we are faced with today. . . .

"An adaptation is seldom seen as an improvement, even when based on legitimate premises. . . . The need to preserve sexual reproduction, the superfluity of the existence of different genders, the inequities that resulted from the concentration of power in a sex that was nothing but a vehicle for a portion of all genetic information, the need for drastic demographic measures to ensure human survival, the indications that our worst enemies were preparing for a renewed attack—all these factors were compelling enough for us to draw the inevitable conclusion. . . .

"A change was called for, and we heeded the call. . . . A change that put a definitive end to the imbalance between the sexes, so carefully cultivated by men. . . .

"The adaptations called for now could be interpreted as measures imposed by authority. . . . But I assure you, your situation will improve, because the concept we applied in developing our new way of life was based on biological evolution. . . . We must return to life on a small scale, to a world in which anonymity is virtually ruled out and we can all fully explore our creativity and ambitions, in the service of our talents and desires. . . . We need to abandon the superorganization, the concentration of humans in unnaturally great numbers. . . . We promote the return of the village and the opportunities it presents for social contact. . . . We are reaffirming the importance of individual survival, so that everyone can see to her own welfare. . . . We are stimulating cohabitation in temporary couples, just like the nomadic ancestors whose way of life lies deeply anchored in our genes. . . .

"Those who wish to live differently are free to do so. . . . Our only desire is to stimulate. . . . We are well aware of the importance of individual variability. . . . We are not striving for total uniformity, for variation is essential, even within species. . . . We do not wish to hobble the individual with ill-considered directives prompted by some urge to exercise total control or misuse people for the purposes of personal ambition. . . .

"We will, of course, bring down the cultural and technological pillars of old, unfounded institutions, such as the military-industrial complex. . . . The major attainments of cultural evolution, education and medical care, will be preserved as rights, contributing to the optimization of individual survival. . . . We will also preserve scientific achievement in the fields of fertility therapy and reproduction. . . . We will give every woman the opportunity to reproduce as long as she wishes. . . . Such biologically sound intervention will lead to the more efficient transfer of genes to the following generation. . . ."

Diana paused for a moment and took a deep breath. "For all these reasons, I am counting on your trust. . . . For all these reasons, I ask your support in overcoming the difficulties bound to rise along the road to a society founded on sound principles. . . . For all these reasons, I ask your patience for any efforts required of you in the course of this adaptation. . . . For all your understanding, I can only express my gratitude."

Kristina couldn't believe it. This was the first time she'd ever heard Diana ask for understanding, the first time she'd seemed anything less than totally resolute, the first time she had ever admitted that her program might not automatically receive a place of honor in human history. But what was even more striking: this was the first time Diana had ever been less than honest.

Until now she had only brought up points she believed in with all her heart. Now she'd lied, definitely on purpose. Her plea for an anarchistic society was not based on any urge to ensure the primacy of individual talent. Not so very long ago, in less public circles, Diana had questioned the concept of unbridled freedom and absolute individualism by noting that not even genes could be unrestrainedly selfish.

Diana viewed genes as the true driving force behind the rise and survival of all life on earth. She belonged to the school of scientific thought that regarded species, including humans, as biological machines built by genes to duplicate and pass themselves on to following generations.

Genes require a body, unicellular or multicellular, to reproduce. But even genes have to work together to build and control the body needed for their survival. Genes operate according to laws and rules, use promoters to regulate their own activities, use complicated feedback mechanisms to switch on other genes, and work together to ensure the expression of a great many characteristics. Genes are organized.

Diana's plea for anarchy and freedom was prompted largely by her inability to keep things under control, particularly at an international level. As time went by, she had become less and less interested in the progress her program was making in those parts of the world beyond her immediate grasp, even though she was still kept informed of specific trends and movements. The virus was the only creature big enough to take on the world. Maybe Diana wasn't really interested in global control; after all, her major goal had been achieved: the elimination of a sex she regarded as superfluous.

Her appeal for understanding had to be related to the problems Jasmine was facing. "He might be able to save the program," that's what she'd said about the man who had broken into the secret wing. But just how dramatic were the problems they were facing? With this last speech, Diana was clearly hedging her bets; things might go a great deal less smoothly than she had supposed.

Not long ago, Kristina had also discovered that Diana's drive for a revival of village life wasn't prompted by any conviction that living in a village would make people happier, just because it reflected the social life-style of their ancestors. No, she had apparently hesitated a long time before taking that step. Because even she was convinced that it was easier to control people when they were concentrated in one place.

Her promotion of village life was largely based on the fear that, within a—humanly speaking—short period of time, her genetically manipulated anti-male virus would be resilient enough to start attacking women as well. Spreading the population over a great many locations, with transportation between them almost impossible, should reduce the women's vulnerability to a surprise attack by the virus.

Kristina was shocked when Jasmine told her that. She'd always assumed that Diana blindly trusted the creature that came to life in her test tubes.

There was another favorable side effect to relocating the population: news couldn't travel as fast. The few media still disposed to action were in the hands of women loyal to Diana and her program. It had been a smart move on her part.

Environmental disasters had accompanied the removal of the male half of the population, but little was heard about them. There had been enough unrest as it was. Several tankers ran aground after their crews had contracted the virus at sea and died before they could reach port. Some of the potentially hazardous industrial installations hadn't been shut down in time. Small groups of female engineers were now traveling around to deal with plants gone haywire.

Kristina knew of explosions in at least two nuclear power plants—rumor had it that one of them had been blown up by its general supervisor, who wanted to punish the world for what had been done to him. Diana paid little attention to these disasters: radioactivity couldn't be seen or felt, no one was taking readings on a regular basis, the expected rise in cancer and congenital defects would never be linked to the program. Accidents like that could only become catastrophes when they leaked out and caused a chain reaction of protest. Splitting up society into small units suppressed large-scale discontent.

Furthermore, Diana always emphasized that the elimination of a large part of industry would have long-term beneficial effects for both humans and the environment. The civil wars of the 1990s had demonstrated that. Once the polluting factories had been shut down, fish quickly returned to rivers in which no one could remember anything ever having lived. That kind of news had made the rounds, especially because most villages were built along a river or stream.

Female anglers. Kristina wondered what the city women would think of that.

When it came to informing the women about her program, Diana's timing had been less than perfect. The announcement had come too soon, but as more and more women became ill, Diana's hand had been forced by the mounting fear of infection. Around 1 percent of all females—X-Y women and others—were killed by the DIANA virus. Even more of them fell ill from stress and a weakened immune system.

Diana felt she had to calm them down, tell them they were safe: her program was designed to keep them from being destroyed along with the men. She used television to spread the news, and she'd hand-picked women from the media to do the job for her.

A few days after the first cautious announcement, a great cry went up to put an end to these Angels of Death who were ruining the world. There were still too many men around capable of physical resistance. A half-sick pilot crashed his jet bomber into the television station that had spread the message. There were male reprisals against defenseless women, incidents that were virtually unavoidable before units like Kristina's were set up.

Diana had counted on mobilizing female army officers to carry out such missions, but they resolutely resisted all assaults on men: as products of a man's world, they had probably been subjected to too much training and discipline.

Women also raised their voices against the changes. Furious women held demonstrations that degenerated into rioting so destructive that soccer hooligans, farmers and mine workers would have looked up in amazement, had they still been able to do so. Crowd psychology seemed to whip even women up into a state in which reason and calm were swept away, and there were almost no law-enforcement officials left to keep things under control.

Women also murdered other women. The TV celebrity who first spoke of DIANA was one of those assassinated by a female. Diana had the attacks investigated, and came to the conclusion that they were largely the work of older women whose sons had been killed by the virus. She turned a blind eye to such sporadic female resistance, in the conviction that it had a biological basis. She attributed it to women who had borne only sons, and who feared that their efforts to transfer genes to the following generation had been thwarted by the extermination of their offspring. Diana quickly assured the public that reproduction would remain operational. Women whose offspring had all been male would receive priority in the forthcoming fertility program, thereby safeguarding their genetic interests.

It was only a matter of time before the opposition died out. The program seemed so perfect.

And now, suddenly, this note of demurral. When Kristina commented on the moderate tone of Diana's speech, Jasmine reacted in irritation. She said she'd noticed nothing of the kind, but that it had to be a lie. Diana would never show such a marked change of attitude in public without consulting Jasmine first.

Kristina had her feelers out. It was time to find out what was behind all this skittishness in the lab.

"We know why the alarm didn't go off when the non-inactivable broke into the laboratory," Jasmine said in a look-what-we're-still-capable-of tone. "The apocrine glands in his armpits don't function normally, although we found no histological defects. Tissue samples from his armpits show that his glands produce pheromones, but don't emit them. There may be something wrong with the bacteria responsible for converting testosterone into odorants like androstrenol. His armpits don't emit those odorants, so the sensors didn't pick him up. But there were androstenones in his saliva. That's probably why the alarm went off when he vomited."

Jasmine was obviously pleased with this explanation. It was at least something for her to be sure of.

"Have you discovered why the virus didn't get him?" Kristina asked. She'd decided to start leaning a little on Jasmine.

Jasmine shook her head. "We're not there yet, but we're working on it. We ran him through a sperm test. His sperm production is higher than average, and his spermatozoa are extremely vital and mobile. His testicular tissue shows no deformation. Last night we did a laparoscopic inspection of his abdominal cavity. His adrenal glands seem to be in order, and all the ducts are intact. We also made a chromosome chart; right number, right shape, everything was normal.

"We're using the sequencer now to stratify the genetic information on his Y chromosome, but it could take a couple of days before the results are in. We have to isolate the target gene for the virus and unravel its genetic code base by base. There must be a defect in the gene, something that doesn't obstruct normal functioning, but somehow makes it unrecognizable for the virus. A real stroke of luck for him: a mutation that has no effect, but protects him against the virus. I think we've been worried for no good reason. This isn't the first time we've come across strange genetic defects that make men immune.

"The wild thing about this one, though, is that he's not sterile. He's fertile, exceptionally so. Diana is already worried about that. I don't think she'll let him live any longer than absolutely necessary. We all know about her aversion to fertile men. I wonder whether she'll crush this one in his cage too."

My father was the first person to die in my immediate surroundings. He had almost died once before, from a massive heart attack, when I was still at college. It hadn't made much difference to me at the time. I was going through a difficult period in my life, and I didn't care much about our relationship. But once he recovered, he seemed changed: he became pleasant to be around, and the older he got, the better things went.

That was why it was such a shock when he started going downhill. It began with muscle spasms, first in an arm, then in a shoulder, then his back muscles would cramp or he wouldn't be able to move his legs because his muscles had seized up on him. The doctors were baffled. His heart was affected, too; his pulse became increasingly irregular and his stomach would sometimes contract so violently that his food jetted out. It was horrible to see, especially since he was fully conscious the whole time and the doctors couldn't get the spasms under control.

An inexplicable failure of the physiological mechanisms ensuring the proportional distribution of energy over muscular tissue; that was the diagnosis they came up with after long hesitation. But it came too late for my father. He had died of a coronary; his heart had reacted to the increased muscular activity by pumping out more blood and then, after a few weeks of incredible strain, had simply collapsed.

My father's struggle with death had been horrible—my mother and sisters refused to have him put out of his misery until the very last moment—and images of his painfully cramped face raced through my mind as I lay on the floor of the cage, trying to fight off the pain in my body by concentrating on other people's traumas. It didn't work. I had four incisions in my body, one under each arm and two in my abdomen, and I was exhausted. I kept slipping irresistibly toward madness. Every time a door opened I was overpowered by terror, fear of the procedure to come, even though the walls had remained in place ever since the injection knocked me unconscious.

My father was also the first person I saw die from the epidemic. Hundreds and thousands followed, a nightmare peopled with living corpses, full of dying men taken to hospitals where no one knew what to do with them. Orders were given to take them straight to the crematories. But the crematories couldn't deal with the supply either, even though they burned at full capacity around the clock.

To get rid of the bodies, the authorities then requisitioned industrial incinerators, waste-processing facilities and foundries. They had even gone so far as to reduce the volume of the corpses before incineration by pulverizing them with heavy machinery, or running them through industrial meat grinders. In their desperate attempts to dispose of the bodies quickly and halt the spread of the epidemic, they went to macabre extremes.

The images of the first corpses to be dumped into a boiling mass of molten metal—it was all on TV—were branded in my memory. The bodies melted away the moment they touched the bright-orange liquid. Later I witnessed hundreds of scenes that would have disgusted me if I had read about them or seen them on TV; but it was easier to cope with the cruelties of the real world than with stories told by others.

The hopelessness of the situation finally resulted in a slackening of the struggle to get rid of the corpses. Biologists pointed out that water was ideal for disposing of bodies. This insight was gained from impact studies on an unexpected source of organic pollution: the washing into Lake Victoria of something like one hundred thousand Rwandan corpses in the mid-1990s. Simulations showed that the lake had recovered quickly from the eutrophication. Scientists had calculated that the biomass of a dead hippopotamus was roughly equal to that of a hundred starved Rwandans, and that nature was able to break down the biomass of a hundred thousand corpses within a period of two months.

Armed with these results, bodies of water everywhere were converted into mass graves. Thousands of corpses were dumped into deep clay pits and giant quarries. Entire stretches of rivers were dammed with weirs. A ban was placed on swimming, and on fishing, but not everyone complied; fish grew fat in the lakes of the dead, and people could be quite abstract about death when it came to their own survival.

As soon as it became clear that the virus had no effect on them, women were called in to help dispose of the bodies. Especially nurses were mobilized, for the hospitals soon gave up all hope of doing anything for the victims except ending their suffering with a fatal injection. This procedure was later adopted by body collectors when they came to pick up patients who had been written off. The victims were put out of their misery with increasing promptness.

When the morphine and other potentially fatal painkillers began to run out, consideration was given to providing an economically sound basis for euthanasia. It was even suggested that large warehouses be converted into gas chambers, an idea that—due to its historical connotations—met with violent protest from the Jewish lobby, which remained active to the very end.

But all resistance was trampled underfoot in the hurry to get rid of the virus carriers. There was no room for humanity in a world that threatened to exterminate *us*.

The large-scale elimination of patients created absurd situations, usually caused by ill-considered bureaucratic measures that led to bodies simply being dumped. The authorities responded by setting up mobile teams to collect abandoned corpses; the primary effect was the abandonment of even more bodies. Heavy fines were levied to punish such lawlessness, but never collected.

The elderly in particular resisted the mandatory destruction of bodies. The political authorities didn't worry much about respecting the religious preferences of patients or their relatives—a God who would let this happen to his creatures shouldn't be mollycoddled anyway. A lot of people had therefore buried bodies in their gardens, where they were sometimes dug up by dogs or pigs.

I remembered a picture of a gnawed scapula sticking out of a bed of asparagus, and a farmer's wife who had taken the body of her husband, who had tyrannized her all her life, and hung it in the vegetable patch. The crows and ravens had a field day—crows knew from long experience that where there was a scarecrow, there was food aplenty. The unfortunate farmer was soon picked clean, causing his wife to remark that he had finally made himself useful by keeping the birds off the vegetables.

The spread of the epidemic was accompanied by the rise of a certain cynicism regarding illness and death. At one point, anyone going out for a walk would encounter more bodies than living souls. After a while, though, death ceased to be a part of everyday life. The epidemic had passed its zenith.

The smell of death was something I never got used to. Fresh bodies all looked the same, with that same drab color that helped elicit indifference, but they all emitted the same spent odor as well, like overdone cauliflower in white sauce served up in some foul soup kitchen. Even in the cage, my memories of the smell of corpses racked my body and made me gag.

I realized that my time had come. Breaking into the laboratory had been a mistake. My intuition had seriously misled me. I was going to die. No one cared about me, the women who worked here were only interested in certain parts of my anatomy, and the way they treated me made it clear: once the experiments were over, they were going to kill me. The prospect still scared me, but I was too weak to react physically, like some of my fellow sufferers in the other cages. I no longer had the energy to resist. I let pain pull me under, and it was breaking my will. Unfortunately, complacency did nothing to relieve my fear of death.

They left me alone that day. Three times someone came to the cage, three times a tray was slid under the door, and three times I left it untouched. The mere thought of food made me even more nauseated than I was. The third time, though, I knew night was coming—the lights in the laboratory never went out—and twelve quiet hours would follow. In the mood I was in, even a shabby prospect like that made me feel relieved.

I actually started to believe that you could live through prolonged imprisonment without incurring permanent psychological damage. It was simply a matter of adjusting one's priorities; at this point, my main priority was to be left alone, so my body would have a chance to recuperate.

Not long after the last tray had been shoved in, I heard the laboratory door open again. Quietly this time, without the usual bang. I broke out in a cold sweat. I silently counted the footsteps as they passed the other doors. This visitor was coming for me, I could tell; the steps kept getting closer. I lay on my stomach, peered through the slot and saw that I was right. The footsteps stopped in front of my door, and I saw the toes of two canvas tennis shoes pointed in my direction.

I braced myself for the irritating hum of the walls moving in, but everything was quiet. Then a hatch opened. I looked up and saw that it was the one at eye level.

A soft voice whispered: "I want to talk to you."

I didn't budge, even though I knew she could see me. The voice repeated its message, a bit more forcefully now. I said nothing.

"Suit yourself," the voice said. "If you're not willing to talk, I'll start the walls and then you'll have to look me in the eye. If you don't want to talk then, you'll be pulverized. It's up to you."

I slowly struggled to my feet and looked through the bars into the bluest eyes I'd ever seen, blue eyes beneath a blaze of yellow-blond hair—the woman from the Mad Maxes.

"What did you see in the secret wing?" she asked in a whisper.

I remained silent, not knowing what to do, but her patience was running out.

"Listen," she said. "Tomorrow you die. Only abnormal men, only the ones whose genes have to be manipulated before they can do anything with them, are kept alive around here. You're fertile, which means you're suspect. Maybe I can do something for you. But then you'll have to help me, too." Her voice sounded tough.

"What could you possibly do for me?" I asked weakly.

"I let you in here by mistake," she replied. "Maybe I'll let you out again."

I was wary, my body suddenly alert. Was she serious? "First let me out of the cage, then I'll tell you what I saw," I tried.

She grinned. "I'm going to let you out of the cage anyway," she said, "because I need you. I want you to come with me. You have to knock out the computer that controls the alarm in the secret wing. I can't get in there, but the sensors won't pick you up. I need to find out what's going on in that wing, and you have to help me. But first I want to know what you saw. I have to be sure it's worth it. Breaking into that wing is dangerous for me, too."

She was going to let me out of the cage. This was my chance, no matter how shaky I felt. I was raring to help her. "I saw monsters," I told her in a whisper. "Dozens of them. All children, in a room full of aquariums with little fish."

"Monsters?" the woman asked quietly.

I nodded.

"Boys or girls?"

I wasn't sure about that. The only child I'd had a good look at seemed to be a girl.

"How old were they?"

That was hard to say. They weren't toddlers, in any case. But the child I'd seen was so horribly misshapen that I couldn't really pin an age on it. A hydrocephalous head with empty eyes, attached to an emaciated body with skinny little arms and fat legs with thighs like pumpkins. I described the child.

The woman breathed a deep sigh. "I was afraid of something like that," she said. "This is going to be bad news."

The biological weapon behind DIANA was perverse in its ingenuity, a masterful combination of impact and deception. Genetic engineering techniques were used to introduce a gene into an inactivated smallpox virus. A gene that coded for one of the recombinases, enzymes Diana had discovered herself. These simple but difficult-to-detect proteins could recognize a preprogrammed segment of genetic code and tinker with its characteristics: recombinases see to the exchange of those characteristics between different chromosomes, inserting some and removing others. They add the spice of variety to living organisms.

That in itself was an amazing scientific discovery, because recombinase had not yet been identified when Diana made her program public.

But it was only the beginning. The manipulated virus had to be made selective enough to attack only men. The most obvious solution was to program it to attack the Y sex chromosome, which is found almost exclusively in males. Diana succeeded in building a recombinase that recognized a segment of the genetic code on the Y chromosome, then snuck in the viral material to where it could begin its destructive work.

Developing the virus's lethal character was the hardest part of the operation. It no longer caused smallpox; that would have been too simple. The obvious thing was to have it interfere with the normal operations of a gene on the Y chromosome and kill its bearer by preventing the production of a protein necessary for survival. But the Y had no genes suitable for that purpose. In the course of evolution it had lost almost all its genes, except for those needed to make a man out of an embryo.

The biological weapon had to be powerful enough to strike hard and in a way that would not allow it to be immediately linked to any known disease, let alone a given chromosome or gene. The confusion had to be as complete as possible, the effects so drastic that the virus could never be unmasked before it had accomplished its task.

The solution was found on the *X* sex chromosome, which contains thousands of active genes. Normal women receive two *X* chromosomes, one from both father and mother. One of the two—the choice is up for grabs—is then inactivated, to keep females from having more active genes than men with their short *Y* chromosome. The inactivated chromosome produces no proteins. A gene on the chromosome itself, called the "*X*-inactivation center," does the job. This gene codes for messengers that switch off most of the genes on the chromosome, without targeting those on the other *X*. No one knows how they do this, or why they don't go on to inactivate other chromosomes. But that knowledge was not essential to DIANA. The clue was to switch on the inactivation center on the *X* chromosome that every man inherited from his mother.

As a result, thousands of genes on the *X* ceased to manufacture the substances needed to maintain life. Inactivating a man's only *X* chromosome obviously had a dramatic effect. The *X* bears genes coding for pigments that make vision possible, genes controlling the receptors of energy molecules or sex hormones in the walls of cells, for enzymes that maintain muscle strength and the release of energy across muscle cells, for messenger molecules that coordinate nerve stimuli, substances that keep tissue-digesting enzymes in check, for proteins used to translate genetic code into useful products or limit the quantity of cholesterol in the blood, proteins that bond with growth and metabolism hormones from the thyroid and manufacture a portion of the blood's coagulants. A list as long as your arm.

The virus had a dramatic effect, because no single biological function was spared. That was why it was so hard to trace the true nature of the epidemic. There were no clear connections with a specific ailment. The victims could die of a whole range of causes, depending on which tissue the virus struck first.

The brilliant thing about DIANA was the way the virus was programmed to nestle in the Y chromosome, so it affected only men, but exercised its fatal power through the X.

The gene Diana targeted on the Y chromosome was called AZF, an acronym for "azoospermifactor"; it was a gene responsible for manufacturing sperm cells. If this gene was defective, the bearer would ejaculate semen with no sperm cells in it. A defect on this gene also misled the virus and made the bearer immune, because the recombinase smuggled in by the virus no longer recognized the code. That's why most of the men who escaped the virus were sterile.

The virus was engineered to insinuate itself into the AZF gene, and it also induced sterility in the men it infected. Once the virus had forced its way in, the gene followed its instructions and made only a very specific form of protein that attached itself to the inactivation center on the adjacent X chromosome. That inactivation center in turn released messengers that switched off the rest of the genes on the X. The men who escaped the virus were called "non-inactivables," because the inactivation center on their X chromosome could not be stimulated.

The idea was ingenious, and it worked almost perfectly. The greatest disadvantage for the DIANA program was that the AZF gene only became active at puberty. Boys were not susceptible to the deadly effects of the virus until around the age of ten. If that hadn't been the case, DIANA's deadly weapon would have made even shorter work of the male population. But the last surviving boys were gradually coming of age. The virus was unrelenting.

"What's so important about the fact that those were girls I saw in the secret wing?" I asked Kristina.

She didn't have to think about her answer. "If they were boys it would mean that problems had come up with the biological weapon

197

program, the way you constituted a problem when you showed up. But since these are girls, it must be something else."

I wanted to know what.

She hesitated for a moment. "It could be," she ventured, "that the virus has succeeded in attacking young girls. But that doesn't seem very likely. For the time being, I'd say that Diana and Jasmine's fertility program probably doesn't work as well as their epidemic did."

I didn't get it.

"In the longer term, that would mean that women are about to be eliminated as well," she said brusquely. "I'm afraid they were better at destroying life than they are at creating it."

She unlocked the door and let me out of the cage. Only then did I see the Kalashnikov hanging from her shoulder. "Do you take that thing to bed with you?" I asked sarcastically.

"For someone who's a total wreck, you've got a pretty smart mouth," she replied. "But don't kid yourself. I won't have to kill you if you make any trouble. I'll just leave you alone. You'd never get out of here anyway. So it's in your own best interests to help out."

We walked past the other cages and heard the men smacking their lips and growling in their sleep. "Strange people," I remarked.

"Most of them never were normal," Kristina said. "Diana only spared genetically defective men. The ones in here are eunuchoids and freaks who grew up as girls because they didn't start producing testosterone or grow anything like a penis until they were in puberty. They ejaculate through an opening at the base of the penis, not at the tip."

When we got to the exit, Kristina tossed me a lab coat that was hanging over a chair. I put it on reluctantly, still feeling naked. "I'm sorry, it's all I've got," she said casually as she opened the door, peered around and stepped outside.

I asked nervously what we would do if someone saw us.

She only laughed. "Our noble scientists are so afraid of having their secrets uncovered that almost no one is allowed on the premises after dark. The few women walking around here now are from my unit, so they won't say a thing. The laboratory where you men are kept has a conventional security system, because sterile men won't trip the DIANA alarm. But that doesn't apply to most of the other buildings. There are no guards in the most important labs, because they might nose around. Those buildings are guarded with sensors. Only a few people have the cards you need to log in at the entrance. Depending on your security clearance, the card either turns off the sensors for the rest of the day or gives you just enough time to get to your office or the lab. I always thought that was strange. I've been trying to get my hands on one of those cards for months, but I can't. That's why I need you."

She suddenly stopped in her tracks. "What about that army of yours?"

"What army?"

She told me about Ellen's slip of the tongue.

"There isn't any male army," I confessed rather hesitantly, wondering at the same time whether it was a smart thing to admit. "I wanted to make Ellen think I could do something for her son, and I figured it would be easier to convince her if she thought I wasn't operating on my own. Apparently it worked."

Kristina nodded. "That's pretty much what I thought," she said, then walked on.

The cool evening air and excitement did me good. Adrenaline is a wonderful substance. The incisions in my abdomen and under my arms still burned, but I seemed to be regaining some of my confidence. Outdoor life had toughened me. I'd become hardened to things that would once have knocked me for a loop. The pampering of the welfare state made people overly sensitive to suffering and pain.

When we reached the entrance to the laboratory with the secret wing, Kristina told me to hide. She spoke to the watchwoman seated at her post along one wall and sent her off on an errand. Then she explained how to find the central computer and turn it off. She gave me a flashlight, because the lights would go when the computer was turned off, and told me to hurry. She needed enough time to nose around in the wing, and it would take a few hours to start up the computer again and wipe out all traces of our visit.

I began feeling uneasy as soon as I walked into the building. Something was wrong. I listened tensely, but didn't hear a thing. Sneaking warily along the corridors, I came to a narrow stairway leading down into the basement, where I had no problem finding the computer and the switch to turn it off. The lights went out immediately. I clicked on the flashlight and went back upstairs.

Kristina was already inside, waiting. I whispered to her that I had the feeling there was someone in the building, but she just started walking down the hall toward the big wide doors. She took the Kalashnikov from its sling and held it out in front of her. She signaled to me to turn the wheel and open the door. She was so adamant about it, I didn't hesitate. I pulled on the wheel and the door slowly swung open. Kristina swore and stuck her finger through the trigger guard of her machine gun.

I stuck my flashlight in the door and peered into the room. In the circle of light stood a woman. She had a pistol trained on us.

"The social interactions in nature are only a reflection of social interactions at the genetic level. Each individual—gene or organism—is naturally determined to do its best to transfer itself successfully to the next generation, but cooperation is possible, if need be.

"Parasitism, however, is just as deeply ingrained in life. Even at the genetic level, turncoats and swindlers exist. They jump from chromosome to chromosome, hiding out, shifting from one place to the next to avoid being recognized as profiteers. Genes that simply distribute copies of themselves that are no good to anyone; genes that are carried on to the next generation amid the flow of useful information without doing anything themselves; genes that make absolutely no contribution to the proper functioning of the body in which they reside. These genes will never become truly important: bodies containing too many parasites and profiteers cannot optimally reproduce, and are disqualified by nature.

"Such vermin, however, do not form the greatest threat at the genetic level. Here and there genes pop up that cannot reconcile themselves to the social contracts, that behave manipulatively, mainly just to make themselves indispensable. Genes that resent the fact that their counterpart on the other chromosome has ended up in half the reproductive cells—when the sex cells are formed, the chromosomes from the mother and the father are mixed and separated into two sets.

"Every gene has a fifty percent chance of ending up in the sex cell that achieves fertilization and produces an embryo. Some genes, however, refuse to go along with the toss of the dice. They rebel against the possibility of exclusion from the next generation, and start fiddling with genetic mechanisms, to avoid being left out of fifty percent of all fertilizations.

"Genes that manipulate reproduction to ensure that only they end up in the embryo provide themselves with a huge strategic head start. Some genes have been successful at it. There are genes that smuggle a fatal element into all reproductive cells, an element only they themselves can defuse. Embryos that develop without the manipulative gene simply die off.

"Other genes produce a chemical weapon that destroys those sperm cells carrying the chromosome on which they're not found. Just after the Second World War, an obscure medical journal published a report about a family in which a Y-killing gene seemed to be at work, a gene on the X chromosome that shanghaied the Y or destroyed all sperm cells bearing it. The woman who told the story to the physician publishing the report was the ninth daughter of a woman who was, in turn, the sixth in an all-girl family. Within two generations, the family produced seventy-two women and not a single male. The rare Y-killer knew no mercy."

Jasmine suddenly stopped talking and broke into heart-rending sobs, weeping without tears, a wolfish wail that seemed to come from her stomach. "Goddamn it, Kristina," she screamed. "Murder and war are ingrained in nature all the way down to the genes. Turncoats and murderers surface at the slightest careless manipulation and try to monopolize reproduction. DIANA's tenets seemed so clear, the program was a perfect piece of design, the ideas were backed by experimentation. But nature went and misled us, shamefully misled us. She let us go ahead, then hit back as soon as we went a step too far."

She pounded her head with her fists. "She doesn't need us, Kristina, she just let us go ahead and exterminate ourselves in our exuberance. She just watched, the way we just watched the men die. She's so much more cunning than we are, and she has no heart."

Jasmine was going crazy. A sound mind couldn't bear the responsibility for two and a half billion deaths and the possible extinction of the human species.

It was Jasmine who had held us at gunpoint in the laboratory. It had been a tricky situation there for a moment: Jasmine was extremely unbalanced and capable of shooting just to have herself gunned down, a sort of sublimated suicide. But Kristina kept calm, telling her this was definitely the wrong moment to do anything stupid, that she had to realize that now was the time to intervene, to try and save whatever was left to save. She reminded Jasmine that she knew exactly how DIANA worked, and was therefore one of the only ones who could help turn the tide.

Jasmine didn't react at first, but her arms started shaking. After a few long minutes, she lowered the weapon. Kristina didn't even take it away from her, just led the woman over to a chair next to the wall of aquariums and started searching the laboratory. The monstrous children were all girls of about ten, badly deformed children who Jasmine said were from the first generation conceived by fusing two egg cells. DIANA's fertility program had also resulted in a high incidence of miscarriages. The bodies of many of the expectant mothers refused to pump time and energy into cultivating genetic monsters, and rejected the embryos outright. Nature didn't invest in mistakes.

"The percentage of healthy girls we can produce is very low," Jasmine explained somberly, "especially when you count the spontaneous abortions. Some of the girls are born without defects. They come into the world with no disorders, genetic or otherwise, at least up until the age we've been able to observe them—none of them have reached adulthood yet. But we've recently received indications that the healthy girls start developing defects at puberty that make them sterile, among other things."

She suddenly grabbed hold of Kristina and screamed: "We're destroying our own species."

Kristina eased her back onto the chair and calmed her down. Jasmine went limp as a rag; there was no more strength left in her body. "More and more women impregnated by DIANA have started coming back with complaints," she said feebly. "So far mostly miscarriages, because the midwives who go out to the villages are under strict orders to take away the girls born with defects before their mothers see them. Some of the women don't put up with that though, especially the partners who weren't pregnant and aren't exhausted from the delivery. They become furious when they see the monsters we've conceived with their eggs. A few midwives have been beaten up by enraged mothers. The murmuring is becoming more widespread; an uprising may be on its way.

"And Diana is so intolerant. Last week a distraught mother came here to complain about her daughter's health, which was going downhill fast. The woman was very persistent, so after a long time we took her in to see Diana. Diana was so irritated by her moaning that she shot and killed her right on the spot. It was the first time I ever saw Diana kill a woman. I didn't know how to deal with it. That's when I realized that the news about the failure of the fertility program would leak out before long. Diana seemed very evasive when I asked her how she planned to avert the crisis. In fact, she acted like she didn't even care. It was suddenly all up to me."

But Jasmine had absolutely no idea how to start a rescue operation, or why the children developed genetic disorders. She had eliminated one option, however. The problem could hardly be blamed on the fact that fertilization wasn't carried out by a sperm cell that had to outstrip millions of competitors and so prove itself the fittest. The effects on the children were too widespread to be blamed on the elimination of the competitive element in an artificial fertilization, on the fact that a cell had never had to prove itself.

Nor did she think these were merely the side effects of imprinting, a process that selectively expressed certain genes in the embryo, depending on whether they came from the father or the mother. To get around such side effects, one of the two egg cells was cultivated in testicular tissue, a technique that had worked perfectly with laboratory rats.

"I'm afraid we interpreted those results a bit too optimistically," Jasmine admitted. "Of course, we were less concerned with the rats' welfare than we were with our girls. Tissue immersion is apparently not enough to eliminate the disastrous effects of genetic imprinting in humans. We started noticing that when an increasing number of reports came in about children with serious mental deficiencies or other genetic defects traditionally linked to the selective loss of genes from one parent. Time bombs planted by nature to punish a sex that couldn't resist the temptation to go solo."

But even such drastic measures weren't enough for nature. Too many girls were being born with defects that had nothing to do with the known effects of neglected genetic imprinting. This was what had set off Jasmine's monologue about mutinous and murderous genes. She was convinced that spermatozoa contained some ingenious substance in their genetic material to keep embryos from developing normally when not conceived with the help of male reproductive cells. Genes monopolized by sperm, like those coded to form the placenta an embryo needed to draw life from its mother.

"The immersion method helped us avoid that pitfall," Jasmine said. "But I don't understand why the female genes allowed the males to win such an exclusive right. It couldn't be so hard to develop a mechanism that would bust that male monopoly. Maybe the female genes had resigned themselves in the course of evolution to the inevitability of a battle between the sexes, maybe that's why they were so tolerant towards the males' drive to make themselves irreplaceable, just like women themselves."

Jasmine admitted that it had been a serious mistake not to take this into account. It seemed so obvious to her now. "Sperm was faced with the risk of becoming superfluous at every phase in evolution," she explained. "All it did was contribute a quantity of genetic material, but it was largely dependent on the female's efforts to transfer its genes to the following generation.

"In the plant world, there are many examples of genes that have degenerated into perverse sexual manipulators. Even though they tend to make use of cross-pollination for reproduction, most plants are androgynous; they have both a female pistil and male stamens. A pitched battle goes on in many plants between man-killing genes in the blossom and those that counter such rebel activities. The man-killers try to make the plant invest as much energy as possible in the pistil, because this provides a better chance of producing offspring. It guarantees that more genes will be passed along to the following generation than the tactic of the stamens, which simply spread their pollen all over the place. The man-killers have no faith in pollen, so they do everything possible to repress the activity of the stamens.

"Those plants able to throw up an efficient defense against these genetic rebels have an advantage: they can profit from reduced competition between pollens. Plants in which man-killers have achieved dominance no longer produce pollen. So the pollen from plants that have invested in stamens can fertilize more pistils and improve the plant's chances of reproducing. Everywhere the phenomenon was studied, this genetic warfare balanced out into a status quo. In corn, for example, two reproductive repair genes compensate for the activities of two stamen-killers; in tobacco, eight pairs of these genes keep each other in equilibrium."

Jasmine was silent for a moment, deep in thought. "Of course, a system like that would be useless in humans," she continued. "We're not hermaphroditic, so we can't favor a female half by paralyzing the male side. But the mechanism illustrates how far genes will go in their drive for optimal reproduction.

"Genes don't think. They're short-term operators, unaware of the danger some of their actions pose for their own future. In some ways, they're just as naive as we were when we launched DIANA. They rely just as blindly on the benevolence of Mother Nature. But nature isn't a caring mother. Nature is hard: it's everyone for themselves and the Devil take the hindmost.

"I'm becoming convinced it was the endless struggle between individual genes that made sexual reproduction so improbably complex. It wouldn't surprise me if the Red Queen hypothesis for the existence of sex, the hypothesis of the queen who ran just to stay in place, really does have its roots in the need to maintain a genetic head start on parasites. But the machinations of genes to repress their sexual counterparts and stay in the running may have made sex the victim of its own success, a prisoner in the spiral of ever-increasing complexity.

"I believe that a genetic war between the sexes can also be fought in species that aren't androgynous. Clearly, male genes have developed ingenious mechanisms to keep from being overshadowed by their female counterparts. If that wasn't the case, the males of many more species would have been pushed aside by females in the course of evolution. The failure of our fertility program is probably to blame on a mechanism intended to reinforce maleness. There must be a vitality factor in sperm without which an embryo can't develop normally."

"Such as?" Kristina asked.

Jasmine shrugged. "I have absolutely no idea," she sighed. "We've been looking for it for years. Maybe it's in the genes carried by the head of the sperm cell, or maybe it's just a chemical substance that travels along with it. It wouldn't even have to penetrate the egg nucleus; it could just stay behind in the tail and do its work from out there."

She pointed to the aquariums. "These fish are my last hope," she said. "If they don't reveal their secret, we're sunk."

Kristina let no grass grow under her feet. Diana had the key. She had awarded herself the exclusive right to rule over male reproduction, because she didn't trust other women who could get their hands on sperm. That's why she kept a collection in her own apartment, Jasmine said, frozen in liquid nitrogen. A private sperm bank, and it had to be saved. The women needed variation. It was too dangerous to use sperm from only one man.

Jasmine was convinced that she could modify the sperm and make it immune to the virus, which was probably still around and very active. She had seen the initial results of the sequence analysis of my Y chromosome and was sure I was the carrier of an almost imperceptible defect on the AZF gene that the virus was programmed to attack. A defect that had no effect on my sperm production, but misled the virus. With some simple genetic engineering, she felt, this innocuous defect could easily be grafted to the sperm cells from Diana's collection, or added to growing embryos. Jasmine felt that such engineering techniques were still a blessing to mankind, as long as the necessary caution was applied. Science could make the new men immune to the virus as well.

Mankind need not despair. It wasn't too late. In principle, a teaspoon of sperm was enough to bring the world population back to its pre-DIANA level, if anyone would want to see that happen. Assuming, of course—but assumptions concerning nature's generosity were clearly dangerous to make—that every sperm cell was capable of generating viable offspring. Jasmine wasn't so sure about that anymore. She thought, for example, that the kamikazes—the soldier sperm cells that attacked strangers—would not make good fathers, that only the real speed demons were predestined to excellence in fatherhood. But, for the time being, that wasn't the point. The point was that a minimal amount of sperm was needed to keep women from being wiped out as well.

The experiment with the fish had been a long shot. Jasmine read about the mollies in the journal *Science,* soon after she'd realized that things were going seriously wrong with the reproductive part of DIANA, that men seemed to have taken out a genetic insurance policy against attempts to eliminate their sex. She had hoped to find a loophole by isolating the vitality factor in sperm, or by taking it from an embryo, making a synthetic copy of it and adding it to the culture of testicular tissue in which some of the eggs were immersed before fertilization. But despite the constant experimentation with the test men in her cages, she'd found nothing to account for such a vital role.

Then one of her assistants showed her the article in *Science.* It was about a species of fish in which the males mated with the females of a related species that had no males of its own. These females produced only daughters, whose genes came exclusively from their mothers. Fathers, therefore, were superfluous. Yet the embryos of the female species could only develop after contact with sperm from a male of the species that reproduced sexually, even though this contact did not result in fertilization. The fish sperm therefore contained some element essential to prompting normal embryonic development in a species that had itself nullified the mandatory male contribution.

The article said nothing, however, about what that essential element might be. The researchers had only looked at why the males wasted their sperm in the development of females that weren't even their daughters. For some unclear reason, the females of the species with two sexes seemed to find their own males more attractive when they had done their best for the fatherless children of their distant relatives. The males could translate this power of attraction into greater opportunities for mating with females of their own species, and therefore into a higher genetic yield.

It had been incredibly difficult to get hold of the fish. Jasmine had cursed the consequences of DIANA. She had no idea how to trace the scientists who could tell her where to find the fish. It took her weeks to contact people who understood the urgency of her request. It took forever to come up with a way to keep the fish alive long enough to fly them over, and even longer to find a pilot willing to make a difficult trip just to pick up a few fish. The promise of financial reward hadn't helped much. If any element in the DIANA program had worked perfectly, it was the elimination of the black market; cash had therefore lost much of its power of persuasion. After a great deal of fuss Jasmine had finally found a pilot who consented to make the flight, but only after the woman had been reunited with her sisters.

It had taken months of hard work and lobbying, but she finally had a collection of fish of both species. Most of them had survived the transport. There seemed to be enough animals of all three sexes to set up a successful breeding program.

But the damned fish refused to reproduce. Not a single youngling was born. Jasmine had gone to the trouble of finding out everything there was to know about mollies—a real task in a world plagued by faulty communications—but she still couldn't get the fish to produce offspring. In desperation, she finally dissected a few of the males for analysis, but that didn't help either. Now she didn't know what to do.

I couldn't believe what I was hearing. The fate of the human species had been dangling from someone's ability to prompt stupid little fish with a special reproductive system to have sex.

Kristina hardly batted an eye when I said that. "If that was the stupidest thing that had happened around here during the last few years, wouldn't we be lucky," she said bitterly.

We left Jasmine in the laboratory and crossed the complex to Diana's quarters. Kristina wanted to arrest her, but we had to take her by surprise. Jasmine had told us that Diana refused to accept the fact that her program was failing. She refused to admit that she couldn't turn nature to her own purposes with impunity, that the male sex she hated so badly was no aberration, no obsolete vestige of the past, but an essential element in nature, an element smart enough to develop mysterious mechanisms to defend itself against an attempted genetic coup.

Jasmine was afraid Diana might even destroy the sperm supply she was holding if she saw that the problems were leaking out, if people began realizing that only her sperm could save the world.

I had Jasmine's pistol and Kristina wanted me to go along. She was afraid Diana wouldn't be alone. It shouldn't be too hard to break into her apartment. Kristina knew the way, and she knew how to short out the alarm system, a classic electronic one. The night was warm, so she figured at least a few of the windows in Diana's quarters would be open.

She was right. It took her some time to decide which window to crawl through. Diana was probably asleep. The cryogenic vat with sperm was in the big room, the one with the black butler statues, in a yellowish-white tub topped, Jasmine said, by a rather inconspicuous statuette of the goddess of the hunt—since the start of her program, Diana had not entirely resisted the urge to a certain megalomania.

We had no trouble getting into the room. Kristina whispered to me to stay in the hall, so I could help out if anything came up. She snuck into the room and had started nosing around when suddenly a door swung open and Diana rushed in. She had on her bathrobe, but she was wide awake. She realized right away what was going on; before Kristina could point the Kalashnikov at her, she grabbed a black box attached to a wire on the lid of the tub and shouted that she would blow the whole thing up unless Kristina handed over her weapon.

A detonator. She'd wired the tub with explosives. She must have sensed that the end was on its way, that she couldn't keep up the deceit and self-deception much longer. She was prepared for that failure, and determined that if she went, the remaining half of mankind would go with her, all within a single generation.

Kristina froze, the barrel of the Kalashnikov pointed at a spot on the wall halfway between her and Diana. She glanced quickly in my direction. Diana was standing with her back to me. I pointed the pistol, but couldn't bring myself to shoot her in the back, no matter how much I'd wanted to when I was lying in that cage, groaning with the pain her program's experiments were causing me. Now that I was no longer suffering and in seemingly no mortal danger, I couldn't pull the trigger.

While I was trying to summon up hatred in my mind, to bring myself to kill the woman who had liquidated half the population of the world, one of the hall doors suddenly opened. A tall woman in a thin nightgown came into the hall, saw me and shrieked. Kristina snapped her Kalashnikov down at Diana and fired, but she was too late. Diana hit the detonator and the tub exploded. The sound rang through the building.

Kristina was thrown against the wall and sank to the ground. I rushed over to her, saw that her eyes were closed, and began patting her cheek.

She looked up at me and smiled. "Not much of a lady killer, are you?" she said quietly, then turned serious. "Was the tub destroyed?"

There was almost nothing left of it. Expertly blown up. Diana's girlfriend came into the room in a panic and shrieked again when she saw Diana's badly mutilated body on the floor. She hadn't survived the exploding sperm, or Kristina's bullets.

Kristina struggled to her feet. She was bleeding in a few places, but they were only flesh wounds. She walked over to the tall woman and led her into the bedroom. She had her lie down on the bed, then phoned one of her people to have her send over a few women to clean up the mess. "It's about time I started looking for another job," she said after she hung up. "I'm not cut out for this kind of thing. It's more of a man's job."

Then she looked me in the eye. "But it's no job for you. Why didn't you shoot her when you had the chance?"

I didn't know what to say, I just stood there abashed. Why hadn't I pulled the damn trigger? It couldn't be that hard to kill someone with a machine.

Kristina didn't stay mad for long. She reached out and touched my arm. "Maybe you wanted her to blow up the vat," she said. "Now you're the only fertile man left, and you're immune to the man-killing virus. You should be able to make yourself useful. All over the world."

I grinned. After the milking-machine experiments of the last few days, it would take a while before I was any use to anyone. "Well, then pamper me," I suggested. "Who knows when I could come in handy."

She shook her head. "No, not me, buddy. That would be too much of a good thing. I believe in the power of exclusivity. I couldn't share a man with anyone. And certainly not with the rest of the world. But don't start getting any big ideas. Women aren't going to throw themselves at your feet for your sperm. Our fertility programs will take over your pressing male responsibilities soon enough.

"Plus there's a fundamental law of evolution we shouldn't forget here. It says that, in the long term, every imbalance in the ratio of the sexes—no matter how extreme—will ultimately return to equilibrium, to fifty-fifty, because the rarer of the sexes will have disproportionate reproductive success. You won't be the world's only operative male for long."

But I would be for a while. The only Adam in a world full of Eves. The ultimate genetic dream, patriarch of a large part of mankind for generations to come. I finally understood why I'd been so keen on staying alive.